DEADLY ADMISSION

LILY ROCK MYSTERY BOOK THREE

BONNIE HARDY

ON THE OTHER HAND BOOKS

eBook ISBN: 978-1-954995-04-8

Paperback ISBN: 978-1-954995-05-5

Hardback ISBN 978-1-954995-90-1

Cover Design by Ebook Launch

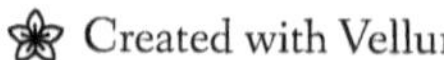 Created with Vellum

GET A FREE SHORT STORY

Join my VIP newsletter to get the latest news of Lily Rock along with contests, discounts, events, and giveaways!I'll also send you *Meadow's Hat*, a short story set before book one :)

Sign up on bonniehardywrites.com/newsletter

*I dedicate this book to songwriters who cajole, warn,
and confront us with our behavior
and its effect on future generations.*

"Teach your children well"
-Graham Nash

PROLOGUE

Is it down there? Yes, there's the body. Splayed out like a chicken ready to be cut into pieces before grilling. One leg looks funny, angled away from the torso. Must be broken. Only matters if he's alive.

He isn't. He couldn't be after that shove and the distance. I can still hear him yell. Must have been a surprise, being tripped and then shoved into an abyss.

Wait. I see movement...is that his head?

No. Just my imagination.

There's no way he lived after that fall. Now what? What do I do? I must stop looking. If someone comes up on me like this, they may assume I pushed him over the cliff.

I'm going back to the dorm.

Go on, one foot in front of the other. Faster. You can do this. Run, get away from the body.

I didn't see a thing.

That's what I'll say to myself and to anyone who will listen. With repetition my account will sound even more convincing.

"I didn't see a thing," I'll say. "I was hiking and then returned in time for dinner." Just that simple.

That's my truth, and who will deny me my truth?

Not gonna think anymore, just keep running.

Oh look, a couple of students up the path. I'll stop and catch my breath. I'll look like a normal hiker. Normal except for one thing: I saw a person fall to his death careening over a cliff.

CHAPTER ONE
ONE WEEK AGO

Friday

"Do you care where I keep my dirty clothes?" Sage held a pillowcase, stuffed to overflowing, in both arms.

"I bought a couple of new laundry baskets and put them in the laundry room." Olivia smiled at her sister. "Coffee is ready, do you want to take a break?"

"Meet you on the deck," called Sage over her shoulder.

In the kitchen Olivia bent down to pat Mayor Maguire. "Hey, doggo, ready for your breakfast?" She glanced at the coffeepot. *Drip, drip*, the last drops filled the carafe. Placing two mugs on the counter, she opened the bottom drawer where she kept the kibble.

"I have moo-food for you today," she told the dog. He waited with a smile, his tongue hanging out the side of his mouth. "We finished the cluck-food yesterday, remember?"

Mayor Maguire took a step toward his food bowl.

"Tired of my chitchat? Don't worry, I've got the food

right here." She bent over to place the metal bowl on the floor. "Eat up, big guy."

He makes me so happy—a dog who's never picky and always appreciative.

Olivia turned toward the counter. Filling each mug nearly to the top, she leaned over to deeply inhale. *Ahhh, the perfect roast. Sage's favorite and mine too.*

With one mug in each hand Olivia made her way toward the great room. She set one mug on the stone mantle above the fireplace. With her free hand she punched the button, and the floor-to-ceiling glass door swept open. Picking up the mug, she walked outside.

"I've got the door," called Sage, only steps behind.

Olivia placed the mugs on the table between two cushioned chairs as the door closed behind the two women. She sat down, casting her eyes upward. Tall pine trees rose from the earth. At the very top she could see the uppermost branches sway gently in the breeze. Looking through the woods she caught sight of Lily Rock, the town's namesake. In the early morning sunshine the alabaster surface of the rock shimmered, casting off sparks of light.

This is the best way to begin a day.

Sage plopped down on her chair, reaching over for the mug.

"Is the coffee hot enough?" asked Olivia.

"Perfect," replied Sage.

There was no need for conversation as the two sisters sipped coffee. They both took in the beauty, enjoying the silence. Several minutes later Olivia finally spoke. "I am loving this cool weather. Fall feels right around the corner."

"My students broke out the puffy jackets this week—that's my official sign that we are finally getting into the new semester," replied Sage.

"How are your new boarding students working out?" Olivia had assisted Sage on moving day, directing parents and teens to their dorms and to the cafeteria. "It's been at least two weeks since I've been over to see how everyone is getting along. The Friday before parent weekend must bring a few complications."

"All is well. No one is complaining about the food, at least. That's what usually brings the parental phone calls. You know the ones. 'Why isn't Amy getting her vegan lunch?'" Sage used a high voice to imitate a typical phone call from a parent.

Olivia smiled. "So remind me, your new chef is named Cookie?"

"Yep." Sage put down her mug. "You haven't met Cookie, but off the top of your head, what do you think a person named Cookie looks like?"

"The first thing I thought of was Mrs. White in the old Clue board game. You know, dressed in a fluffy apron, in her sixties with white hair."

"Nope." Sage's chin dipped as she hid a smile.

"So tell me. Who is this Cookie?"

"He's not a woman to start with."

Olivia's eyebrows raised. "Really? I assumed with a name like that..."

"You assumed wrong. Cookie is a man in his fifties. He wears a military haircut. You know, close-cut over the ears. Plus he has a goatee and a mustache."

"Cookie is a nickname?"

"Right. His named is Charles Kravitz. He was a culinary specialist in the Navy before retiring. Everyone called him Cookie, so the name stuck."

"And he cooks vegan? I never thought of the Navy as the kind of organization that catered to special diets."

"He reluctantly cooks vegan," Sage admitted. "I've had to use my most persuasive arm-twisting to get him not to swear at the students who need special meals."

"A whole different group than the Navy," laughed Olivia. "What other kind of special meals is Cookie expected to produce?"

"Oh, you know, the usual. Some students are lactose intolerant, so no dairy for them. A few don't eat gluten, so Cookie has to be careful with wheat and even with baking so that the gluten doesn't spread to the non-gluten goods."

"Now that's a challenge!" Olivia admitted.

"Running a school often comes down to what the kids eat and how clean the bathrooms are. If I can get past the first month without too many complaints, then I have the chance of keeping my job."

"The Old Rockers wouldn't fire you over gluten in the bread! At least not with Meadow on the board."

"You haven't heard?" Sage's voice dropped as she squirmed in her seat. "The Old Rockers no longer run the academy like the old days. They appointed a new separate, independent board of directors for the Lily Rock Music Academy; we had our first official meeting last week."

"I hadn't heard." Olivia took the last sip of coffee. "I've been working on Marla's estate, you know, getting things ready to quitclaim the property."

As she spoke, the glass door behind them slid open. Olivia looked over her shoulder to smile at the tall man in a flannel shirt.

"So that's where you are. I've been trying to call," he said, grinning back.

"Hey, Mike," called Sage. "Pull up a seat."

By the time he dusted the tree pollen off the chair, Olivia returned with another mug of coffee and the pot. "I put the usual cream and sugar in yours," she said. "And here's some more for you," she added, refilling Sage's mug.

Michael's deep-blue eyes took in one sister and then the other. "This new roommate arrangement seems to be working out for you both. Can't remember when I've seen either one of you look more relaxed."

"I'm loving it," admitted Olivia.

"Me too," agreed Sage.

"So are you both ladies of leisure, what with Marla's estate and the inheritance getting settled? I imagine there's a nice lump sum after you pay the attorneys." He shook his head. "Maybe it's time to let the old ways die, to quote Bradley Cooper. You can pour all your efforts into the band."

Olivia sat back down before explaining. "As wonderful as that sounds, the estate still poses a few challenges. Of course, splitting the house would have been the biggest one, but all I have to do is quitclaim to Sage and that's settled. After that we can move forward with evaluating what's left."

She continued, "We split everything down the middle. When all is said and done, we'll both have a small income along with the investment of the house. But we still have to work for everything else. Maybe one day Sweet Four O'Clock will pull in enough income," Olivia sighed.

"There's enough money not to totally panic if one of us gets laid off, but not so much that either one of us can actually thrive without another job," added Sage.

"Is that how you see it?" questioned Michael, looking at Olivia directly.

"The perfect balance. I start my next temp job in a week," she added, a teasing note in her voice.

Michael sat up in his chair. "News to me," he said, scratching the back of his head. "I thought you were staying in Lily Rock awhile longer, or at least I hoped you would, until your band starts touring." He looked dejected, not hiding his disappointment. "So you're leaving. Down the hill to Playa, and who knows when we'll see you again. Just like last time. I thought you'd stay now that you and Sage are roommates."

"Not exactly like last time because my job isn't in Playa. You're not rid of me that easily," Olivia said, reaching over to pat his arm. "I have a job right in town."

A smile started at the corner of Michael's mouth. "So you were teasing me, is that it? You wanted to see if I really cared instead of assuming that I don't. Okay then, what job are you taking? Do tell."

"Janis Jets hired me to help out at the constabulary until she finds a replacement for her last assistant."

"Janis hired you?" gasped Sage, returning to the conversation.

"You gotta be kidding," added Michael. "I never thought Janis would pay you to get involved. She's always complaining about how you nose yourself into her business, and now she hires you to work at the constabulary?"

"She's not just letting me in, she's handing me all the secrets with the computer access and front desk location. I'm her new girl Friday with a nose for crime." Olivia smirked.

"You are not." Sage waved dismissively. "You are a musician who sings and plays the autoharp. You can't help it if people just keep confessing to you all the time."

"It's Olivia's voice," commented Michael. "And her eyes, and the way she just captures your heart. You want to confide in Olivia just to keep her listening a little longer."

Now both women turned toward Michael. He smiled self-consciously. "I'm just sayin', I'm not the only one who thinks Olivia has a gift. Apparently Janis thinks so too, or she wouldn't have hired her as a temp."

Olivia squirmed in discomfort. *There he goes again, telling me how he feels in front of another person...*

In order to change the subject, she turned to Michael. "So I have a job in town. Now you both know." Then she addressed Sage. "Don't you have to unpack and get your laundry organized before work? I'm not Meadow, but if she were here she'd say, 'Time's a-wasting.'"

Sage laughed. "Nobody can do Meadow as well as you. Not quite the same zing, but definitely a tone of knowing what's best. Yes, yes, I'll get going in just a minute. So many phone calls, so little time." Sage didn't move from her chair, her glance finding its way back to the forest beyond.

"Did you hear?" Olivia asked Michael. "Sage has a new chef at the academy whose name is Cookie. Now what kind of an image does a name like that bring up for you?"

Michael put his mug on the table with a grin. "A guy in his mid-fifties with slicked-back gray hair who used to be military."

"You already knew!" Olivia cried.

"Not only heard about him but met him a couple of days ago. I was up at the academy looking at the plans for completing the new concert venue and ran into him. Seemed like a good guy. Don't know if he's a good cook."

"No complaints that I haven't resolved," insisted Sage. She stood, her empty mug in one hand. "Since my laundry won't sort itself, I'd better get going. You two can get along without me." Sage winked at Michael. With a small wave of her hand, she pressed the button to open the glass wall. As soon as the door closed, Michael leaned closer to Olivia.

"Remember the dinner you promised me a month ago?"

Olivia looked down at her hands, feeling her cheeks

grow warm. "I sure do. The one in Playa where you'd be spending the night."

"Now that you aren't returning to Playa, how about a Saturday night dinner in Lily Rock instead? I'll make a reservation for us."

"Who would have a table at the last minute? Parent weekend will make everything crowded."

"I know some people who will make room for us at The Refuge. Been there?"

She'd only heard of the upscale eatery. "I haven't been there yet. It's right up the hill, toward Lily Rock, right?"

"Hidden in the pines, well into the forest. Very private. Very intimate setting, with tables for two nestled into the trees, waiters walking silently on cat feet."

"Did you do the architectural design for the restaurant?" Olivia asked. "Sounds like your kind of place."

"I wish. But The Refuge was built before my time in Lily Rock. The owner did some reconstruction this past year and I think he may have borrowed my ideas from the pub. You know creative consulting doesn't always happen with words." Michael's eyes glowed with satisfaction. "I know the owner and he says his chef is the best on the hill. He'll find us a table for two. Does this mean we're on for dinner?"

"Sure," she said quietly, her heart beating rapidly. "Why not?"

Michael's jaw tightened. *How have I offended him this time?*

His nostrils flared for a moment, his voice conveying disappointment. "Just a why not? I've been waiting so long to take you out. I suspect you're not as excited as you were a few weeks ago."

She looked up, her eyes taking in his open expression

and the intent gaze directed straight at her. She sighed. *He is irresistible.*

"I want to have dinner with you, it's just..." Her voice dropped away. *How can I explain my feelings when I don't know them myself?*

Michael stood up, stretching his arms over his head. Olivia took a moment to look watch a squirrel chase another squirrel up the trunk of a tall pine tree.

Animals have it easier. They see what they want and they go for it. Why do my feelings go from off to on? No wonder he's impatient.

"Don't worry. I'm taking this slow. It's just dinner. Nothing more," Michael assured her, a calm expression returning to his face.

The knot in her stomach released. Still hesitant, she said, "I'm not very confident about moving forward. I wish I were better at this."

Michael leaned closer to her chair. He kissed the top of her head as she inhaled deeply. His scent, the lingering smell of citrus and mint, left her head reeling. She grasped his hand, holding it in her own.

He knelt down in front of her chair, placing both of his hands on her knees. "Honey, you don't have to be confident. I will carry my certainty for both of us until you catch up. I plan on being the perfect gentleman until you give the word."

A smile crept to her lips. *I like this, handing over my emotions to him, at least for now.*

"I'm still a bit confused," she admitted to Michael. "With the job and Sage moving in, especially if I plan on staying here in Lily Rock; I'll have to give my landlord notice in Playa. It's a lot to think about."

Olivia closed her eyes for a minute and then opened

them. He remained on his knees, waiting for her to speak first. Then he leaned in ever so slightly.

I'd better say something or he's going to kiss me and then who knows what I'll do.

She blurted out the first thing that came to her mind. "Dinner sounds amazing. Let me know what time works, so long as it's after six. I have to rehearse with the band in the morning and then check in with Janis that afternoon."

He patted her knees with both hands and then rolled back on his heels. Strong legs lifted him to his full six feet. "Good. That will work. I'll text you with the timing."

As Olivia rose to her feet, Michael opened the glass door. Mayor Maguire lay spread out on the sofacushions, his chin resting on a pillow. He faced the fireplace, eyes closed, though his ear twitched a greeting.

Olivia sat next to the dog, running her fingers through his curly neck fur. "Time for a snooze after breakfast?" She reached over and gave him a big hug.

Mayor Maguire licked her hand, his tongue rough on her skin.

Michael called out to the dog, "Hey, Mayor. Want to go for a walk this morning?" His voice lifted at the end, causing the dog to stop licking Olivia's hand. He bounded off the sofa to stand in front of Michael, who leaned over to give him a pat.

Mayor Maguire's joyful bark echoed throughout the great room as he spun in circles before heading toward the front door.

CHAPTER TWO

After a hasty breakfast, Olivia drove to the Lily Rock Music Academy. *Tap, tap, tap* from a woodpecker rose above the rustle of branches. With her autoharp under her arm, she walked to the auditorium. The main entry doors stood open.

Olivia unpacked her instrument first, leaving it on top of the piano. She dragged a stool from behind the curtain to sit on. *No sign of Sweet Four O'Clock yet.*

A few minutes later Sage arrived. "So sorry I'm late. I had a phone call from an irate parent. She wants to pull her child out of the academy because he didn't make first chair in the orchestra."

"Is first chair a political appointment?"

"Not at the Lily Rock Music Academy. We hold auditions behind visual screens. The faculty can't see the player. They select the musician who sounds the best and then afterward, the names are announced."

Resting her fiddle case on the back of the piano, Sage sighed. "A lot of music prep schools give out scholarships and first chairs to the children of wealthier parents. We've been able to avoid that in the past. But now that we have our own governing board, I'm not sure I can dismiss a donor's special request. The board wants to improve the campus, and that means they must court the wealthy parents."

"Hey, ladies," a voice interrupted. Dave Franco stood wearing a Lily Rock T-shirt, jeans, and a pork pie hat sitting back on his head. "Sorry I'm late. I had to help a student with a math assignment early this morning."

Olivia smiled at Dave. *Is the hat a fashion statement or an attempt to hide some premature balding? He's probably mid-forties by now.*

"Where's Paul?" Sage asked Dave. "He called last night and said he'd be here."

"And here I am," said a low voice. Paul, dressed in a T-shirt and cargo shorts, moved toward the stage. He rolled a stand up base behind him. The case was big enough to contain an average-sized person. "A couple of kids asked me some questions outside, which held me up. How are you, Olivia?"

"Just fine, Paul. I see you're still a Christian." She pointed to the large cross that hung around his neck.

"Can't seem to shake ol' Jesus," he admitted. "You have a problem with that?"

"Not at all," Olivia assured him. "I pray the Psalms all the time."

"You go to church?"

"I don't have to go to church to pray."

Paul shrugged. "Can't say I go that much now that I've been gigging more. Sat in on a great jazz combo down the hill last week."

Sage spoke up. "Okay, enough chitchat. I have to get back and soothe the feelings of some more parents. Which tune do you want to warm up on?"

As the rest of the band readied themselves, Olivia heard

voices from the back of the auditorium where a group of teens had gathered. *Must be their lunch hour too. Let's see if anyone likes old-time country tunes.*

Sage began to noodle on her fiddle. Soon Olivia joined, strumming chords on the autoharp. Her right hand picked up a syncopated rhythm as Dave's hands smoothed a back-beat with his conga. Finally Paul joined in, beginning with a slow improvised riff on his standup bass.

An old-time tune, "Will the Circle Be Unbroken", filled the auditorium. The kids in the back stopped talking as Sweet Four O'Clock played and Olivia began to sing.

> Will the circle be unbroken
> By and by, by and by?
> Is a better home awaiting
> In the sky, in the sky?

Her voice twanged in the lower register. It wasn't until she rounded the corner into the final verse that her voice rose, filling the entire auditorium.

At the end of the song a loud clap rang out from the back. "You are amazing," called a boy making his way toward the stage. He offered Olivia his outstretched hand. "Could the Tone Rangers use that song for our set?"

She smiled, taking his hand. "The Tone Rangers?"

"Our a cappella group. I'm Legend Watner, by the way, the bass in the group."

Legend Watner's wearing a dress and I'm not sure if he's a girl or a boy.

"You can certainly compose an unaccompanied arrangement for "Will the Circle Be Unbroken". It's in the public domain, you just have to do a search on the internet. I want to warn you though, the words are very Christian."

"The words are about salvation," Paul added, fingering his cross. "Are you familiar?"

Legend smiled. "Haven't a clue. I just like the tune and the way she sang the words." He pointed to Olivia, who was now aware that Sage was tapping her foot, waiting for their conversation to be over.

"Time for you to get back to studying," she told Legend. "You have a big exam coming up."

Legend shrugged. "I know, but I think this school should have, you know, more relevant classes, like what this band is playing. Not just some old European

stuff."

Sage cleared her throat. "I've heard this complaint before, Legend. We can address your concerns later, but now it's time for class."

"Yes, ma'am."

As he walked back up the aisle, Olivia turned to Sage. "Boy or girl or does it matter?"

"Legend identifies as she/her."

Olivia nodded. "I'll try to remember. This pronoun thing throws me. You must have a lot of that considering the academy is full of young artists searching for their identity."

"Don't get me started. It's hard to remember who is who, and then some students change from one day to the next. I do my best. I think it's important for me to pay attention at the very least."

Dave sauntered over to Olivia and Sage. "Pretty cool when the kids like our style of music. Do you want us to sing at the parent weekend recital on Sunday?"

"It may work." Sage nodded. "I have a few bands lined

up, mostly staff performances. Sweet Four O'Clock would be distinctly different than the others, but then—"

"We've always been different," finished Olivia. "It's our brand."

"I, for one, am looking forward to the parent weekend. I haven't stayed on a campus since I was at Berklee."

"You went to Berklee College of Music?" Olivia's voice filled with respect. "They produce a lot of good musicians. Did you audition?"

"In those days acceptance wasn't hard at all. They had rolling admissions and pretty much took everyone with a pulse who had the tuition. By the first year over half of the freshman dropped out, or if they were really good, gave up on college and went on tour."

"Did you need an SAT score?" asked Olivia.

"I got a great SAT score the first time I took it. Tests have never been a problem for me for some reason.

"Admission isn't like that now," Sage admitted. "All of my students are here to get the best grades and test scores and to audition to get acceptance to an Ivy League school. The seniors, like Legend, spend all their time searching for an original sound. He—I mean she—joined the premier a cappella group called the Tone Rangers as a bass. But lately Legend surprised everyone by shifting to falsetto. Now that she wants to sing the soprano melodies, Abbey's nose is out of joint. She was the original soprano. The group is in turmoil with auditions coming up next month. Not a good sign."

Now I know I don't want Sage's job.

"Honey, you have some real challenges as the school director," Olivia said. "How does a bass become a soprano, I ask?"

"You can talk to Legend about all of that if you like. She's not shy."

"I can check in with her on parent weekend. I don't suppose I can accompany the Tone Rangers on autoharp?" Olivia asked innocently.

Paul and Dave laughed together, pointing to Sage. "Just try to make that happen," said Paul.

"I dare you," added Dave.

Sage grinned. "You know the definition of a cappella."

"That's not even the point," chuckled Dave. "Even if they sing unaccompanied, I'd sure like to see Olivia make the autoharp cool again."

Olivia's voice flared. "The autoharp *is* cool! How dare you!" Her face collapsed into a grin. "Oh, I know. You don't have to answer that. The autoharp is never cool. That's why I love it so. The misfit of folk instruments. Even the banjo has a better reputation."

Olivia glanced to the back of the room where a clock hung above the exit doors. "I've got to go. I told Janis Jets I'd meet her at the constabulary for my job introduction."

"You're going to be a cop?" Dave's eyes widened. "I know you've solved a couple of crimes in the past, but cops—they're a different breed. I had no idea you were going to take up police work seriously."

Olivia held up her hands in protest. "Don't get the wrong idea. I'm just a temporary assistant while Janis finds a replacement. I think the job will only be a few months, then I'll be looking for another."

Dave scratched his head. "I heard you were loaded."

"And that is just rumor. I have—I mean, we have," she glanced at Sage, "a nice house, which is expensive to keep up. There's a little extra income but not much. Gotta have a side hustle to support the music. It's the way of the world."

"I understand making ends meet. That's why I tutor. Linnea and I do our best, but some months we have nothin' left in our account until the next paycheck."

"Money problems?"

"Our landlord is kicking us out in a month. He says it's for renovations, but I know it's because we're three months behind in our rent. He doesn't want to look like a jerk, so he's made up a big excuse. Linnea is upset. She's pregnant, you know."

"Congratulations," said Olivia. "When's the baby due?"

"February some time. I still can't believe I'm going to be a dad."

"I'm sure you'll be a great dad," Olivia assured him. "Your baby will be beautiful, tall and blond and wear stylin' hats just like Papa."

Dave smiled in response, but his eyes did not agree.

He looks really anxious. I wonder if he's ready for this big change in his life. A family can't make it on his bass improv licks and small-town tutoring gigs for very long.

Olivia's phone rang, interrupting her thoughts.

"Where the hell are you," demanded the voice of Janis Jets.

"I thought we said two o'clock. It is Saturday, you know," added Olivia. She glanced at her cell phone.

And I'm not even late.

"I did not say two o'clock. Are you hard of hearing or deliberately obtuse? I can fire you before you even start the job with that attitude." Janis's voice continued to lecture Olivia, as she tuned out. She tuned back in just in time to hear, "You were rehearsing?"

"That's it. Got it in one," Olivia replied.

She's so talkative and intense.

"Stop with the messing around. We have work to do.

Antonia left the place in a mess and I have to fill you in on the latest town shenanigans."

"I will see you soon," Olivia assured Janis, adding, "boss."

"Don't call me that," shouted Jets, "I can't stand being called boss. Reminds me of my first captain, a complete jerk."

"I'll see you in a few minutes." She clicked off the cell phone and slipped it into her back pocket. The last one to leave, Olivia packed up her autoharp. She slung the strap over her shoulder and walked toward the exit.

Olivia parked her car in front of the constabulary. After locking up she walked the short distance over the boardwalk to the entrance. A nudge to her knee made her jump. "Oh hi, M&M. I thought you'd be sleeping by the back door today."

Tail wagging, Mayor Maguire made his way around Olivia and sat at her right knee. "Let's see what our pal Janis is up to, shall we?" She opened the door, stepping aside to let the dog go first. Her gut clenched as she looked around the room. The office looked a shambles.

What a mess! Janis wasn't kidding, she does need an assistant.

Crumpled fast food bags lay in a mound alongside two staplers and a three-hole punch. Papers were strewn across the desk, some tumbling to the floor.

A trash can nearby had been turned upside down, two empty plastic water bottles lying on top. Even the desk chair, spun to its lowest adjustment, faced the blank wall behind the desk.

I know what I'll be doing today.

Olivia looked for a place to store her belongings. She

had to push the contents of the bottom desk drawer to the back to make way for her oversized tote. *Maybe Janis is in her back office...*

When she stood in front of the glass doors that separated the reception area from the cells, the sensor lit up as the glass swished open.

I bet Janis is in her office.

On the walk down the hall, Olivia glanced to the right and left. All the doors of the interrogation rooms stood ajar. As she stepped closer to Janis's office she felt a twinge of apprehension. An unexpected sound caught her attention.

What is that?

A soft voice came from the direction of Janis's office.

She moved closer to the wall, edging forward one step at a time.

"I know, sweetie. I feel the same about you," came a seductive drawl.

Wait a minute, that's not my Janis. I've never heard that tone of voice before.

Olivia shook her head to clear her hearing.

Janis never speaks like that. What happened to her usual harsh repartee?

Olivia felt a cold chill run down her spine. As she lifted her hair off her neck, the most ominous sound of all flowed from Jets's office. Something Olivia never dreamed was possible assaulted her ears.

Janis Jets giggled.

No way, I must have heard wrong.

Then it came again, a chirp then a string of them, like a bird's warning call.

At that moment, her heart in her throat, Olivia knew for certain: *The world is coming to an end.*

Once she regained her composure, she moved toward

the giggling sound, determined to find out what had gone wrong. The rolling giggles kept coming at her, growing louder as she approached.

Olivia stood in the doorway. Her jaw dropped at the unexpected sight.

Jets's back was turned, giving Olivia a chance to suppress a gasp. Gone was the usual tidy bun at the back of Janis's neck. Instead, thick wavy hair tumbled to her shoulders, layered to perfection in a mass of curls.

I had no idea she had that much hair, and look, those are blond highlights.

Olivia kept her silence, holding in her shock.

Unaware that Olivia watched her, Janis continued. "I know, baby. I have to go back to work. But listen, I hired an assistant, and she can run things so that we can get away around Halloween. Does that work for you? I hope you can wait that long." Janis laughed, the deep growl of seduction rolling from the back of her throat.

"Stop it!" giggled Janis. "You are incorrigible."

"Ahem," Olivia cleared her throat.

Janis's chair swiveled around. Her gray eyes grew round when she saw Olivia. "Just a minute," she said to the person on the other end of the line, "I have someone in my office. Can I call you back?" Janis clicked off her cell phone.

"'Bout time you got here. I've been waiting."

Olivia shrugged. "Looks like you had plenty to do."

"You're the one with plenty to do," Jets retorted. "I want the reception area cleaned up as soon as possible. Tonight, if you have to. How can I do business with that mess?"

"Nice outfit," Olivia noted.

Jets wore a plunging blue top that exposed part of her cleavage.

"Looks like you've been outdoors, you know, with the tan and all." Olivia swept her hand over her own blouse.

"I have naturally olive-toned skin, I'll have you know. It just doesn't show in my uniform."

"Speaking of uniform, what happened to the blue blazer, and where are you hiding your weapon in that outfit?"

Janis stood, pushing her shoulders back. "If you must know, I came right to work."

"Sure you did," Olivia smirked. "Your leather pants add a whole new dimension to your police presence, I'll give you that. Is this a new look for cops?"

Tongue in cheek, Olivia. Don't give in to giggles. Is now the time to mention the thigh-high leather boots with chunky heels?

"Why would you say that?" Janis tugged at her skin-tight black pants, adjusting the waistband. "I'm just a little dressed up, that's all."

"How long have you been 'just a little dressed up'?" inquired Olivia, her eyes still innocent.

Janis ran a hand through her flowing hair. "Enough about me. Time for you to get to work." From the corner of her eye, she looked longingly at her cell phone. "I have an important call to make, so you can take this trash can and start sorting out that reception desk. No one has sat there in some time."

Olivia full-on smiled. "I think I saw a rodent underneath the stack of papers munching on an old cheeseburger wrapper."

"Look at you, Ms. Amateur Sleuth. Nice work. Go away. I've got things to do right now." Janis sat back down behind her desk, reaching for her cell phone.

Olivia waved, easing her way out of the doorway. *Sure*

she has things to do. Like call her boyfriend or girlfriend back and finish the conversation.

Five o'clock came and went as Olivia looked at each paper on her desk. Her cell phone buzzed. "Ready for dinner?" asked Michael before she had a chance to say hello. "Pick you up in five minutes..."

She nearly dropped the phone. "I forgot about our reservation." Then she hastily added, "I'm not avoiding our dinner. I came in for a quick chat with Janis and she put me to work. Have you seen the constabulary office lately?"

A big sigh brushed past her ear. "I haven't been to the constabulary in a couple of weeks. Every time I call Janis, she doesn't pick up. I was hoping she'd finally taken some time off, you know, for a vacation. I pictured her in uniform, with her weapon hidden in her waistband behind that navy blue blazer, somewhere on the beach."

Olivia laughed. *Do I tell him what I saw?*

"It is a bit of a challenge thinking of Janis Jets on vacation. Before today I always thought the bun was fake, stuck on with tape and a chewed piece of gum."

Michael snorted. "All kidding aside about Janis, Lily Rock has been pretty quiet since the last time you stirred up trouble."

Olivia knew he was right. "I really am sorry about our dinner plans. Can I make another reservation in a couple of days for us?"

"I'll make the reservation since I know the chef. But Olivia...I won't wait forever. I want to step up our relationship and I think you do too."

"Of course you do. I want to have dinner, Michael. I do.

It's just that something is off with Janis." She heard the worry in her own voice.

He inhaled quickly. "What do you mean something is off?"

"Did you know she has shoulder-length wavy hair with blond highlights and that she wears leather pants?"

"She does not!" he retorted. "The next thing you're gonna tell me is that Janis goes out on dates."

Olivia waited, letting his assumption sink in.

"She goes out on dates?" Michael's voice grew warm and filled with wonder.

"Yes, she does. But that's not the worst part." Olivia gulped, and then added,

"Janis Jets giggles. She giggled, Michael, to someone on the phone."

A low sound erupted from the back of his throat. He growled, "We've got trouble right here in Lily Rock. Maybe it's time for me to get down there and check things out for myself."

CHAPTER THREE

Sunday

"What do you want?" Olivia mumbled into her cell phone. "I said I'd be there before eight o'clock. It's only 6:30. Don't you have something better to do?"

Janis Jets's throaty laugh met Olivia's ear. "I need your help, so get up and get dressed. I'll pick you up in fifteen minutes sharp."

"No you won't! Getting up this early on a Sunday is not in my job description."

"Who cares about your job description? Crime is not contained to a nine-to-five job. I want to check out the academy. Some guy's been calling me about an assault. You've got fourteen minutes left."

Click went the phone. Olivia slid out of bed. She had the shower running and her hair washed before the doorbell rang. She turned off the water and stepped out of the shower, and with a quick tap, she texted back, *I'm nearly ready. Give me five more minutes.*

By the time Olivia arrived downstairs, she opened the door to find Janis Jets holding two paper to-go cups with lids and sleeves. Janis paraded past Olivia with Mayor Maguire nipping at her heels. Olivia closed the front door behind them.

When she entered the kitchen Janis had already arranged the coffee cups on the table. Nearby, Mayor Maguire leaned into her thigh, his face hopeful.

Jets held a cookie shaped like a dog bone just above the mayor's head. "Good doggie," she said, as drool dribbled down the mayor's chin. "Want this bone, don't ya? How about a high five?" Mayor Maguire tapped her palm with his paw. She wiped the drool from his jaw and then tossed the bone in an arc, the dog snapping up the treat.

"I have to interrupt this little training session to ask an important question. Is that coffee for me?" Olivia pointed to the second paper cup on the table.

"Black like you like it." Jets nodded.

"Did Mayor Maguire sleep with you last night?" Olivia reached for her coffee, removing the lid as the steam rose up to her nose.

"The silly hound must have spent the night with me. I don't really remember, except that he met me at my truck this morning, insisting on a ride in the passenger seat. Then I had to roll down the window to keep him from smearing the glass with his snotty nose."

"I wondered why he didn't stay with me," Olivia mused aloud.

"He likes me better," Jets said with authority. "But he did hitch a ride to see you this morning. I'll give you that. Plus the last time he came over for a visit, my cat rebelled. I haven't seen Joanie since he cleaned out her food bowl yesterday, his tail wagging like he owned the joint."

Her cat is named Joanie? Why haven't I heard about this before...

"Where do you live, by the way?"

Janis patted Mayor Maguire's head, ignoring Olivia's question.

Two murders later and I have never asked Janis anything personal. I guess I thought she lived at the constabulary and slept in one of the cells. I'm a bad friend.

Finally Janis spoke. "Never mind, Nancy Drew. I live close to town over the other hill. You're not invited to my house ever. Just so you know."

Olivia felt the hair raise on her neck. "Why not? We're friends."

"No, we're not. I keep telling you, I'm your employer, not one of your pals."

"You're just mad that I never asked before, about where you lived."

"Don't flatter yourself. Your disinterest in my personal life works entirely to my advantage. I don't want people to know where I live or who I hang out with."

"Even friends?"

"Did I not just answer that question a minute ago? I don't have friends in Lily Rock. Now drink up. We have work to do at the music academy. Some bossy guy called me at six a.m. because he wants to press charges against one of the students."

Olivia took the last sip of coffee, appreciating the warmth running down her throat. "Okay then. I'm ready. I'll grab my purse and we're on our way."

Jets rose from the table, Mayor Maguire looking directly at her. "No more treats for you," she grumbled.

Olivia slung her purse over her shoulder, following Janis out of the kitchen. With the door locked behind her, she moved quickly to catch up. Jets and the mayor were already seated in the front cab of the truck. Olivia opened the back door, sliding into the seat.

Jets backed the truck up, and then shifted into first gear. "You settled yet?" she called over her shoulder to Olivia. "I didn't hear the click of your seat belt."

Olivia checked the seat belt one more time as Janis headed toward the main road.

By the time they reached the music academy, the choice areas under the shade of trees in the student parking lot had already been taken. Olivia leaned over the seat to speak to Janis. "Where are the students?"

"Hopefully getting an education," answered Jets.

Olivia sighed. "I'm just trying to figure out what the Lily Rock Music Academy does on weekend mornings. It's been ages since I've been in high school."

Jets guided the truck into a parking space near the foot-path to the admissions office. She put the vehicle in park and opened her door. "They can spend all morning in bed for all I care. That's up to their parents."

Boy, she is crabby.

Olivia opened her door from the back seat just as Janis opened the passenger side for the dog. He jumped down, landing on Olivia's shoes.

"Ouch."

The dog looked up at her. He sniffed her shoes as if to apologize. Before he trotted away, he gave her hand a quick lick as if asking forgiveness.

Janis Jets walked ahead and stood in front of the main

office. Before trying the door handle, she stepped to the side and stared into the front window.

"Looks like all the suspects are lined up and waiting for the interrogation," she commented.

Mayor Maguire pushed the door with his nose. When it didn't budge, Janis turned the handle. Olivia followed Janis and the dog into the office, stopping in her tracks.

Four teens sat against the wall, each holding a cell phone. Olivia's eyes shifted downward to their feet. All four students wore identically styled hiking boots, clearly from the same manufacturer.

I know those boots. Designed for trails and hiking—really pricy.

"Here doggie doggie," called one young female who reached a hand down to wait for Mayor Maguire to come closer.

Olivia recognized Legend Watner from the day before. She looked the calmest of the four, a slight smile on full lips. *She does look like a girl with that peasant blouse and long hair. If I ignore her broad shoulders and slight beard, I think I can remember to say she/her.*

Next to Legend sat another male. He wore jeans and a black T-shirt that said *Johnny Cash* on the front. His worn hiking boots interested Mayor Maguire, who ignored the outstretched hand to sniff at the laces.

"Mayor Maguire likes you," commented Olivia.

"I guess," responded the sullen teen.

A girl stood up first, stretching out her arm. "My name is Abbey Court, I'm the soprano and leader of the Tone Rangers. I'm cisgender, so my pronouns are she/her." She turned and pointed to the kid on her left. "This is Raleigh Ulrich, our tenor. Their pronouns are they/them."

Raleigh fondled Mayor Maguire's ears, reaching to his

back haunch to scratch near the dog's tail.

Abbey continued the introductions. "That's Anais Butler, our alto, and she uses she/her as well." Abbey's voice dropped to a disdainful growl. "And the guy sitting on the end is Legend Watner. He thinks he's a soprano, but he isn't. Pronouns don't change that even if I have to call him a her."

Olivia gulped. *This is going to be hard to figure out. I have two girls who identify as she/her, and two guys, one who identifies as she/her and the other with they/them.*

Janis Jets interrupted. "I don't give a rat's tail what your pronouns are, I'm gonna call 'em as I see 'em, and I see two boys and two girls. End of discussion."

Olivia flinched.

Abbey's cheeks turned bright red. "I'm she/her and that's all that matters to me. Go ahead and diss the rest if you dare. Not my problem."

Olivia gulped.

Janis stood taller. "Call all the lawyers you want. Now then, which of you smacked the other one and where's the proof?"

Abbey flung her left shoulder back. With a graceful swoop she pointed a manicured index finger toward Legend. "He—I mean she—slapped me on my face." Her arm dropped. "I have photos and my dad will be here in a few minutes so that we can press charges." Her voice smoothly shifted from authoritarian to wheedling.

Janis looked Abbey up and down. "I don't see any damage on your cheek. But that doesn't matter, show me the photos."

Before Abbey could respond, an inner office door opened. Sage stepped out, a grim look on her face.

"I just got off the phone with Abbey's father," she

announced.

"That's who I've been talking to this morning," Jets said. She looked at Abbey, then back at Sage.

"Don't say anything until Abbey's dad shows up with the lawyer," Sage warned all of the students.

"We're tired of sitting here," responded Abbey with an exaggerated shrug.

"I'm hungry," added Raleigh, rubbing their chin. "Let's go get some lunch and then we'll come back."

"I don't trust you four with the rest of the students," Sage said. "If you start fighting again, we'll have chaos in the cafeteria."

"It's okay, Ms. McCloud. We won't fight anymore, will we?" Anais looked at the other teens, then back at Abbey.

"I don't care what you say. My father paid for tuition and I'm entitled to three meals a day. Let's go, Anais." Abbey opened the door, taking Anais by the elbow.

Janis Jets intervened. "Okay, so let those two go first. Then Olivia can accompany the other two in twenty minutes. That will keep them separate."

Sage sighed while Legend and Raleigh nodded, glances dropping back to their phones.

"Before you go to lunch," Jets directed her gaze at Legend, "I want to know what possessed you to smack that entitled little twit. I mean, you must have known she'd be trouble."

"It's a music thing," mumbled Legend. "I said I was sorry right away, but she wanted to make a big deal out of it. I only want to help the Tone Rangers."

Jets shook her head, turning toward Sage. "How can four singing nerds get so riled up that they smack each other around? I just don't get it."

Sage explained to the baffled Jets. "The Tone Rangers

are a highly competitive group. They're known for precise harmony and everyone expects them to get early admission to an Ivy League college. Just one wrong note at a singing competition might lower their chances."

"Knock us out of early admission is more like it," clarified Legend. "You probably don't know, but a cappella singers get accepted to prestigious colleges. It's not as good as sports, but almost. A cappella is at least as good as lacrosse and rowing."

"So this is all about getting into college. Not just getting in, but getting admitted earlier than the rest..." Jets shook her head. "What's the hurry? A big waste of time, if you ask me. Why not take one of those gap years and see the world a bit before you tie yourself down to four years of drudgery?"

Sage held her finger over her lips. "We can talk about all of that later. Right now I want to walk Raleigh and Legend to the Curated Cuisine to get some lunch."

Jets rested her hands on her belt in front of her stomach. "What is a Curated Cuisine?"

Raleigh spoke first. "That's what they call the cafeteria." They smiled at Janis, showing two rows of invisible braces.

"Idiots," mumbled Jets under her breath. "Since when is school cafeteria food supposed to be a gourmet experience?"

"I heard that, Janis. Obviously you have not dined with us recently," came Sage's tart reply.

Olivia felt her cell phone buzz in her pocket. "What's up?" she answered.

"I came by for coffee this morning. Where were you?" asked Michael.

"Janis got to me first. We're at the music academy. One of the parents is filing a lawsuit against a student. They called Janis, and as the new assistant, I guess she thought nothing of pulling me out of bed early this morning."

"Not the explanation I expected." Michael chuckled. "Give me a few minutes and I'll come up and join the gang. I don't want to miss Janis taking down an elite music student before lunch. This should be good."

"Better hurry. We're heading to the Curated Cuisine in a few minutes, and the fur is already flying."

"I can be there in ten minutes. Save me a place in line," laughed Michael.

"I gotta take a call," Janis Jets said, looking at her phone. "Go ahead with her and they. I'll catch up with you."

Olivia winced at the obvious misuse of pronouns.

She really has to stop doing that. They're just teens trying to figure things out.

Sage and Olivia emerged from the footpath, Raleigh and Legend following close behind. Olivia spotted Abbey and Anais right away. They were first in line at the Curated Cuisine. Other students dressed from pajamas to jeans to sweats stood behind. At the end of the line Olivia recognized Michael Bellemare.

"You're here already!" she exclaimed. "I thought you'd take longer."

He turned around, a slow lazy grin coming over his face. Stepping away from the line, he walked toward them. Legend and Raleigh took the opportunity to peel themselves away from the adults, cutting in with a guy wearing blue jeans and a black hoodie.

"I missed you," he said with a wink. "I'd have been here sooner. I thought faculty would get a separate entrance, so I went around to the back."

Sage interrupted. "I get in line with the students and I recommend that the faculty does the same. That way we get to know our community outside of the classroom."

"Very egalitarian of you," mumbled Michael. "Except I'm hungry. Didn't get my usual muffin and coffee this morning." He glared at Olivia, who winked back at him.

"I hear some of your students come from wealthy families," Michael commented.

"They do. That girl over there, her father wants to file the police complaint. His name is Simon Court. Heard of him?"

"I've met Simon Court. He's a real estate developer in Los Angeles."

Sage's eyebrows raised with a question.

Michael shrugged. "I submitted an architectural bid for one of his properties. They didn't pick my design, said it was 'too outdoorsy' for his vision."

"You don't look unhappy about that," commented Olivia.

"Nope. People don't have to like my designs. I'd prefer to part as friends at the beginning before we get into contracts. If they don't like what I do after that point, it's tricky to back away without hard feelings and lost revenue."

Isn't he the business professional.

Olivia took his arm and gave it a squeeze. Michael smiled down at her, his eyes bright with appreciation.

By the time they'd made it to the front of the line, only a handful of students stood behind them. "Hey, Olivia," came a familiar voice.

"Brad May," she laughed. "So you work here now?"

"I work where I can, kind of like you," he explained, a blond strand of hair falling over his face as he looked at his clipboard.

"How are things working out for you this week?" Sage

asked, sounding all business.

"Things have been okay. It's only part-time, so I can put up with a lot." Brad looked around, his gaze stopping on a compact man eyeing him from the kitchen entrance. "My boss is pretty uptight." Brad dipped his head toward a stone-faced man who watched him intently.

"And just so we understand each other...no weed on campus," Sage added.

Brad's smile dampened. "Oh right. No weed on campus. I smoke on my off hours. I especially don't distribute here. I can't contribute to the delinquency of minors."

Michael and Olivia burst out laughing. Sage's expression remained serious.

"You can move ahead," Brad told them. "The empty tables are near the door."

Once admitted into the room, Olivia stopped to look up and around. "This isn't your design, is it?" she asked Michael.

"Not mine, but quite nice. Check out all the serving stations."

Sure enough, tables with linen cloths had been arranged around the space so that students could serve themselves, optimizing crowd control. Next to each table was a sign held by a tripod stand.

"Vegan, gluten-free, vegetarian with dairy, baked goods," Olivia read aloud. "When I went to college we had special days. You know, pasta Monday, tuna casserole Tuesday." Olivia began to laugh. "I remember a small salad bar that got skimpier as the week progressed. By Saturday you only had wilted lettuce and a couple of tomatoes to choose from." She turned toward Michael and Sage. "What happened to Thursday hotdogs and Friday mac and cheese?"

Sage laughed. "We're not in culinary Kansas anymore,

Dorothy. Come along, I want you to meet our new chef."

Walking away from the hungry students, Sage pointed to a swinging door on the back wall. Dressed with a hair net and a crisp white shirt, a familiar man stood behind the dirty dish drop-off. Olivia took another look.

"Thomas Seeker got a job here?" Olivia asked incredulously. "I hope he left his camera at home."

"He did," answered Sage. "Mom advocated for him on the condition that he'd not take any photos of the students without permission."

"Is Meadow still dating Seeker after all of their problems?"

Sage sighed. "The heart wants what the heart wants. I think she feels sorry for the guy. You know Mom."

I wonder if the academy board of directors knows that Sage has hired the town weed dealer and the Peeping Thomas of Lily Rock. This could go so wrong in so many ways. Sage has a big heart.

After Thomas Seeker got through the doorway, Sage gestured for Olivia and Michael to follow. She walked up to a man leaning over the vegetarian main serving table, looking at each vegetable. When he stood up, he folded his arms over a chambray shirt, his ice-blue eyes taking them in.

Sage stepped up first. "Cookie, I brought you a couple of friends to meet." She ignored his grim expression.

"I see," he said.

"This is Olivia Greer, she's my sister and bandmate."

He nodded, arms still folded across his chest, eyes surveying the dining room.

"And you know Michael already."

Sage put her hand on the man's shoulder. "This is Charles Kravitz, or Cookie, as we call him. He's our culinary specialist."

Michael reached out his hand to shake. Cookie reluctantly released his arm fold to take Michael's hand. Olivia watched the men, knuckles turning white. *Who's gonna let go first?*

Michael released his hand but not before giving Cookie a cheeky smile.

Olivia sighed.

"Is there any chance I could get a word with you?" a voice from behind Olivia said.

A tall man in joggers and a T-shirt wearing an arrogant grin stood by the kitchen door. He spoke to Sage, who smiled back.

Olivia felt her gut clench. Michael said, "Simon Court? I believe we met in Los Angeles a few years ago."

Court blinked at Michael but then leaned toward Sage, his face flushing. "I don't remember. I came here to talk to the cop. She ducked out of our agreed meeting but must be around here someplace. I'll just talk to you instead!" Court faced Sage. "As head mistress or principal or whatever they call the gal that runs this place, you're doing an abysmal job."

"I'm the academy director," said Sage.

"Yah, well, I'm here to sue you and this school if you don't immediately boot out that kid who assaulted my daughter. She's the soprano for the Tone Rangers and that's that."

"That would not be possible," Sage said politely, ignoring the man's tone bond attitude.

"It's possible if I say it is. I'll be bringing up this situation at an emergency board meeting before parent weekend, just you watch."

Court stomped away, his aura of entitlement palpable.

CHAPTER FOUR

Monday

Over the breakfast table the next day, Olivia stared into Michael's dark eyes. "Do you believe that Simon Court guy? I thought about him all night, the way he threatened Sage and how she didn't say a word in her own defense."

"But she did maneuver him out of the dining room before the students could get involved," commented Michael. "You've got to give her credit for that." His hand engulfed the mug of hot coffee that he held in front of him. He smiled across the table as Olivia waved her hand over the steam coming from her coffee mug.

I feel so at ease with Michael; our early morning coffee connection gets me ready for my day.

She glanced at her kitchen timer.

The muffins must be ready.

Covering her hand with a mitt, Olivia reached into the

oven, pulling out twelve lightly browned muffins. She touched the top of one, smiling in satisfaction.

All done.

She placed the hot pan on the counter. With a rounded metal spatula, she eased two muffins from the tin, taking care not to break away any of the edges.

"The edges are the best part," she told Michael, setting a plate before him.

"Do I smell chocolate chips?" he asked, picking away a crispy part before popping it in his mouth.

"I added pecans to the chocolate chips, your favorite."

She handed him a napkin. They munched in silence until Michael wiped his fingers. Then he took a sip of coffee while Olivia broached the first topic on her mind.

"I liked watching Sage yesterday. She has some skills with irate parents, knowing when to talk but mostly when to keep quiet. I wonder how the argument with Simon Court turned out... I didn't get to talk to her last night. We keep missing each other. In fact, I see less of her now that we live together." Olivia sighed, staring into her coffee mug. "That Curated Cuisine surprised me with all of those food options. And what did you think of the new cook?"

A mischievous smile came to his lips. "Did I win the handshake contest? I think I won the handshake contest... No, I'm sure I won the handshake contest."

"You released first, but he rubbed his red knuckles for a long time. You definitely won. Men are so funny." Olivia smiled.

"And you think women aren't?" Michael responded dryly. Then his grin widened. "But I am glad you were a witness to the handshake win."

Olivia smiled at Michael's playfulness. Then she picked

up her cell phone, which had been lying facedown on the table.

As much fun as it is talking to him, I better get going to work.

"Thanks for coming by this morning, but I have a crabby boss waiting for me at the constabulary."

"Sure, consider me gone." Michael glanced toward Mayor Maguire's empty food bowl. "I wonder what the mayor is up to?"

"No sightings of M&M this morning. For what it's worth, he seems to be hanging with Janis and her cat named Joanie. At least that's what she told me. I found out that Janis is a self-proclaimed cat person."

Michael scratched his head. "How did I not know that?"

It's not just me. Even Michael draws a blank when it comes to Janis Jets's personal life.

"By the way, any idea exactly where Janis lives?"

Michael's brow wrinkled. "Janis just pops up like one of those flat sponges that instantly expand when you add water."

"I feel like a bad friend," admitted Olivia. "Before she hired me at the constabulary, I thought we were close, but now I see I know nothing about her. I mean, when she giggled and showed up in those leather pants, I was really unnerved."

Michael laughed. He dabbed at his mouth with the napkin. "Stop it. You must have known Janis had a personal life. I wouldn't feel bad, she's just a private person."

"I still feel like a bad friend," Olivia said, not persuaded by Michael's logic.

He gulped the rest of his coffee before setting the empty mug back on the table. "I don't feel like a bad friend, just one who minds his own business."

And there you have it, the difference between men and women.

As Michael rinsed his cup in the sink, Olivia looked out the window. "We're having dinner this Saturday, right?"

He turned to face her. "I got the reservation. Don't stand me up again."

Olivia opened the back door. "I'll be ready this time. I heard the food at The Refuge is farm-to-table fantastic."

When Olivia arrived she found the door to the constabulary unlocked. Once inside she walked straight to her desk to tuck her purse into the bottom drawer. She placed her cell phone by the computer.

A text from Janis showed up on her screen.

I'm in my office.

Me too.

Then she began where she left off the day before. Most of the paperwork had already been sorted. She shuffled through all but the last, whose letterhead caught her attention: Riverside County Sheriff's Department.

Dear Ms. Jets, Thank you for applying to the job of chief of police. We look forward to your interview scheduled on Monday.

Olivia's heart pounded in her chest. She immediately jumped to conclusions.

Janis is leaving Lily Rock. Unthinkable!

Swallowing back the lump in her throat, she nervously slid the paper back and forth on the slick desktop.

Now that I've read that letter, should I confront Janis or pretend I didn't see it? I am her assistant, not her friend, at least for now. Maybe that's why Janis went against her better judgement and hired me. When the next police chief arrives, they may want to let me go and hire a new permanent assistant. This has happened before in other temp jobs.

She looked at the paper, holding back every instinct to crumple it into a ball and toss it in the wastepaper basket.

Pulling a fresh manila file from her desk drawer, she filed the paper inside and then shoved it back into the drawer.

Maybe that will take care of it. Janis will assume she didn't get an interview and forget the whole thing. Olivia's head began to throb.

Too easy. This paper probably is a follow-up to a previous email.

Closing the drawer with the thrust of her right foot, she looked up in time to see a person standing in the doorway. Olivia swallowed back her irritation.

He's like spoiled milk. Enough to make me gag.

Simon Court stared her down and then looked around the room, taking in the small table in the corner, the four chairs, and the plain walls. "Kind of simple here," he said, "not unlike the rest of the town."

He's looking for trouble, I just feel it. Stay calm, Olivia.

"How can I help you?" she asked, remaining seated behind her desk.

Court's head swiveled back to stare at her. "I'm here to file a complaint with the chief of police."

"Are you speaking for yourself or on behalf of a client?" asked Olivia politely.

He might be an attorney. How would I know?

Court responded in a curt voice. "None of your business, is it? You're just the secretary."

That would be administrative assistant, you conde-scending dumb-ass.

Gulping back annoyance, Olivia kept her voice neutral. She reached into the middle drawer of her desk. "Here is a form. You can sit over there to fill it out." She clipped the paper to a board and gestured with her head toward the corner where the small table stood empty.

"Get me the chief first. I don't have time to dillydally around here. I'm heading back down the hill right away for an important conference. Like I said, call the chief."

She smiled, ignoring his tone of voice. Picking up her cell phone, she texted Janis.

Simon Court is here to see you.

Be right there.

The doors swished behind Olivia as Janis Jets stepped through. She walked closer to Olivia's desk, resting her left hand on the corner. "How can I help you today, Mr. Court?"

"You didn't show up yesterday, so I didn't have a chance to express my personal grievance at the bodily harm inflicted upon my daughter right at her own school."

"I did try to find you later," explained Janis, "but you were out smoking cigars with Charles Kravitz. At least that's what I was told when I asked one of those Tone Rangers. I didn't want to interrupt an important consult."

Olivia gulped. *Does he even know she's insulting him?*

"I've heard men need bonding time," Janis added without a glimpse of a smile.

Good for you, boss.

Court rocked back on his heels. He selected his next words carefully. "You can't treat me this way. I warn you."

"I guess I can treat you however I choose," said Jets, "'cause I already did. I'm a busy woman and I've forgotten the details of your complaint. Why don't you write everything down on that paper and I'll get to it when I have a minute."

Court's voice hissed in response. "How about hell no. I'm not filling out any form. You listen to me and you listen very carefully. My daughter Abbey was assaulted by another student and you'd better do something about it now, or I'll make a few phone calls and that school and this town are going down.

"My daughter took a photo." Court reached into his pocket, then found the picture on his cell. "Look at her cheek." He handed the phone over to Janis. She stared and then handed it to Olivia, who looked for herself and then handed the phone back.

Janis explained as if to a child. "Okay, the photo is of concern, if it's for real. But it only takes some makeup and lighting, and the whole thing might be Photoshopped. I can take this to my experts to determine its validity, but it might take several weeks. Were there other live witnesses, like the person who supposedly took this shot?"

Court's voice rose. "Her entire quartet was there. The other two will give testimony to her abuse!"

A slow smile came over Janis's face. She leaned toward him. "That may be, Mr. Court. But I'd check with them before you stick your neck out. According to my sources, the other two are just as angry with Abbey and they thought the smack was justified. So you see, your witnesses may be construed as collaborators, if you get my drift."

"This is an outrage! Those simple-minded teenagers don't know the trouble they're in now. My daughter is the only truly qualified one of the four. I should know, I'm on the admission board to the Lily Rock Music Academy."

"What do you mean truly qualified?" Olivia jumped in. "All of those kids have talent and grades."

Janis glared at Olivia, holding her mouth tightly closed.

I should have kept my mouth shut.

Court took a step closer to the desk. Leaning over, he sneered into Olivia's face. "You have no idea how kids get accepted into private high schools. It takes grades, talent, and clout. I'm the clout behind every music student in the Tone Rangers. I have guided their parents on the trajectory of their children's education from kindergarten through high school. My families get into the best colleges, with early acceptance, ahead of everyone else."

"Is that so?" Olivia muttered, looking at her desk to avoid his intimidating gaze.

"According to my source, your daughter is quite talented," mused Janis Jets aloud. "She's the leader of the Tone Rangers and throws her weight around. I wonder where she learned to do that?"

"I mentor Abbey every way I can," Court said.

Olivia kept her eyes fixed on her desk, waiting for Janis to reply.

As if deflated by his own words, Court took a deep breath. "I've changed my mind. We won't file charges this time. But I warn you, if it happens again, that music academy will be removed from the list of elite high schools, and you won't have any students by the time I'm done. I have—"

Janis interrupted, "I know, you have clout. We get it. But if there isn't anything else, I need to get back to work."

Court huffed in disgust. He spun on his heel and left the constabulary.

Janis immediately turned and spoke to Olivia. "He threatens a lot, have you noticed?"

"I think he might be as influential as he says, and it worries me."

Janis dismissed Olivia's opinion. "Oh, he's all bluff and no bite." Then as if reconsidering she asked, "What exactly are you worried about?"

"Mostly about Sage and her job," admitted Olivia. "The new academy board of directors, with Simon Court as president, may fire Sage and find another director. I'm also worried about the Court-Kravitz connection. Do you think they're pals? Maybe Cookie uses their cigar moments to share gossip about the school."

Janis shook her head in disgust. "Come on, what would Cookie have to tell the likes of Simon Court? He could out a vegan to his mommy, I suppose. That would make headlines. Music Academy arrests student who eats an egg."

"People are allergic to certain foods," insisted Olivia. "Some people are lactose intolerant or have celiac disease and can't digest gluten. Not everyone eats meat. You shouldn't be so snarky about food issues...or gender identification either," retorted Olivia.

"Blah, blah, blah. I'm so tired of everyone having a special diet that they talk about on and on. I like people who eat what they eat and who keep their upset stomachs to themselves."

In your day parents didn't shell out fifty grand for high school tuition every year. They have a right to ask for special diets.

Annoyance rose in Janis's voice. "From the special diets to the special gender, I don't know why I even keep trying here in Lily Rock. I'm feeling more and more that I don't fit, at least not like I used to. I can't even get the right pronoun, let alone give a damn about someone's culinary selections. Give me a break."

Janis spun around as the glass doors swished open. She took a quick exit, mumbling to herself.

I get it now. Janis doesn't feel appreciated in Lily Rock. No wonder she's looking for another job.

Later Olivia locked up the constabulary and walked toward her parked car. Once behind the steering wheel, she texted Sage. On my way for our band rehearsal. See you in ten.

Olivia turned the key in the ignition.

I wonder what the beef is with those Tone Ranger kids... Could Abbey's forceful leadership be putting them on edge, or has Legend's new idea actually put the a cappella group off balance?

The winding roads and the smell of pine helped calm Olivia's nerves. She rolled down her driver's side window, the breeze brushing past her face. By the time she parked in the faculty lot, she felt much better. Once inside the double doors of the auditorium, she spotted Sage opening her fiddle case.

"I'm here," called Sage. She stood down front near the piano.

Olivia walked down the middle aisle.

"How are you?" she asked Sage first.

"Doing fine," Sage answered, her voice sounding anything but fine.

Olivia took a deep breath. "I've been thinking on the drive over, so before I forget, I have an idea. What if I help out this afternoon with your students, starting with the

Tone Rangers? I'm curious how they sound. Are they as good as they think they are?"

Sage nodded. "Sure, that can be arranged. I can introduce you as guest faculty. You can listen to them and coach. Give a master class to brainstorm music ideas. I can't pay you though, until your contract is cleared with the board of directors."

"Not necessary." Olivia smiled. "Simon Court..." Her voice trailed off.

I almost told her about his threatening behavior at the constabulary. But now that I'm an employee, it may be a breach of confidentiality.

Sage prodded her. "You were saying about Simon?"

"He's kind of a character," Olivia said.

"You were there in the cafeteria. It's like he's searching for any excuse to start a fight. I actually ran into him on the hiking trail this morning. He's a fast runner, I'll give him that. At this altitude he's in excellent shape."

"Was he wearing one of his jogging outfits?" asked Olivia with a smile. "He doesn't dress the part of big executive. Worn athletic shoes, along with joggers and a T-shirt. I would have thought he'd dress to impress."

"At least he's not a poser," laughed Sage. "He's a good runner. Like I said, I saw him myself."

Olivia agreed. "I'm not surprised he's an athlete. Being in good shape, that would explain his high energy."

"A moving target is harder to hit." Sage smiled.

Olivia looked around the auditorium. "Where are the guys?"

"Dave texted. He's caught in traffic coming up the hill."

"And Paul?"

"He's vaping behind the building."

"I'm here," called the bass player from the back of the

auditorium. "It will just take me a minute to set up." He strode toward the stage.

"I'm here too," added Dave from the side door closest to the parking lot. "Man, so many motorcycles this morning coming up the hill. Sorry I'm late."

"Don't worry. Sage and I never see each other at home, so we had time to catch up."

Sliding her bow across the strings, Sage began to tune. Olivia soon joined, humming under her breath. After her voice warmed up, she began singing. By that time Paul joined with his bass. Only Dave paused to listen, his hands suspended over a large conga drum.

When Olivia eased off the last note, Dave spoke. "You have an amazing voice. Every time I hear you sing my heart rises up to my throat. Reminds me of when I'd go to confession as a kid. I want to tell you everything I've ever done or said."

"I've been told people want to confess when they hear me sing," Olivia admitted. "I don't understand how that works. I guess it goes into the category of blessing and curse."

"Her superpower," Sage added. "If you like that sort of thing."

Dave laughed. "I'm not sure if I like it or not, but I sure feel the urge to get everything off my chest."

They were interrupted by the sound of voices bickering.

"I'm not going to do any new arrangements before we audition for early admission," came a shrill voice from the back of the auditorium.

"New arrangements would only improve our chances. I'm telling you we'll stand out and get early admission if you'd only be more flexible," came another voice.

Sage looked at Olivia. "I invited the Tone Rangers to

listen to our rehearsal." Then she turned to Dave and Paul to explain. "Afterward Olivia's gonna work with them for a bit. You're welcome to stay."

"I'll stay," said Paul immediately. "Do I get to eat dinner at the omnivore table afterward?"

"I'm a pescatarian myself," said Dave. "But I'd like to stay."

"Pescatarian?" asked Sage.

"I don't eat meat, but I do eat fish."

"A throwback to your Catholic fish-on-Friday days?"

"As a matter of fact, yes. My parents were pretty religious and we always ate fish sticks on Friday night."

As the voices grew louder, Abbey Court's could be heard over the others. "Come on, we're here to listen, remember."

As usual, Anais followed right behind Abbey as they made their way toward the stage.

"We don't have all day!" Sage urged the students.

Legend wore a long skirt and a button-down shirt, with scuffed hiking boots. Raleigh also wore a maxi skirt with a small pattern of roses.

I wonder if they coordinate their outfits. I used to call my girlfriend the night before when I was in high school. Sometimes we'd trade. Marla loved that lavender sweater of mine. In some ways high school hasn't changed that much.

CHAPTER FIVE

Tuesday

After her cleanup the day before, Olivia started work with a sense of confidence. She took time to admire her tidy desktop, her polished computer, and her cell phone waiting close at hand.

I beat Janis to work. I know, I'll make coffee. Yay me!

In the back room, she poured water into the reservoir of the coffee maker. She scooped fresh grounds into the basket, measuring out a full ten scoops with her plastic spoon. After some jiggling, the basket filled with coffee slipped into place. She tapped the On button. All of these automatic actions gave her time to think about yesterday afternoon.

Once Sage agreed that Olivia would make a good music coach, she'd wasted no time telling the Tone Rangers about the master class.

At first they reminded her of cats, circling and rubbing against each other. Claws showed right from the start.

"My name is Anais," the youngest told Olivia, shyly ducking her head.

"You're the alto, right?"

"That's right. I'm not very good, but I've been working with a voice coach."

"I sing alto too, or at least that's the register where my voice is most comfortable. What are your pronouns?" Olivia was pleased that she remembered to ask.

A light smile crossed Anais's lips. "Oh, I'm cisgender. I identify as she/her, but that's no big deal, you can call me whatever works for you."

Abbey walked forward, standing between Olivia and Anais. "I hear you're running a master class for us. What makes you think that you qualify as an a cappella coach? You're an autoharp player, at least that's what I heard."

Olivia glanced away from Abbey, giving herself time to brush off the insult.

"Since I was already on campus, Ms. McCloud invited me to coach the Tone Rangers this afternoon. With the parent weekend performance coming up, she thought you could use a good polish with a professional musician."

"Whatever," Abbey said. "Maybe you can tell that she/her over there that falsetto will bring us way down with the judges. We're not the Bee Gees after all."

"We could cover the Bee Gees," argued Legend. She stood near the piano, looking over a music score. Legend held up sheets with handwritten notes. "I've worked it all out right here. Shift the melody to the falsetto voice, bring the harmonies closer together, and we'd have a new sound, a chance to be memorable, not just mundane."

"'How Deep Is Your Love'," said Olivia, the corner of her mouth turning up. "You could cover that song and it might work."

"That's exactly what I've been telling you," insisted Legend. "We can't sing Indigo Girls forever."

Legend folded the music sheets and made her way toward Olivia. The mid-calf flowered skirt flowed around slim legs. She had small breasts under her peasant-style blouse. Unlike Anais, Legend stood to her full height, shoulders back with chest thrust out, proud of her appearance.

The fourth Tone Ranger sat in their seat, waiting for Olivia to take notice. When she did, they smiled tentatively.

"Hi, Raleigh," Olivia opened the conversation. "You sing tenor. Do you have an opinion about the music arrangements?"

"I think—"

"Who cares what they think?" Abbey interrupted. "I'm the lead singer. I make the music choices. And I say we stick with traditional voicing."

"How about we talk later, when we can find some time?" She smiled at Raleigh, who ducked their head back to the cell phone they held in one hand.

"Why don't you four sing for me," Olivia suggested. "Then I can hear and see how you work together." She placed a chair in front of the piano, gesturing with her hand. "I'll sit here. You form a semicircle and warm up. I'm all ears."

A chuckle came from behind the piano. Olivia peeked around to find Dave Franco sitting with Paul George. Dave gave her a thumbs-up.

"You guys stayed for the master class. I wasn't sure you really meant it earlier. Now is the time for feedback, before we get too much closer to the recital. Let me know if I miss anything."

The Tone Rangers stood in a semicircle. Abbey counted them off, "One, two, one, two, three, four."

Anais sang first. "I'm tryin' to tell you something about my life."

She sang with more confidence than she spoke, the first line of the Indigo Girls's hit, "Closer to Fine".

The coffeepot stopped sputtering, bringing Olivia back to the present. She could still hear the Tone Rangers singing in her head as she filled her mug.

They're good, really good. The master class went well. I actually enjoyed working with them.

The hot burner sizzled as she replaced the carafe.

Olivia walked down the hall, heading to the reception room. Past the sliding glass doors, she sat behind her desk. The computer, booted up and ready, showed Mayor Maguire's face. "Welcome to Lily Rock," the sign above his head read.

She found herself humming the Tone Rangers song again.

There's something about yesterday's master class that's intriguing me—not so much about the music, more about the social dynamic. Mostly about Abbey's tone of superiority, and how Anais and Raleigh didn't even get an opinion.

Olivia clicked on her email. Before she could read any messages, she heard the front door open. To her surprise Anais Butler came through the door. Her shoulders slightly slumped, she made her way to stand in front of Olivia's desk. She spoke in a hesitant voice, her eyes looking to the right corner of the room instead of at Olivia.

"Hello," Anais said.

"Can I help you?" asked Olivia.

"I hope so." She said.

"I wanted to mention this yesterday, but I didn't have the courage...you know, with Abbey there."

"It is difficult to get a word in edgewise with Abbey."

Olivia nodded in agreement. "Do you want to bring over a chair? We can talk now."

Anais shook her head. "No, I don't want a big conversation. I want to drop out of the Tone Rangers, but I'm afraid to tell Abbey."

That's it! That's what my mind has been circling. I sensed her unhappiness. The problem is that if Anais quits the group, then all of the Tone Rangers will suffer. They will be one alto short of an early admission.

Olivia walked around the desk to stand in front of the girl. "I think this conversation requires us to sit down, so let's go to the break room. I can get you some coffee or water."

Anais shrugged. "I guess so," she said reluctantly.

"Let's go," Olivia said before Anais could change her mind.

The glass doors, activated by the sensor, slid open. Anais followed Olivia as the doors swished closed behind them.

Once she'd settled Anais into a chair in the break room, Olivia poured herself another cup of coffee. When the girl's eyes followed her actions she asked, "Do you drink coffee?"

"Not me," said Anais. "Abbey would kill me. She says it's bad for the vocal cords."

"I've never heard that one before. I know smoking is bad, but I had no idea about coffee." She took a long sip just to prove her point. "Water then? There's some sparkling in the refrigerator. Help yourself."

The girl didn't get up. Instead she crossed her right leg over her left.

Thrust into the new role of teen counselor, Olivia took the seat across from Anais. "So why would you quit the Tone Rangers? You have a strong voice and you sing on pitch, perfect for a cappella."

Anais hid a smile. "That's nice of you to say. It's just the Tone Rangers are way too good for me. They're all going someplace. I just sing for fun. I'm not even sure if I want to go to college, let alone get early acceptance."

Olivia felt confused. "Just for clarification, why would your parents send you to such an expensive high school if you're not sure about college?"

"My parents don't care what I do after high school. It's my grandparents who want me to go to college. They have a big emotional investment in my future. Gran didn't get to go to university, and Granddad dropped out to make money for his family."

"I see. Will any of your family be here for parent weekend?"

"That's why I want to get this decision out in the open as soon as possible. My grandparents will be here, and I thought you could tell Ms. McCloud and then it would be done."

Olivia sat back in her chair, taking a long look at the teen.

"You say it's your idea to quit, but I wonder if there isn't some other motivation."

Tears formed in her eyes. "Abbey is so critical. She never compliments me about my singing. I know I'll pull her down and she won't get early acceptance, and then it will be all my fault." Anais sniffed, rubbing the back of her hand over her eyes like a small child.

"Abbey is critical," admitted Olivia. "But she's critical of everyone, not just you. I worry more about Legend quitting. She's the one Abbey is out to get."

A big sigh escaped the teen's lips. "We may get through the recital on Friday, but once Legend gets her way, then

Abbey will turn on me. I'll be next. I'd rather quit before that happens."

Once Legend gets her way...

Olivia placed her arms on the table. She leaned forward, her voice filled with persuasion. "How about this idea? I'll work with you on a few issues—the quality and volume of your voice. We have some time before parent weekend. Then when your grandparents come, you can talk to them, if you still want to quit. I think you have a confidence problem, not a musical one. What do you think?"

"I don't want to upset my grandparents. They show up for everything," admitted Anais. "They also pay my tuition. But I guess your idea makes sense."

"I'm happy we had this talk," Olivia said. "But now I have to get back to work. Don't you have classes?"

Anais stood. " I have one free absence before it affects my grade. Thanks for your help." She smiled at Olivia.

"Hold on a minute. I'll walk down the hall with you," said Olivia. She rinsed her coffee mug. Anais followed her back to the reception room in silence.

"See you at rehearsal," she called after her.

Anais walked toward the door. "Bye, Olivia."

Sitting behind her desk, she checked her phone—a missed call from Janis Jets.

She touched the name on her redial list.

"Are you at the constabulary?" came Janis's demanding voice.

"Been here for over an hour," answered Olivia serenely.

"I've got some business down the hill. Will be back after lunch, anything to report?"

"Nothing going on here."

"Not even a guy filing an assault form on behalf of his daughter?"

"You mean Simon Court? I haven't seen him." Olivia clicked on her computer to check email. "Nor has Court filed anything electronically, so far as I can see."

"Maybe he feels better now that he's threatened us. All bark no bite, that's my take."

"I don't quite agree," said Olivia. "I think he bites when your back is turned. Just saying."

"I can see that," said Janis.

She didn't argue with me?

"Just so you know," Olivia said, "I'm heading up to the academy during my lunch break. I'll have my cell phone if you need anything."

"Okay then, see you later." Janis Jets ended the conversation.

If I weren't her employee, I'd ask her what's wrong. We'd go out for a meal and talk it through like we used to. But now I can't cross that boundary.

Olivia poked her head into the music academy office. She glanced at the empty row of chairs against the wall. *No one in trouble this time.* Even the three doors in front of her remained closed, giving the reception area an eerie quiet.

Olivia noted the signs near each inner door. "Sage McCloud, Academy Director" looked the oldest, the edges of the plaque slightly tarnished. "Rydell Cox, Academy Guidance Counselor" looked newer, the brass plaque still shiny. On the right side of Rydell Cox, an empty sign had been left, indicating a vacant room.

Much to Olivia's surprise, the middle door suddenly flung open, revealing a compact man in his early forties wearing a put-together navy suit.

Is he actually wearing a wool blend in this climate?

The man's necktie screamed expensive silk, and the diamond-studded tie clip spoke dollars and cents. Olivia gulped.

"May I help you?" asked the self-important man.

"I'm looking for my sister." She pointed to Sage's closed office door. "I'm Olivia Greer," she added.

Perfectly straight white teeth smiled at her. "Oh, you're the one who did the master class yesterday with the Tone Rangers. We haven't met." He extended his hand, engulfing hers with his own.

"Is Sage around?" Olivia looked toward the principal's door.

"She's at the Curated Cuisine with the students," he explained. "I'll give you a campus tour and show you the way."

She turned to Cox. "Actually I've been here many times. Is giving tours in your job description?"

He stood back, eyes appraising her carefully. "Keeping the students safe is my highest priority."

She felt the hair raise on her neck. Before she could respond, Rydell Cox walked across the room. He turned the doorknob, then stepped back and held the door for her.

Without directions Olivia headed toward the path leading to the main campus. It wasn't until she turned to see if Cox followed her that she felt a familiar nudge at her knee. Mayor Maguire waved his tail in greeting.

"Hey, M&M. Long time no see." The dog circled her feet and then stopped at her left leg, sitting down and waiting for her next move.

"He's your dog?" asked Cox.

"Kind of," commented Olivia, "at least for now." She patted his head, feeling the usual calm she experienced in the dog's presence.

Cox picked up the conversation. "Sage has taken on a lot of responsibility as principal and head teacher at the Lily Rock academy. She's done a good job so far and I'm grateful that the new board of directors offered me a contract. I think my hiring may be a sign that the academy is moving up the prep school tier here in California."

"If they're moving up, as you say, it's because of Sage's hard work," commented Olivia dryly.

Cox clenched his jaw. "Oh of course, Sage's work, but it may be time to pass the baton. That's what I'm picking up from the board of directors. Time to give up some of her control and let a real professional take charge."

"I'm wondering why you're telling me all of this," she asked.

"So you can pave the way," he promptly replied. "I've tried to warn Sage, but she won't listen. She jumps from project to project and doesn't give me time to present my case."

Olivia gulped. "This is a conversation for the school board to have with Sage," she told him firmly. "But I wonder why you're so eager to push my sister aside, you being new here and all."

Rydell Cox waved Olivia off with his hand. "Oh no, I meant no harm. I'm just a visionary. I see the future and I wanted to give you a heads-up, along with your sister, of course."

The conversation stopped as they approached the open doors of the Curated Cuisine. Brad May stood with clipboard in hand, just as he had before.

"Hey, Olivia," Brad drawled, ignoring Cox. "Sage is in the kitchen."

Cox looked Brad up and down, reaching out to snatch the clipboard. He examined the list. "You're supposed to check off the students who have eaten lunch," he grumbled, flipping to the next page, "or breakfast. How long have you neglected proper notation?"

Brad smiled. "If someone doesn't belong at the academy, I know right away."

"But you have to keep track of every meal. We charge by the plan and when students go over their month's allotment, we charge extra. It's your job to keep track."

"I'm not a computer," mumbled Brad.

Mayor Maguire took the opportunity to leave Olivia's side to sniff a piece of food on the sidewalk.

"That dog isn't allowed in the food area," Cox insisted.

Both Brad and Olivia laughed.

"I'm sure M&M isn't allowed, but he's always welcome." She walked through the entrance with the dog right by her side.

She left Cox behind, hearing his voice lecturing Brad on the finer points of checking people off a list.

"Come on, doggo," Olivia called to M&M. "Let's find Sage."

Only a dozen or so students stood at the serving tables, piling food on their plates. Olivia noticed all four of the Tone Rangers sitting at a separate table in the back of the room. Instead of stopping to chat, she focused on the swinging cafe doors that led into the kitchen. Sage's voice caught her attention first.

The doors smacked against Olivia's back as the mayor slid underneath. Cookie Kravitz looked over as Sage continued to talk to him, her voice filled with laughter.

Cookie tapped Sage's shoulder and then leaned over to whisper in her ear. Sage laughed again. "You crack me up," she told the man.

He's quite the charmer, Olivia noted.

Today Cookie wore carefully tailored jeans and a snug-fitting shirt the exact color of his blue eyes. "Hey, guys," Olivia called out. Sage smiled in her direction.

"Janis released you for lunch," she observed. Walking around the counter, Sage reached out her arms to give Olivia a hug, leaning down to pat Mayor Maguire's head.

"She did. Looks like you've already eaten." Olivia pointed to an empty bowl on the kitchen counter.

"Oh no, Cookie was sharing his recipe for split pea soup. He used to work at the White House as a chef."

"My secret ingredient helps," Cookie said. "Let me get you a sample and see if you can figure out what I add that's different."

Olivia's stomach growled. "Great. I'm hungry. Bring on the soup."

Standing over a large kettle at the center counter, Cookie dipped in a ladle, coming back with a thick green liquid that he tipped into a nearby bowl. Reaching under the counter he grabbed a hunk of bread, which he placed on another plate.

"Here you go, tell me what you think," he said, setting the bowl and plate before Olivia.

Olivia didn't need to be asked twice. She took a nearby spoon and lifted some of the green contents to her lips. A fusion of vegetables and warmth hit her mouth. "This is amazing soup," she declared at once. "I thought I didn't like pea soup until this." She took another spoonful.

"It's the secret ingredient," Cookie assured her. "My grandma taught me and I've never told anyone else." He looked down at Olivia's feet, nodding to Mayor Maguire. "How about a chunk of bread, doggie?" Cookie pulled a sizable piece off the loaf, tossing it to the dog, who caught the offering in the air.

Sage clapped. "Well done, Mayor Maguire."

Olivia held up her last bite of bread. "And if I'm not mistaken, this is a freshly baked baguette."

"Yep, I bake every morning."

Olivia nodded, her mouth full of delicious goodness.

"I've got to go now," Cookie said, "but be sure to stop in any time, you two." He glanced at both sisters with his intense blue eyes before turning toward the back counter.

"He's a good hire," Olivia commented as she accompanied Sage out the back door.

"He certainly is. I got his name from the new guidance counselor. Cookie was by far the most qualified applicant."

"I met Rydell Cox. He talked nonstop about the school."

"He does go on a bit. I don't know how I feel about him yet."

Olivia looked down at her side. Mayor Maguire trotted next to her left knee as stray bread crumbs dropped from his chest fur to the ground. She felt tempted to tell Sage what she thought about Cox. But then she stopped herself from speaking.

For once I'm going to mind my own business.

CHAPTER SIX

Wednesday

At the constabulary the next day, Olivia felt restless. By
11:30 her stomach growled. *Is it too early for lunch or am I
just bored?*

Before she could decide, Janis walked through from the
back. She stared at Olivia and then shook her head. "You
look like a teenager from the music academy," she muttered.
"Shorts and those boots, not exactly professional."

"Do you want to check my homework?" Olivia turned
toward her computer.

"It's been dull in the office since you arrived. I have to
admit I thought you'd bring more chaos, but so far it's gotten
calmer. Why don't you go ahead and have an early lunch?
I'll text you any issues that come up."

"Why thank you, Officer Jets. I assume you meant that
as a compliment, me not bringing any more chaos."

"I guess I did." Jets shrugged.

The phone in Janis's hand lit up, giving Olivia the chance to lean closer just in case she could catch the name on the screen.

Aware of Olivia's interest, Janis Jets quickly held the phone to her ear. "Yep. Okay. Sounds good. Tonight then." Janis let out a high-pitched giggle. "You're incorrigible..."

Janis is blushing. I don't believe it. First the giggle and now this!

Removing the phone from her ear, Janis held it against her khaki pants, screen side away from Olivia's keen gaze. Then she patted her hair with the other hand.

She's the one who looks like a teenager primping for her gentleman caller.

The cell phone buzzed again. This time the ringtone caught Olivia's attention. "You're the one that I want...ooh, ooh, ooh."

A song from Grease? *Really?*

Janis looked at the screen with a smile, nestling it back to her left ear. She didn't speak. Olivia could hear a male voice on the other end of the connection, but not so clearly that she could distinguish who had brought the smile to her boss's lips.

Janis walked past the sliding glass door toward the back rooms, still holding the cell phone to her ear.

Olivia shut down her computer, heading to the front entrance.

I'll pick up a sandwich and eat on a bench in the park. The weather is beautiful.

Once outside she walked briskly down the boardwalk, dodging the gaggle of tourists that was seemingly unaware of blocking the street and walkways. Stepping to one side, Olivia said, "Excuse me," even though she didn't mean it.

As she passed by she heard, "Look at the cute fur cap." A

mother pointed to a window of the Lily Rock Mercantile. Her small son feigned interest as a strawberry ice cream dripped down his wrist onto the boardwalk.

Olivia ducked right to avoid a woman with two toy poodles. The dogs were dressed as sailors, with matching striped T-shirts and red scarves.

The residents of Lily Rock had varying degrees of impatience with the tourists who frequented the town. The most irritating part about visitors was that they walked in the middle of the street, stopping wherever they were to chat and appreciate the quaint village vibe.

In order to keep civil, most of the Lily Rock residents affixed permanent grins on their faces when going about their daily business, especially on weekends. The smiles dropped away as soon as they stepped inside a familiar shop or eatery. That was when the complaining would begin.

"Hey, Olivia," Suzanne greeted her from the pickup window of the Village Pie Shoppe. "The tourists are particularly ghastly today, don't you think?"

Olivia rested her arms on the outdoor counter of the takeout window. "Just ghastly," she imitated Suzanne's use of words and inflection. She leaned into the takeout window, her smile dropping as she rubbed her cheeks with her fingers. "I thought my face would freeze there for a moment. Lots of tourists today. Is there a prize being handed out for the best dog costume?"

Suzanne smirked. "So you saw the poodles? I'm sure Mayor Maguire is hiding. He doesn't like dogs in matching attire."

"I didn't realize the mayor had an opinion about canine dress, but I'm willing to agree." Before Olivia could give her order, she heard someone clear their throat from behind. Olivia turned around.

"Hey, Thomas," she greeted the man, noticing that his black hat lay flat on his head, making him look more like a mid-century undertaker than a photographer. His camera bag, slung over his shoulder, bumped against his thin body.

"I have a job and I'm in a hurry," Seeker's lips pursed.

"You can go ahead of me," offered Olivia. "But aren't you working through the lunch hour at the academy?"

"It's my day off. I work Friday through Tuesday," Seeker stepped neatly in front of her.

"I'm happy you found a part-time job. Since I've got a long lunch hour, feel free to go ahead."

"Thanks," said Seeker. He reached his hand up to tip his hat.

I wonder if he's still sneaking around taking photos of young women?

When Seeker finished his order he stepped aside, making way for Olivia. She nodded to him, leaning into the window. Suzanne stood ready with her tablet and stylus pen. "One vegetarian sandwich on whole wheat, with a bottled water," Olivia said. She paid Suzanne and then stood to the side to wait with Thomas Seeker.

"I wanted to tell you, the Sweet Four O'Clock concert last week was fantastic," Seeker said. "I took some photos, and if it's all right with you, I'd like to submit a few to the *Lily Rock Gazette*."

"Look at you, asking my permission," said Olivia. "I give my full approval for you to submit them to the local press. Thanks, Thomas."

The awkward man reached into his camera bag. He pulled out a business card and handed it to Olivia. "Meadow helped me design the new card," he said proudly. On the front was Seeker's contact information. On the back he'd written, "Fun Photos Upon Request."

Olivia pointed to the back. "Is that your new brand?"

"Yep, that's the one Meadow helped me with," he said. "She thinks I can stay out of trouble if I ask people instead of, you know, how I used to do things before."

That Meadow. She sees the best in everyone and gives people second chances too.

"Thomas Seeker," called Suzanne, shoving a box across the takeout counter. Seeker stepped forward, lifting his hat one more time in Olivia's direction.

After he hurried away, she stepped up to the empty window and leaned in. "I assume I'm next," she called out to Suzanne's retiring back. In a minute the young woman returned with her order, the paid receipt pinned to the top with a toothpick.

"Here you go," Suzanne said, sliding the box toward Olivia. Then she reached down, pulling up a water bottle. "And here's the drink," she added, plunking it on the counter.

Olivia took her food in one hand and the water in the other as she made her way across the street to the park. Recently redesigned benches lined the winding paved paths, shaded by carefully tended giant sequoias.

Just a few years ago, after some behind-the-scenes negotiations, the park land had been leveled. Only the stately trees remained. The Old Rockers hired two famous arborists to assess the health of the sequoias and to recommend care. The town council approved a request for new rail fences to be built in order to keep people away and from trampling the root systems of the precious trees. The short rail fences allowed an easy view of the trees but blocked access to foot traffic.

The trees had been neglected for years. It wasn't until they built the park that the sequoias started looking healthier; to keep them that way, the Old Rockers had provided signage: "Keep away from the trees and stay behind the fences."

Olivia sat on an empty wooden bench, placing her takeout container on her lap. She lifted her sandwich from the box, overhearing loud voices. Looking over her right shoulder she saw Simon Court in his usual nondescript running garb. He sat next to none other than Cookie Kravitz.

Olivia scooted to the end of her bench.

Maybe I can hear what they're saying.

"Thanks for getting away from campus during lunchtime."

"Not a problem. I left the place in capable hands." Kravitz's voice carried the best.

"Did you get my email?"

"I did, that's why I wanted to talk to you. I think you're right, Court, there are some conditions that need improvement at the academy. Sage doesn't expect enough from the students and babies them when they bring her excuses. That wouldn't happen in the military, I can tell you."

"Not happening under my supervision either," said Court. "The Tone Rangers will get early acceptance because I've directed their lives and promised their parents. It's up to us to make sure that happens."

"You must care a lot about the next generation to take on four random teens," replied Cookie.

"Oh, I get paid, believe me."

"So you have more of an investment than I thought, not just because you're Abbey's father."

"Abbey takes care of herself. My job is to make sure her a cappella group is the best, so I make it happen for the other three. I contact parents and explain how I work. They meet my asking price too, which leads to my need for this conversation."

Olivia took the last bite of her sandwich, her mind tumbling with information. *Does Sage know about Court soliciting help from the academy cook? It feels like Cookie is spying on the students.*

As she crumpled her bag into a ball, Court continued to talk in a loud voice. "I want you to send me regular texts about how the kids are doing. And then make sure those kids are happy with the right food. They're a picky bunch, I have to admit." He took something from his pocket. "Here's the key I told you about. Keep it safe. I'll leave a bag with the items for you to use when necessary."

"Got it," said Kravitz, who took the offered key, shoving it into one of the loose pockets of his cargo pants.

Olivia stopped chewing. Spotting a trash can behind the benches, she slowly stood up so as not to attract attention.

If I throw my stuff into that bin, I bet I can hear them better. Of course, I risk being seen.

She walked a short distance, taking deliberate steps to keep out of sight behind their backs. When she reached the trash can, she looked over to the bench where they sat.

They're gone. What's that on the ground?

Olivia dropped her trash into the can and then walked closer to the bench where Court and Kravitz previously sat.

Something shiny sparkled in the dirt beneath the bench. She bent over to retrieve a key and a key ring. Slipping the ring over her index finger, she walked briskly away.

This must be what Court handed Cookie. When he stood up the key must have fallen out of his pocket without him realizing.

. . .

Back at the constabulary Olivia put her purse in the bottom drawer of her desk and then briefly checked her email. One request for a public gathering at the park caught her eye. She forwarded the form to Janis Jets for final approval. When the form did not come right back, Olivia took a moment to process.

I need an excuse to talk to Janis about her odd behavior.

She stared down. The key in her hand looked small, more like a locker key than one for a door. Olivia turned it over in her fingers.

This is my excuse!

She found her boss sitting behind her desk talking on her cell phone.

"Gotta go. Someone wants me." Janis clicked off the cell. "What's up?" she asked Olivia.

Olivia held out the key with the ring attached, then dropped it on Janis's desk. "I found this under a bench in the park while I was eating lunch."

I'm not telling her about Court and Kravitz. We both can keep secrets.

"And..." Janis asked, her tight mouth indicating impatience.

"Do we have a place to put lost items?"

"We do. In your bottom drawer," Janis said as if speaking to a child. "Take out your purse and put the key there, why don't you. Any other burning questions?"

"Are you dating someone new?" Olivia blurted, her eyes wide.

"And that's any of your business because..."

"I thought we were friends and you might want to, you know, share a little with me."

Janis's jaw tightened. "I do have some news for you, but it isn't about my boyfriend."

She has a boyfriend. Not a girlfriend, but a boy, or a man; I hope he's a good man.

"You're the One That I Want" echoed in her mind.

Staring at Janis, Olivia realized the time had come. "I saw you had an interview with the Riverside Police Department. There was a paper."

"I figured you'd seen it. I was waiting for the right time to talk with you."

"Did you get the job?"

"I don't know yet," answered Jets. "I do think it's time for me to move out of this small town and spread my wings a bit."

"So it's not about the gender thing?"

"What gender thing?" Janis's face showed surprise.

"You s-stumbled over the students' gender pronouns," stammered Olivia. "I just thought you were leaving because of stuff like that."

"I've already signed up for gender sensitivity training, if you really want to know," sighed Janis. "I'm a bit slow at some stuff, but I do care about those kids getting a good education."

She continued to explain, "I don't fit in Lily Rock anymore, and frankly I'm becoming way too friendly with the people. I need to protect and serve. This small-town police gig is wearing me out."

Olivia's stomach dropped. "Okay then, I guess you've made your decision. Let me know when they get back to you."

"They may not hire me."

"Oh, they will. You're the best, and anyone can look at your record and see what an amazing job you do."

Olivia quickly spun around, taking a step toward the

door. *I'm not going to cry in front of her.* She brushed away her tears.

"Hey," she heard as she rushed down the hallway. "You forgot your key, and stop sniveling. It makes me want to puke."

Pulling herself up, Olivia bit her bottom lip to stop crying.

Good ol' Janis. She hates a scene and she's giving me a good kick in the behind.

Olivia spun around and walked back to take the key from Jets's outstretched hand. "Right, I'll put them in the bottom drawer...boss."

"Don't call me that!" hollered Janis.

Back at her desk, Olivia stuffed the key back in her pocket.

The Curated Cuisine hummed with students as the staff prepared for early dinner.

Olivia avoided the line, making her way around the building to the back of the kitchen. She found a guy rolling a dolly, which was stacked with cardboard boxes. He balanced his load against his hip to fumble with the doorknob.

Olivia stepped closer. "Here, let me get the door for you." She waited for him to pivot the dolly and back his way through the opening. He smiled in thanks.

She stood inside, taking advantage of the hustle and bustle to look for Cookie without being noticed. There were piles of food lined up on the prep counter. Each vegetable had been cut into strips or bites, making it easy for a person to pick up with tongs and place on their plate.

A stack of sliders sat next to the vegetables. Olivia

sniffed. *Pork.* The next prep counter displayed three-layer cakes, two with chocolate frosting and one with vanilla. Next to the cakes were several plates of cookies. Olivia looked longingly at the one on top, crispy brown on the edges, chocolate chips oozing, still warm from the oven.

Would they miss a cookie if I grabbed it really quick?

"I see you are admiring my baked goods," commented a man's familiar voice.

She turned to face Cookie. His piercing blue eyes looked her over in one long glance. A spotless white apron circling his cargo pants looked as if he'd just taken it from the dryer.

"You've got very blue eyes," Olivia commented, regretting her observation immediately.

I hope he doesn't think I'm coming on to him.

Cookie stared even harder at Olivia. "The better to see you with, my dear. It's the hair and the eyes combo. That's why they call me the silver fox."

"Two nicknames: Cookie and the silver fox? Most people just stick to one."

"I am not most people," he commented dryly, "as you have most likely ascertained already."

Olivia nervously cleared her throat and tugged at the metal key ring. "I think you dropped this in the park?" She dangled the key.

With one smooth move he slid the key from her hand and dropped it in his apron pocket. "I thought I saw you in the park eating lunch. Good thing you picked this up." He gestured toward the dessert counter. "Have a cookie as my way of saying thanks."

Olivia was not distracted. "Why were you chatting with Simon Court?"

Cookie's jaw tightened. His eyes narrowed, giving

Olivia the full force of his icy blue glare. "Court and I knew each other back at school. We ran into each other here at the academy, had some catching up to do."

"Which school was that?" asked Olivia.

"The Naval Academy. I cooked there for a year. I started as an enlisted culinary specialist, then became an officer, and retired as a captain. Took twenty years."

"That's why you have two names. Cookie for your enlisted job and Silver Fox when you became an officer."

Cookie's face softened. "I never thought of that, but yes, I think the two names go along with my two careers. You're smart."

"Mostly I'm nosey and I wanted to get your key back."

"Since you just happened to see it drop," Cookie added, suppressing a smile.

Olivia blurted, "I don't like Simon Court. It shocked me to see you together talking."

He took a deep breath before answering. "Stay away from Court. He's not to be underestimated."

She leaned forward for a closer look at his face. "I'm hard to warn off. Just ask anyone in Lily Rock. I don't intend to stand by and watch my sister's school get caught up in some kind of scandal."

He shrugged. "I have no idea what you're talking about. Gotta go now. The students have run out of vegan options."

Olivia eyed the cookie plate one more time before she left through the back door.

I wish I knew what that key opened. But I do have a plan B.

Only then did she unzip the side pocket of her purse. She reached inside to feel the duplicate key she had made at the hardware store.

I'll ask Sage. She might know.

CHAPTER SEVEN

Thursday

Olivia unlocked the constabulary and turned off the alarm. She secured her purse in the bottom desk drawer, then switched her computer on, giving it time to boot up as she surveyed the room and desk.

After attending to a few emails, she unlocked the sliding doors with her card key. *Time for coffee.*

On her way to the break room she glanced into Jets's empty office. Without the officer the constabulary felt empty.

I suppose I might as well get used to her absence.

A twinge of sadness hit her every time she thought about Janis leaving Lily Rock.

She's such a permanent fixture for this town, not just for me.

Flipping on the light to the break room, Olivia stood at the sink. Pushing aside boredom she rediscovered satisfaction in her routine. She rinsed the carafe and then filled it with fresh tap water. Pouring the contents into the reservoir at the back of the coffee maker, she snapped the lid down, then fitted a new coffee filter into the plastic basket. Next came the measuring. Counting to ten, she spilled rounded spoonfuls of ground coffee into the filter. Her hand froze in midair.

"Hey, assistant, can I have some of that?"

Olivia smiled. After she finished the last spoonful of grounds, she slipped the basket in and turned to face her boss. "Almost ready," she said with a smile.

Dressed in her official uniform of khaki pants with navy blue blazer over a white shirt, Janis smiled back.

This feels like old times.

"Good to see you this morning, boss. I trust everything worked out okay yesterday?"

"Yep, all is good." Jets looked over Olivia's shoulder at the brewing coffee. She shifted from foot to foot as if she had something else to say.

"Want to sit down and chat for a bit?" Olivia asked.

Instead of sitting, Janis looked Olivia up and down. "Bring me some coffee, would ya? You can find me in my office."

Stung by the rejection, Olivia did her best not to look disappointed.

A few minutes later she arrived in Janis's office doorway holding a mug of coffee in each hand. Janis did not look up; she peered at her computer instead. "Just set it down, I'll get to it later," she said off-handedly.

Olivia complied, taking her own mug with her on the way out of the door.

When she saw Michael standing at her desk she felt better. As soon as he saw her, he shoved his cell phone in his pocket with a grin. "I miss our morning coffee at your house, so I dropped by to ask you out to lunch."

Thoughts of Janis's dismissive behavior vanished. She looked over her desk.

No more clutter, so why not go out to lunch?

"Great idea," she told Michael. "Speaking of food, are we still on for Saturday night dinner?"

Michael nodded. "I got a table for two outside with an outdoor heater and privacy."

"Will we dress up?" inquired Olivia, feeling her heart flutter.

"The Refuge doesn't require anything fancy, but maybe a little dressy," suggested Michael. "It's kind of a big occasion for us, finally going out on a date. I can wear a jacket, but no tie. Hate those things."

"No tie. That tells me everything. I've got the perfect outfit."

Michael glanced around the reception area. "Things are looking tidy and organized." He turned toward her desk. "Any new robberies or murders to solve? You've been here for nearly a week."

Olivia thought for a moment. "This new role as the constabulary temporary assistant puts me out of business as the Lily Rock amateur sleuth."

I could tell him about Janis leaving, but she may walk in any minute.

"We can talk more at lunch," she added. "I should be ready around noon."

"Sounds good. By the way, no Mayor Maguire. Has he abandoned you again?"

"I think he's staying with Sage for now. At least that's where I left him yesterday, walking with her back to the academy office."

"I heard there was a complaint filed by a parent," Michael said.

The Lily Rock grapevine strikes again.

Olivia sighed. "Not filed, at least so far. Simon Court came here and threatened Janis. I was a witness. She's not too concerned."

"I'd keep away from him, he's not a nice guy," Michael frowned.

"I would, but it's not possible because I'm coaching his daughter's a cappella group."

"How did you get roped into that?"

"I volunteered with Sage's approval. She thinks the Tone Rangers need an impartial listener who knows music, and she also knows that I come cheap."

"How about we pick up the conversation at lunch?" suggested Michael. "I've got a few errands to run before then."

"Good idea," she agreed.

"Be by to walk over with you around noon."

Michael waved, turning the doorknob in his hand.

She faced her computer for the second time.

Olivia took the rest of the morning to clean out old messages. Before she knew it, her phone registered quarter to twelve. She sent Janis a text.

Leaving for lunch, be back in an hour.

By the time she shut down the computer, Michael had arrived. Olivia didn't wait for a reply from her boss.

When they stepped out of the door toward the Village Pie Shoppe, Olivia heard a slapping sound overhead. "What's a helicopter doing in Lily Rock?" she exclaimed.

Michael held his hand over his eyes, staring into the sky.

A helicopter circled above the center of town.

"Kind of interesting, feels like we're under surveillance. Maybe they're looking for drugs." He took her hand.

"Should we alert Brad?" laughed Olivia.

"Let's walk away from the noise," he shouted as the helicopter came closer. "Let Janis worry about her town."

Janis has other things on her mind. She probably won't even notice a helicopter hovering over the park.

Sandwiches ordered, Michael leaned back in the booth. "So what did you want to say that you couldn't mention earlier? Start at the beginning."

She took a moment to sip some water, then put the glass down. "This is so weird being an employee for Janis. It's like she's a totally different person and I don't know what I can talk about and what I can't."

Michael reached across the table to take both her hands into his warm grasp. "On the one hand," he raised her left hand with his, "Janis can be standoffish. On the other hand," he raised her right, "she'll act like your best friend if she thinks she can get information to solve one of her cases."

Olivia laughed. "That was a good Janis Jets imitation, I'll give you that. The one hand, other hand bit." She relished the calm she felt, her hands in his. Then gently tugging away from his grasp she unwrapped her utensils and placed the napkin on her lap.

"This may sound odd," she confided, "but I have to sort out what I can tell you and what I can't, now that I'm Janis's assistant. I'm walking a fine line here." She grinned. "At least until I figure it out, I'd best zip it up." She held her lips tight.

Michael did not disagree. "I get it. We were a team with Janis and now you're an employee. They need a Hippocratic oath like medical people have, only it applies to police work."

"They probably have an oath," Olivia said thoughtfully, "but I don't know the details. I'm just going on instinct."

As soon as she finished her sentence, the waitress arrived with their meals.

Later that afternoon Olivia locked the back and front entrances to the constabulary.

I don't want to be late for the Tone Ranger master class. I'm nervous about them and the school. Probably a good idea to keep listening so that I can share my concerns with Sage.

She hurried out the front toward her parked car.

On the drive over she thought about her lunch with Michael, remembering the rest of their conversation.

"The Tone Rangers seem nervous about the recital for parent weekend," she'd said, "plus I got the funny feeling they weren't telling me everything. Anais showed up at the constabulary. I feel like a dorm advisor. I wonder who these kids have to talk to about their problems."

Michael had listened attentively, nodding while holding her hand over the table.

She pulled her car into a space at the far end of the lot. Grabbing her autoharp from the passenger seat, Olivia stepped out of the car as she heard people arguing.

Several yards into the woods, two people occupied a wooden picnic table, sitting across from each other, face-to-face.

Olivia closed her car door and locked it, making her way toward the voices.

Better keep out of sight.

She ducked behind, keeping close to the trunk.

The person, back toward her, looked like a student. Even from a distance Olivia saw clenched fists.

Looks familiar, but I can't tell from the back.

Once she got closer, she recognized the man facing her direction.

That's Dave Franco.

Her eyes shifted as she tried to identify the other person.

He may be talking to one of the Tone Rangers.

Dave spoke in an insistent voice. "You know we have to practice taking the test. Your dad hired me to help you get a better score."

Olivia felt a prickle down her spine. She glanced over each shoulder, and then quietly stepped away from the tree to see if she could edge closer to hear more of the conversation.

I am such a nosey person.

The student spoke loudly. "My dad doesn't know what the hell he's doing. He trusts you to make me a good test taker. I do okay on my own, at least then it's not cheating. You're helping me to game the system."

"No, no, Raleigh," came Dave's soothing voice. "You've misunderstood your dad's intentions. He hired me because I help a lot of students improve their SAT scores to get into better colleges. He only wants what's best for you."

Raleigh pounded their fist on the table. "No, that's not really what this is about. As soon as I got into junior high, Court sent me to his psychologist to get some tests done. They claimed I had Attention Deficit Disorder or something. Then the school gave me special deals. I could take more time than the others on tests. I could take an extra week of study. They kept giving me more and more special treatment. My friends were so jealous. Heh, friends...I don't even have friends anymore. Not since Dad and Court got together to get me into Harvard."

Dave leaned over the picnic table to assure the distraught student. "It's okay, Raleigh. You've got this. We'll keep practicing for the test. Pretty soon it will be so easy you can take it in your sleep."

Fists unclenched, the teen hung their head. They swung both legs from under the picnic table to stand up.

I can pretend that I just arrived. Now's my chance.

Olivia walked closer to the bench.

"Hey, you two, how are things going today?"

Dave smiled, his hand nervously adjusting his pork pie hat.

"Hey, Olivia. We're good. Doing some tutoring with Raleigh." He tapped their arm. "Say hi to Olivia, Raleigh."

Raleigh sighed. "Hi, Olivia, it must be time for the master class."

"As a matter of fact I am here for the Tone Rangers," Olivia said cheerily. "You're an amazing tenor and I'm sorry I haven't directed my attention to you so far. I guess you should be complimented. I have nothing to add to improve your performance."

Raleigh shared a slight smile.

"If I remember correctly, your pronouns are they/them."

Raleigh nodded, their smile deepening to a look of appreciation.

"Thanks," they muttered. Raleigh reached over to pick up their tablet. "I better go now so that I can be there for the master class. Nice talking to you."

"See you in a few minutes," she said.

As Raleigh hurried toward housing, Olivia sat down in the place they'd occupied.

"I heard you guys arguing, so I just held back."

"I saw you hiding behind the tree," admitted Dave.

"Hey, that was my Nancy Drew moment. Nancy often hid behind trees to overhear conversations."

Dave shrugged. "Don't worry about eavesdropping. We were pretty loud."

"The Tone Rangers concern me, so nervous and highly strung. I remember when I was in high school; I didn't care as much about performance and getting an early acceptance. The kids today are under so much pressure."

"I know I didn't care about achievement. This is a new generation. A lot is expected of them, and on top of that, the kid has some issues."

"The dad hired you?"

"I got a referral from Rydell Cox in the fall. A lot of parents want their kids to max out the admission tests and get early acceptance in their senior year. One of my superpowers is test taking. I'm just good at it, always have been. So I help the kids here at the academy, which gives me some extra income. Like I said before, Sweet Four O'Clock isn't my only gig." He smiled at her.

"I am not surprised at all. Everyone in Lily Rock looks for part-time jobs just to keep up with the cost of living. And anyway, you said you're having a baby."

Dave's smile faded. He looked down for a moment, then back at Olivia.

"I'm worried about finances," he admitted with a nod. "I'm worried about a lot of things. It wasn't my idea to have a baby."

"I didn't have a dad growing up, but I'm sure you're going to be great. You can teach the kid drums. What kid doesn't want to play with sticks and be a rock star?"

"I hope you're right. My wife thinks I'll do okay, but I worry. My dad was not a great role model, let's just leave it at that." Dave glanced at his cell phone. "It's time for your master class. Do you mind if I sit in again?"

"No problem," said Olivia. "Why do you care so much about a cappella singing?" "I was clueless about a cappella until this fall. I mean, four kids singing without accompaniment...how would that get them into college? But since I tutor the kids, I thought it would be a good idea to see them doing their thing. Plus I was told by Cox to pay more attention. According to Cox the academy board of directors takes great pride in the success of the Tone Rangers. If they all get early admission into prestigious colleges, the rating for the music academy will rise. Then next year they'll draw even more applicants. Then they can raise their tuition."

"Sure," said Olivia. "You tutor all four? How did that come about?"

"After Rydell Cox referred me, their parents called me individually. I started tutoring them before school started, back in July. A lot rides on the college admission test scores. Assuming they keep up their grade point averages, there's a good chance all four will get early admission."

"You're an important cog in this wheel of getting admitted," commented Olivia. "We're the same, you know. I coach the music, you coach for testing."

Now on his feet, Dave looked away. "Not exactly the same," he said softly. Before Olivia could inquire further, his voice perked up. "See you later. I'm going to grab a water and then I'll meet you in the auditorium."

"Behind the piano," laughed Olivia.

"That's right." He grinned. "I'm incognito." He adjusted his hat. "Basically I don't want to interfere. You're very good with the Tone Rangers. I saw that right away."

Olivia felt her cheeks warm.

That's nice of Dave.

She waved as he walked away.

She made her way toward the auditorium, her autoharp under her arm.

"Thanks for arranging the chairs," she called out to the Tone Rangers who had arrived earlier. "Hey, Raleigh," she added as the teen rushed through the door.

"Anais did it," Abbey said. "She's always the one to kiss up to the teacher."

Anais's chin tucked toward her chest. "I guess so," she said softly.

"Just leave her alone, would you?" Raleigh glared at Abbey.

Abbey rose up on the toes of her worn hiking boots and faced Raleigh. "You aren't the leader of the Tone Rangers and Anais needs to grow a backbone." She stamped her foot and then turned away.

No one disagreed.

"Let's get going. I don't have time for this coaching stuff, especially from a woman who plays autoharp," Abbey added impatiently.

"That's because you've never heard her sing," said Dave, stepping in from the exit. "Olivia Greer has an extraordinary voice and you're lucky to have her as a coach."

Abbey shrugged, dismissing Dave with a sneer. "What do you know...you're an average percussionist who tutors kids on how to take tests. Your opinion doesn't matter to any of us. Just do what you're hired to do."

Olivia's gut clenched.

She's so hostile and just like her father.

Olivia looked over to Anais, who stared back, her eyes pleading for help.

"That's enough of the bickering," Olivia scolded the group. "Let's get to your first song for parent weekend."

Olivia pointed to the empty chairs as an invitation to sit down.

All four Tone Rangers complied.

After the last note of "Closer to Fine", an Indigo Girls classic, died away, Legend spoke. "We haven't tried the falsetto register yet. I know it's not the same arrangement as usual, but it might add some interest for the listener."

"We don't care about the listener," Abbey said. "We only care about the judges, and they are very conservative. They don't want boys dressing as girls, let alone singing in falsetto."

"I don't agree," Legend said. "I think the judges want to hear something fresh, and a falsetto voice in an Indigo Girl song might be the best way to get their attention and set ourselves apart."

As the two argued, Olivia looked at Anais, whose eyes filled with tears. Before she could ask the girl her opinion, Anais rose to her feet, running from the auditorium.

Abbey continued to argue, "I am the leader of this group and I say no falsetto. End of discussion."

Legend's eyes dropped as she ran her hand over her skirt. Instead of continuing to make her point, she clamped her mouth shut, nervously folding and unfolding the fabric over her lap.

Raleigh turned to Legend. "Let's get out of here. I'll meet you at the Lily Rock trail in ten minutes. We can hike the crest."

"Sounds good," replied Legend.

Raleigh paused for a moment and then turned to Olivia. "Are we done with the master class?"

"We're finished for today. When you two hike together, do you wear those skirts?"

Legend flipped her skirt for the second time to show off the worn boots. "We've got boots that are made for hiking."

"That's just what they do," added Raleigh in the perfect imitation of the Nancy Sinatra song.

"And one of these days these boots are going to walk all over you," added Legend in perfect pitch, eyes directed at Abbey.

Abbey froze in her spot, a look of fear coming over her face.

The intention of Legend's song had hit the mark. Olivia inhaled sharply.

Abbey's days as the leader are numbered. If she's not careful Legend will take over before the first competition.

CHAPTER EIGHT

Friday

Before heading to work on Friday, Sage and Olivia shared a cup of coffee in the kitchen. Olivia observed her sister with a smile. *She's feeling more at home.*

"I'm still amazed that you shared Marla's estate with me. You didn't have to do that," Sage's voice was filled with warmth.

Olivia poured her another cup of coffee.

"I think Marla wanted me to share the estate with you all along. Once she realized she was ill and might not recover, she left me in charge of the money. But she also placed her DNA research at my disposal. You're as entitled to the estate as I am, since you and Marla had the same biological father."

"And Marla didn't know any of her other half-siblings," mused Sage. "Still, I think you're great."

Olivia sighed, resting her chin on her palm. Warmth spread through her body.

In Sage's company, everything feels all right.

"I'd like to chat longer, but it's time to get ready for work. Janis expects me right on the dot."

"I'd better get going too," admitted Sage. "Catch up with you later."

Olivia picked up both mugs, which she rinsed in the sink. She followed Sage through the great room toward her bedroom downstairs.

Later that morning Olivia sat at her desk, wishing she were back in their kitchen sharing time with Sage. *I feel like I'm waiting for the other shoe to drop.*

She refocused by opening the top drawer of her desk to look inside. The pencils lined up in order, the longest in the back to the shortest in the front. *Okay, so I'm easily amused.*

The middle and bottom drawers looked equally organized. As for the desktop, it held her cell phone and a calendar desk blotter. The calendar read Parent Weekend. Olivia tapped her fingers on the desk.

As she continued to contemplate her restlessness, the door to the constabulary opened. In walked Meadow McCloud. "Hello, dear," she stepped behind the desk to give Olivia a hug. "Are you busy?" Meadow didn't stop to hear Olivia's answer. Instead she rushed into her next statement. "I have a break from the library and I wanted to ask you a favor."

I forgot Meadow worked next door.

Looking around for an extra chair, Meadow dragged one from across the room to sit on the same side of the desk as Olivia. Straightening her denim jumper around her knees, she leaned forward. "I'm worried about our Sage," she whispered loudly.

"You don't have to whisper," Olivia assured Meadow. "Janis is in the back and I'm the only one here."

A pink color came to Meadow's cheeks. "Oh right," she said in her normal tone. "I forgot we're not in the library."

Meadow continued, "I went to the academy board of directors meeting last night and you won't believe what I heard. One of the students attacked another and her parent may be suing the school. I don't know what the argument was about, but I thought you might know more of the details since I was told the father filed a formal complaint at the constabulary."

Olivia couldn't resist conspiring with Meadow. "Simon Court came by to file that complaint. He's on the board of directors if I'm not mistaken."

Meadow looked grim. "Simon Court is out to get Sage. I feel it in my bones. He holds her responsible for what he calls an 'unsafe environment' fostered by old-fashioned educational paradigms." Meadow used her fingers to quote Simon Court.

"When you say it that way, it sounds really sinister," Olivia admitted. "What makes you think he blames Sage?"

"He said so right out loud at our meeting last night and then the other man, Rydell Cox, chimed in afterward. He's the new staff guidance counselor. He thinks Sage can't stand up to the students, adding fuel to Court's fire."

Olivia sighed. *Court has Cox and Kravitz...*

"I've spoken to Cox. Do you think he wants Sage's job?"

Meadow patted her jumper again. "That's exactly what I think! Cox and Court are in cahoots and I want to put a stop to it."

"So how can I help?" asked Olivia. "I'd hate to see Sage lose the job she loves."

"Especially over a couple of outsiders with outlandish ideas about modern education," added Meadow.

"Have you talked to the Old Rockers? What do they think?" Olivia mentioned the unofficial town council because she knew Meadow was their leader.

"The Old Rockers along with the town council handed over responsibility of the school to the newly formed board. Sage said the parents requested the change. Then the town council added me as a liaison. But I'm basically invisible to Simon Court and the rest. I sit at meetings and no one speaks to me. They ignore my questions. Lately I've taken to making notes and observing."

Olivia smirked. *At their own peril... Meadow wields some clout in Lily Rock, and they probably have no idea.*

"Who else have you told about this?" asked Olivia.

"I've mentioned the problem to Arlo and Cayenne."

"They don't have children at the school, what makes you think they could help?"

Meadow's head shook back and forth. "I'm not so foolish as to think an outright advance on the opposition is the best plan right now. Arlo and Cayenne, working at the pub, know more about Lily Rock than most. Add that to what I pick up at the library and what you hear, now that you're centrally located in the constabulary, and we make our own secret service."

"It doesn't hurt that Cayenne's cleaning service, Mops 4 Us, has access to most of the prestigious homes on the hill," added Olivia. "We do have this covered."

"That too," agreed Meadow. "Cay can pick up all sorts of information just by tidying someone's kitchen. Plus she's so wise. We all know that."

"So you've gathered your Lily Rock Secret Society to

figure out what's happening with Sage and the music academy. Am I the last person you've spoken to?"

"You are the best and the last. You love Sage. I know you'll figure out what we can do to preserve her job. She's a wonderful teacher and organizer. I stand behind her and so do the Old Rockers. These new people don't get to take over the music academy just because they have money."

"I'll let you know what I hear," Olivia assured Meadow.

The constabulary phone buzzed. "Olivia Greer, constabulary office," she said into the phone.

Crying met her ear.

"Who is this?" Olivia asked, chills running up her spine. "Take a deep breath and tell me why you called."

"Olivia," came a sobbing voice. "It's me, Abbey. You have to come quick."

"Take a breath, Abbey. What's wrong, why do I have to come quick?"

Olivia glanced at Meadow, whose face had grown white. "Is it Sage?" she mouthed.

Olivia held up her finger for quiet before she spoke into the phone.

"Tell me what's unsettling you," she asked the sobbing girl.

"It's a body...at the bottom of the Lily Rock trail."

Olivia's heart pounded in her chest. "Do you know who it is?" she asked.

"I don't know. Ms. McCloud told me not to look but to call the constabulary right away."

"Got it," Olivia said, relief in her voice. "I'll alert Officer Jets and we'll be there as soon as we can. Stay calm and close to Sage."

Olivia took a moment to speak to Meadow in an aside. "Not Sage."

Meadow let out a sigh of relief, soon replaced with, "Then who?"

Olivia shook her head, pointing to the cell.

Abbey continued, "The whole school is here, plus a bunch of visitors who arrived early for parent weekend. I'll stay with them."

"Okay, Abbey. I'll tell Officer Jets and we'll be on campus as soon as we can. Where can we find you?"

"At the top of the Lily Rock Crest Trail," Abbey said, breaking down into tears again.

Olivia hung up the phone and glanced at Meadow's stricken face. "It's not Sage, at least we know that. I'd better let Janis know." She used her cell phone from the desk to call.

"What?" asked Jets after the first ring.

"We have an emergency near the academy," Olivia said quickly. "A body found at the bottom of the Lily Rock trail. Call for help came in at 4:30 p.m."

Olivia reached her hand over to pat Meadow's knee, still listening to Janis Jets.

"Who called it in?" demanded Jets.

"Abbey Court, she just hung up."

"Give me a minute and I'll get right back to you." Jets clicked off.

Olivia set her cell phone on the desktop.

Color had returned to Meadow's cheeks. "I'm so happy you came into our lives when you did. Now I'm not the only one to look after my girl."

Olivia leaned over to hug Meadow, her shoulder growing damp with the older woman's tears. Unclasping her arms, she grabbed the buzzing cell phone. Olivia held it to her ear.

"What's our next move?" she asked Janis, skipping the preliminary greeting.

"Meet me at the academy right away. I have a call to make." Janis's crisp voice gave no room for argument.

Olivia reached into her bottom drawer for her purse. "I know you have to get back to the library," she said to Meadow. "I'm going to meet Janis at the academy."

Meadow nodded. "I wish I could help, but maybe it's best that I stay at my job. Please give Sage my love. And Olivia? Be careful. Try to let Janis handle the crime scene."

"I'll watch out for Sage. No sleuthing for me," she assured her.

After ushering Meadow out the front door, Olivia secured the constabulary.

A brisk walk across the park brought her to her old car. She quickly popped behind the driver's seat, shoving the key into the ignition. It turned over on the first try.

Once on the road, she made her way to the music academy, taking the time to think.

Who could be at the bottom of the cliff? For that matter a dead body doesn't bode well for Sage. As the principal of the Lily Rock Music Academy, she'll be held accountable.

By the time Olivia arrived at the scene, Janis Jets had cordoned off the top of the cliff to keep away parents and students. Groups stood by, gathering beyond the orange tape. A brave woman stepped over the tape, walking toward Janis Jets.

Jets glared, anticipating the question. "I don't know who's down there," she snapped. "But when I do I'll tell everyone. Just stand behind that tape and keep calm. We've got officers from down the hill on their way."

Olivia hurried toward Jets, handing her a water bottle. "Thought you might be thirsty," she said to her boss.

"What are you, my nursemaid?" Janis shoved aside the bottle. As if thinking better of her words, she reached over and grabbed it back. "I am thirsty. Thanks."

On the other side of the orange tape, first responders worked with ropes and a stretcher. Each wore a yellow T-shirt marked Lily Rock Volunteer Fire Department in black letters.

"Your guy is over there," remarked Janis, nodding. Olivia instantly recognized Michael bent over the empty stretcher, adjusting straps.

Olivia scanned the responders. "I see Arlo also arrived," she commented. "The last time I saw the volunteer first responders was when they showed up at the fire at the animal shelter."

"That was a doozy," admitted Janis. "But now we have to move quickly. We haven't identified the body and who knows, the person may be alive." Jets paused for a moment, then added, "It would be unlikely, considering the height of the cliff and the time it took to organize a rescue..."

Sounding discouraged, Janis moved away from Olivia to talk to one of the first responders. Olivia watched her in action.

Maybe this job is getting to her and that's why she's been unusually grumpy. She doesn't have her customary composure. Something about Janis is off.

Jets looked back at Olivia. "Drop the sad face. Whatever you do, don't get all sappy on me. Not our first dead body... we've done this before." Jets attempted a smile.

"I was beginning to think you lost your mojo. I saw all those pencils lined up in the drawer. Ridiculous. I admit since you've been working for me it's been awfully dull. But now I feel better. Nothin' like a potential dead body to get the juices running."

Olivia nodded as if she believed every word. Looking past Janis, she saw Arlo join Michael. They carried the stretcher toward the cliff's edge. Within minutes, Arlo's boots slid over the berm, his hands gripping the end of the stretcher. Michael held the opposite side, easing it over the cliff. Then he grabbed a tether in his hand to keep the stretcher from tumbling too fast, potentially knocking against Arlo.

Janis and Olivia stood together, closely observing Arlo making his way down the rocky cliff. Each step he took, Michael released the rope further. Arlo and then the stretcher descended toward the bottom of the ravine.

Finally Arlo jumped the final distance to the ground. He pulled the stretcher with him with a hard yank. Michael watched and then let go of the rope once he knew he'd safely accomplished his descent.

Arlo left the stretcher close to the body. Then he bent over, grasping a limp arm. Placing his fingers against the wrist, he waited.

"He's checking for a pulse," Jets said.

Olivia held her breath. Arlo shook his head, moving his hand to lay fingers on the neck of the body near the carotid artery. After what seemed like forever, Arlo lifted his head and looked up the mountain. His eyes found Janis Jets. He shook his head again.

"No sign of life," remarked Janis Jets, her voice low in her throat.

Olivia glanced back. Now another responder began repelling down the cliff. She maintained an even pace as one foot then the other lodged in the loose dirt.

Olivia leaned toward Janis. "Can you tell who it is yet?"

"Someone will get on a walkie-talkie and let me know pretty quick."

Arlo and the other responder slid the stretcher underneath the body, lifting one side then the other, before covering the person with a blanket. Arlo secured the straps.

"They didn't cover the head. Does that mean there's a chance the person may be alive?" asked Olivia.

"They may have forgotten to cover the face. No pulse means no life," sighed Jets.

As the responders hoisted the stretcher up the cliff, the crowd behind grew quiet. When they reached the top, the rescue team released their burden, laying the stretcher on the ground.

Arlo wiped his face with the back of his hand. Michael came closer, looked down at the dead man, and then turned to find Olivia. She saw the sadness in his face.

Janis walked closer to the rescue team, her shoulders slumped as if dreading the worst news. She turned to all of the volunteer responders who gathered around. "Thanks to all of you. You did a great job today. I'll be sure to mention everyone in the report."

Michael continued to stare at the uncovered face. "He's gone. I think Olivia may know him, one of her bandmates in Sweet Four O'Clock."

Close enough to hear, Olivia's legs began to shake.

Michael added, "Let me tell her. I don't know how well she knew him, but it will come as a shock."

Michael made his way past the rest toward Olivia. He reached to take her into his arms.

"Who is it?" Olivia asked quietly.

"I think...it's the guy who plays drums in your band."

Olivia gasped, yanking away from Michael. "Oh no, not

Dave...he tutored students and was going to have a baby very soon. Oh no, not Dave," she repeated.

Placing one hand on each of her trembling shoulders, Michael asked, "Was Dave an experienced climber?"

"He hiked with his students, but I don't think he did mountain climbing, if that's what you're thinking." Olivia felt stunned.

Michael tilted her chin up to look into her eyes.

She buried her head in his shoulder, wrapping arms around his middle.

As the men shuffled the stretcher to the ambulance, Janis Jets edged closer. "The name on his driver's license is Dave Franco."

Olivia nodded. "That's who Michael suspected."

"Could you make a quick identification for us?" Jets asked Olivia. "Just for an initial affirmation before we take him away."

"Sure," said Olivia.

On her way she noticed Sage standing next to Abbey in the crowd.

"It's Dave, isn't it. I think I overheard someone say they found his wallet," Sage said, her voice scratchy with emotion.

Olivia gestured for her to stand outside Abbey's hearing range. "Yes, it's Dave," said Olivia, choking back tears. "Do you think he—"

"Not Dave," insisted Sage. "He'd never end his life with a baby coming along. He must have slipped on the trail, you know, walked too close trying to get a better view."

Janis Jets came up behind Olivia. "Or maybe someone came along and gave him a nice clean shove. We'll figure it out in the next twenty-four hours, what happened and how. The problem comes when you ask why. Why would a guy lean over a dangerous cliff or why would someone push him?"

Jets turned to Olivia. "That was one of those rhetorical questions you don't have to answer. What you do need to do is identify the body for me and then fill out the paperwork for this incident report. See you back at the constabulary."

"I'll see you there," Olivia said, glancing toward Michael.

Taking her by the elbow, he walked with her to the emergency vehicle. "I'll go with you. One quick look for the identification and that's it."

Once Olivia and Michael stepped forward, Arlo held open the side door of the truck for her to look inside. Dave lay on his back, his eyes closed, his skin a pale white. Olivia blinked her teary eyes and then looked away.

"That's Dave Franco. I almost didn't recognize him without his pork pie hat."

Michael took hold of her elbow again. Olivia inhaled deeply and then pulled her cell phone out of her back pocket to text Sage.

> Going back to work. I'll be late getting
> home. Love you.

CHAPTER NINE

At the constabulary late on Friday evening, it only took an hour for Olivia to input the death and rescue information into the computer. With each detail she felt her heart race faster and faster. Once she pushed Send to Janis Jets, she sat back in her chair. Emotionally spent, she finally had a chance to assess her own feelings. Tears of hopelessness filled her eyes.

Dave is gone.

Olivia tried to remember when she'd felt so detached from her perennial optimism. *When Mom died I felt this way. She was my best friend. I was just getting to know Dave, but I feel the same senselessness in his loss.*

The doors behind her swished open. Janis Jets appeared, her face looking grim. "Have you eaten dinner yet?"

"Not hungry," Olivia said, reaching for a tissue.

"I ordered burgers. They'll be delivered. We have to begin our investigation. You can feel sad later once we've figured out if he jumped or fell or if someone pushed him."

"We?"

"Of course, we. You think I hired you to do your nails and file papers all day? You've got, might I say, certain instincts for eliciting confessions, and I think you'd be an asset on this case. I have a plan."

"You think it was murder then?" Olivia shoved her balled-up tissues into the wastebasket. She sat up in her chair, her mind welcoming a challenge.

Jets rubbed her hand on the back of her neck. "He might have fallen off the cliff," she scratched her head over her right ear. "I don't know how he could have lost his balance in that particular place. Just to make sure, I asked his wife when we spoke; she said Dave hiked the Lily Rock loop all the time. He was familiar with the trails."

"How did you feel talking to Linnea about Dave?" Olivia watched Janis carefully. Her face, immobile, did not give away any emotion.

Jets shook her head, tucking a wisp of hair behind her ear. "Even if Riverside Police made the visit to her house, I was the one who called on what was quite possibly the worst day of her life." The facts, spoken in a staccato delivery, sounded like an addition to a police report.

For the first time, the full impact of Janis's work hit Olivia. Up until then she'd been an observer and part-time help outside of investigations. But today, she saw a different side. A person she knew had died and notifications needed to be made.

I wouldn't want that part of Janis's job for anything in the world. Typing a report doesn't compare.

Olivia inhaled deeply. She dropped another tissue in the wastebasket. "Okay then, I think I am feeling a bit hungry. Did you ask for the burger to be slightly pink on the inside?"

Janis's grim face shifted to slightly amused. "That's the

stuff, first we think food...then if we have another few minutes, we turn to investigating. I'm happy to hear that your nutritional needs have become foremost on your mind. I ordered two hamburgers, slightly pink just the way we like them."

"Food keeps me sane," Olivia admitted.

Jets checked her cell phone. "I'll go back to my office and read your report. You bring the delivery back to the break room as soon as it gets here. Don't dawdle. I like a hot fry, not a soggy one."

Within ten minutes the delivery guy bounced into the constabulary, bringing two brown food bags, complete with grease stains.

"Here's your order," he said, dropping the bags on her desk. "Gotta go." Before she could say goodbye, the door closed behind him.

Since it grew increasingly dark outside, Olivia locked up the entrance to the constabulary. Then she made her way to the break room.

Janis followed her down the hall as Olivia set the bags in the middle of the table. Janis reached in first, handing one burger to Olivia before grabbing one for herself.

Both women sat down, peeling away the paper wrapping. They ate in silence.

Olivia finished her last bite and then gathered the paper wrappers. "I don't want to come back next week to leftover food on the table," she commented dryly to Janis, tossing the trash into the receptacle.

"Didn't I tell you?" Jets wiped a crumb from her chin. "You're not coming back to the constabulary starting tomorrow."

"I'm fired?"

"You're not getting out of this job that easy. I have a

plan. Time to change your work location. I want you up at the music academy day and night, at least for the rest of parent weekend. If we act fast we can figure out this incident before people start leaving.

"In fact, I asked Sage to find you a room at the dorm so that you can eavesdrop on the students, listen and report back. Many a killer confesses over brushing their molars in the community bathroom. You probably don't know that because you're an amateur sleuth."

"I didn't know that," Olivia agreed, imagining herself living in a dormitory room.

A small twin bed with no one talking at me would be so good right now.

"How will Sage explain my presence to the student residents?"

"You're going to be the dorm head. I checked the student housing charter while you were writing your report. Sage emailed it to me as soon as I told her my plan. According to what I read, an adult is required to be present in the dorm, especially in the evening. Plus with a potential campus killer on the loose, I'd feel better if you were there to be a soothing and, of course, a nosey presence."

"Does this mean I have to pack an overnight bag and go undercover? Do I take on an accent and wear a wig?"

Jets smirked. "I think the students know you too well to get away with any phony nonsense. Just be you. Your music cred will be background enough and interesting to the students. Plus everyone knows you're the lead vocalist of Sweet Four O'Clock and that you play the auto thingam-abob, and that you also coach the a cappella group. Not exactly undercover, more like minor celebrity big frog in a very small pond."

"I don't know if I like being compared to an amphibian," muttered Olivia.

Janis ignored her. "Now then, we need to interview all of those Tone People one at a time."

"Rangers," corrected Olivia. "They're called the Tone Rangers."

"Whatever. And then, as if we don't have enough problems, we have to interview their parents. Lots of relatives arrived for parent weekend. I'll handle that part while you mingle with the young." Janis smiled, looking happy with her plan.

"I hadn't thought about all the parents being around. Do you have to interview everyone on campus?"

"My gut tells me the Tone Rangers are at the center of this murder. Let's start with them and see where it goes," Jets stated calmly.

"I already told Sage to break the bad news to the families. I don't imagine her popularity is soaring at the moment. You know she's already in hot water with the school board. I heard all the details from Meadow."

"Did I mention priorities? Sage's job is the least of my worries right now. In a way she could be one of my suspects. She's around that campus all the time."

"You don't really think Sage had anything to do with Dave's death, do you?"

"Between us, I don't. But while you are snooping around the pool of potential pushers off the cliff, I'll do my best to gather evidence. If Dave actually jumped, he hid his depression very well."

Olivia thought for a moment. "Dave did talk to me about his concerns about being a dad. He seemed worried but not ambivalent, nothing that would lead me to believe he'd take his own life."

"That's helpful," Jets said. "Of course, Dave could have fallen by accident. Like I said, a fall would look different to the pros. They'll know. And if Dave was pushed, there will be signs revealed by forensics and the coroner. That's my job, to get the professionals on the case while we still have the students and families available and under our surveillance."

"How long can Sage keep the parents from leaving?"

"I have no idea. It will take some ingenious planning and soothing, because that's what rich people appreciate. Oh, and it will also require good food. I have that Cookie guy already baking his butt off tonight."

"You talked to the chef of the Curated Cuisine about the case?"

"We spoke briefly. He says he'll pull out all the stops with his pea soup and baked bread. Pea soup?" Jets added, scorn in her voice. "Ever since I was a kid I made it a habit to avoid green food."

"Not even a green vegetable?"

"If it's green, it's mean. That was my motto. No green anything, especially salad—the most overpriced item on any menu. Adding protein to a salad has become a fad. Give me the meat, hold the rest."

Not a green vegetable fan. Another thing I didn't know about Janis Jets.

Olivia glanced at her cell phone. Two missed calls from Michael and one from Sage.

"I guess I'd better throw some things into a suitcase for my new assignment," Olivia said.

"Don't forget your toothbrush," Janis added with a sly wink.

. . .

"I'll catch up with you tomorrow at the academy," Michael sounded tired over the phone. Olivia had called to touch base with him before heading to the music academy dorm.

"When Sage finds me a room, I'll text you the number," Olivia added. "What a day, huh?"

"I really hoped he'd be alive when we got the stretcher to him," admitted Michael.

"Dave was a good guy. I was just getting to know him. Janis said she spoke to his wife already," Olivia swallowed back the lump in her throat. "I wouldn't want to be in Linnea's shoes, with a baby on the way. Plus Dave mentioned financial problems to me just a day ago. That would be tough." Tears came to her eyes.

Michael drew a deep breath. "We can help with the finances, at least we can try. I've got a couple of ideas, but I'm too tired to explain them now. How are you doing?"

"I'm ready to drive to the academy and sleep at the dorm. I never thought this would be one of my constabulary assignments, going undercover with a bunch of teenagers in high school."

"You do get around," chuckled Michael. "Don't forget to give me your room number when you find out." She heard a stifled yawn over the phone.

"Get some sleep," she told him. "See you tomorrow."

After Michael clicked off the phone, Olivia had one more call to make.

She found her Recents in her phone and pushed redial.

"Hi," said Sage. "I've been getting your room all ready; it's on the second floor, number 235."

"I'm on my way to the academy."

Sage interrupted. "You know where the building is, but there's a new sign. The dorms are called the Court Family Residence Hall."

"I see," said Olivia. "I guess the Court family donated the funds to renovate the old bunkhouse."

"That's right. I was there when the board decided to let him put his name on the building. At the time I didn't object because I can't afford to annoy Simon Court if I want to keep my job." Olivia heard the desperation in Sage's voice.

"Speaking of parents, how did the families respond when you told them parent weekend would also include the opportunity to watch a police investigation?"

Sage hesitated. "I haven't had time to make all of those phone calls, at least not yet. And I don't know how to tell people without alarming them. Right under my nose one of our tutors dies. I'm not feeling good about all of this."

"I know, honey. You must be exhausted trying to please everyone all the time. I hope Janis has some answers for us soon. I'll be listening to all conversations. Janis seemed to think I'd learn the most in the bathroom brushing my teeth."

Sage chuckled and then sighed deeply. "So much of my work is about appeasing people who donate money to the school. Over the past year I've had my head buried in meetings, keeping my mouth shut. I didn't even see how odd things had become."

"Dave's death is a wakeup call," admitted Olivia. "Something sinister is happening at the school and we'll get to the bottom of it very soon." Olivia wanted to encourage Sage and also let her know that she had her back. "I'll meet you in front of the dorm in five minutes," she added. The phone disconnected.

Once in her car, Olivia headed to the main road. It took less than ten minutes to arrive at the music academy.

Parking as close as possible to the footpath, she turned off her ignition. Her legs ached once she stood on both feet.

Will this day ever end?

Olivia took her suitcase from the trunk and then clicked the fob to secure the car. She rolled her bag toward the dormitory, noting the new sign, Court Family Residence Hall, above the double-entry doors.

Through the glass of the doors, Olivia saw students mingling in the entryway. Abbey and Anais huddled together until Anais caught sight of her; she ran to open the door.

"You got here quick," Anais said breathlessly. "Ms. McCloud told us to look out for you. She'll bring your key up in a minute. Can I help you with your bag?"

"Thanks, that's very kind."

Anais pointed to the stairway. "It's probably the same room as the old head was in, right up those stairs and to the left. The odd-numbered side of the hallway."

Olivia looked around. "Maybe I'll wait here until Sage arrives. How are you two doing? I feel so sad about Dave Franco."

"What a horrible school this is," cried Abbey. She leaned her back against the wall, a scowl on her face. "I told my father I want to transfer right after winter break. Once the word is out that someone actually died here, right on campus at the Lily Rock Music Academy, I'm sure the rest of the parents will pull their kids out. I want to be as far away as possible. You too, Anais." She pointed to her friend.

Anais nodded. "We won't qualify for early admissions now. Colleges avoid any kind of scandal with students or high schools, or at least that's what I heard."

Olivia looked at Anais closely. Why would she believe

the school would be held responsible for an unexpected campus death?

She wanted to quit the group anyway. Why is she pretending to care about early admission?

Abbey pointed. "Ms. McCloud is coming. She must have your key."

Sage let herself in the glass entry door. "Ah good, you're here," she said, giving Olivia a quick hug. "I see you've been talking to your greeting committee."

"We've been sharing our sadness over Dave's death," said Olivia. She left out the part about leaving the academy.

Sage turned to face Anais and then looked at Abbey. "You girls know you can talk to me or Olivia any time about what you saw tonight or your feelings about the accident."

Olivia noted Sage's deliberate use of the word accident. She didn't flinch or disagree. *Better to let the girls think it's not a murder. They'd be even more freaked out.*

Neither Abbey nor Anais addressed Sage's offer.

"We'll be going now," said Abbey, taking Anais by the elbow. She looked over her shoulder at Olivia. "Both of us are on the second floor, so I'm sure we'll be running into each other. But for now I need a walk and some fresh air. How about you, Anais?"

Anais smiled as if pleased to be included. "Sure, that would be great. Bye, Olivia. Oh, and you too, Ms. McCloud," she added as an afterthought. The girls walked out of the doors arm in arm. They headed toward the wooded area, where lamps lit the path.

Once upstairs Sage watched as Olivia flung her suitcase on the twin-sized bed. She pushed her hands into the covers to feel the mattress. "Feels comfy."

When Sage didn't respond, Olivia looked at her sister more closely.

She looks exhausted. Dark circles under her eyes from crying.

"I've got everything from here," she assured Sage. "Why don't you head back home to get some sleep? By the way, is M&M with you?"

"He's waiting back in my office. Every time I pick up the phone or type on the computer he stands up as if he's annoyed. I think my phone has survived four crashes from him bumping it off the desk with his big paw."

Olivia laughed. "That dog knows what's best. Time for you to go back to the house. Take him with you and text me when you get there. We can talk in the morning."

Sage didn't argue. Before she got out the door she turned to tell Olivia, "The showers are that way." She pointed. "End of the hall, take a left."

"I'll find everything," Olivia assured Sage.

Asking questions will be part of my undercover work. Gives me an excuse to talk to the students.

"Right," answered Sage. Before she could step into the hall she heard a low yip. Olivia watched as Mayor Maguire greeted Sage by offering his paw for a shake.

"Hey, M&M," called Olivia.

The dog spun around, moving past Sage. He leapt onto the bed, shoving his head into Olivia's chest.

"Good to see you, boy," Olivia bent her head into his neck, inhaling the smell of dog fur and pine needles. "You go with Sage, but I hope to see you tomorrow."

The dog shook off from his head to his tail. Then he jumped to the floor to follow Sage. Olivia closed the door softly behind them.

She examined her room more closely now that she was alone. The twin bed and a nightstand had been pushed into the corner by the window. Olivia turned down the sheets, appreciating the scent of bleach and lemon. Then she left her suitcase on top of the dresser across the room. A light shone through the window, attracting her attention.

Olivia pushed aside the curtain to look out. A group of students talked in a grassy area beneath her window. Abbey Court stood in the center. Though Olivia could not hear what the girl said, it was obvious by her hand gestures that she felt intensely.

She turned from the window to unzip her suitcase, finding a few necessary items. She grabbed her bag with her toothbrush, shampoo, and soap. After undressing she wrapped a thread-worn bathrobe around her body, cinching the tie at her waist.

Shower kit in her hand and flip-flops on her feet, she made her way to the door.

I'm in search of the showers and my first conversation. Let the sleuthing begin.

CHAPTER TEN

A slice of bright light coming through the curtains woke Olivia Saturday morning.

So early for a weekend, it's only 7:45.

A door slam from the hallway startled her into an upright position.

Someone coming home late or getting up early?

She slid her legs over the side of the bed. After a yawn and a stretch, she pulled jeans and a T-shirt from her suitcase.

Time to get going on the investigation.

With her bathroom kit in hand, she headed down the hall.

No one brushing their teeth this morning...sorry, Janis.

After washing her face, she headed back to her room. Once dressed she made her way out of the dormitory toward the Curated Cuisine. She moved quickly along the path through the woods, inhaling deeply to clear the fog in her head.

A strong cup of coffee powers my concentration.

Olivia could smell eggs and bacon, inviting her closer to the kitchen back door.

The first person she saw was Janis Jets, who held a coffee mug in the air to greet Olivia. Cookie Kravitz smiled from the corner, brushing his hands down his immaculate white apron.

I suspect that Janis is up early interviewing the adult suspects. Look out, Kravitz.

"Is there more coffee?" Olivia glanced around the kitchen, her eyes resting on an industrial-sized machine.

"Out in the main dining room," Cookie told her, "right through the swinging doors. You can find lots of flavors and various milk substitutes. If you want plain old black coffee then the pot's right here." He pointed to the giant silver monstrosity in the corner of the room.

Olivia selected a mug from the stack, she looked at the pot in admiration. It hissed a greeting.

Hello, you beauty!

With a full mug of coffee, she paused and heard her stomach growl. And then the smell of bacon wafted over her, causing her nostrils to flare.

"Would you like some breakfast?" asked Cookie, glancing at her full mug of coffee.

"That bacon smells amazing," she admitted.

"Let me fix you a plate." He moved toward the stack of dishes. Sliding one off the top, he turned to the frying pan, deftly scooping scrambled eggs and three slices of bacon onto the plate. "Here you go," said Cookie, a smile on his face.

That's a man who likes feeding people.

Olivia selected a bacon strip, biting into its crispness and finishing it off as if she'd not eaten in a week.

"I've got toast right here," Cookie said, shoving a basket

toward her. She took the slice off the top and then set her plate on the raised counter. Noticing Janis Jets glaring at her from the other side of the room, she ate quickly, crunching on a bite of bacon before diving into the eggs.

Janis sauntered closer to hiss in her ear. "Besides eating like a starving woman, what's your job this morning?"

Olivia took a sip from her mug. "I'm here to..."

We're not alone. This is part of my undercover act. Even if Kravitz looks busy doing his chief cook and bottle washer thing—shifting clean plates to the dining room and turning over the bacon in the frying pans—he could easily hear our conversation.

"I'm here for the Tone Ranger rehearsal," Olivia said loud enough for Cookie to hear. She glared at Janis Jets.

"Looks like you spent the night in the dorm," said Jets in her equally loud voice.

Oh great, now she's pretending it wasn't her idea for me to be her undercover snoop. That's for Kravitz. I'm supposed to play along.

Olivia swallowed back her irritation. "Sage wanted me to be an RA, at least until after parent weekend."

"What happened to the regular RA?" asked Janis, a smirk on her face.

Is she trying to irritate me? Now I have to come up with a backstory in case Cookie is listening.

"She had to go home for an emergency."

I hope that sounded authentic.

"I see," answered Jets, moving closer to Olivia to whisper in her ear. "When Cookie goes to his pantry to get some paperwork for me, I want to give you some instructions. Just wait a minute." She leaned back, looking at Olivia's empty plate, then over her shoulder as if she had nothing but time on her hands.

Olivia watched Cookie from the corner of her eye as he turned off the burners, taking his cast iron skillets to the sink. "They can cool for a minute while I get those menus," he told Jets.

When he disappeared into the next room, Janis leaned closer to Olivia. "Here's the deal," she began, "I don't want to be seen with you very often. Just now and then, so as not to alert anyone's suspicion that you're actually working the case."

Olivia nodded, her eyes on the door where Cookie had disappeared.

"While we're waiting for the coroner's report, I'd like to interview that Tone Ranger group. This time in an official capacity. I can write down their take and elicit alibis for yesterday at least. Our guy's time of death is estimated to be about two hours before we showed up."

"You were right to interview the Tone Rangers first," Olivia said. "All of them were being tutored by the deceased. I wanted to tell you earlier, but it didn't seem relevant until he was found dead."

Janis's eyebrows shot up. "Is that so? Interesting connection."

"I only know that because I talked to Dave just the day before he..." At the mention of Dave's name, her eyes welled up with tears.

Janis reached over to pat Olivia's shoulder. "I know how difficult this is for you, but just remember, you're bringing information to help solve this case. The information will help Linnea grieve Dave's death and give her a story to tell their child when he or she is ready. Plus if Dave was shoved off that cliff, then your work will bring the killer to justice. That's the story we want Linnea to tell her child when the time comes, that justice prevailed."

Olivia's tears quickly dried up. Setting her shoulders back with determination she said, "Thanks for the pep talk. I'm on it."

Jets nodded. "And go ahead and show your feelings, shed a tear or two. It only makes your undercover work more authentic. Even before my official interview, I want you to meet up with the teens as soon as you can. Get me any information you know by the end of the day. Let's connect around dinnertime. My temporary office location is the space next to Rydell Cox in the admissions office. Bring food. We can eat and discuss."

I'll have to cancel with Michael again.

"I'll be there," she told Jets, sliding past her to snag one more strip of bacon off the counter.

As soon as Cookie came back into the kitchen, Olivia took her empty plate to the sink. As she rinsed and stacked, Brad May came striding through the door, an envelope in his hand.

His eyes lit up when he saw her. "Hey, Olivia," he waved the envelope in her direction. "Simon Court gave me this to give to you. He said he doesn't have your number to text, so this is old school. I told him you'd be wherever the coffee was, and here you are!"

Olivia dried her hands on a nearby towel before grabbing the envelope from Brad. Sure enough, her name had been scrawled on the back. She slid her nail under the flap and pulled out the paper.

"A secret admirer?" asked Janis from across the room, raising her eyebrows at Olivia.

"Looks like it," she muttered.

As her head bent over the paper, Cookie came from his pantry with a clipboard. He handed it to Jets. "Here's what you wanted. I printed every menu from the past two weeks.

You can keep the pen." Olivia noticed his smirk before she read her note.

Please meet me in the student parking lot at 9 this morning.
I want to talk to you about the Tone Rangers
and my daughter's future
at the Lily Rock Music Academy.
Simon Court

Olivia shoved the paper into her back pocket along with the envelope. She nodded to Jets, who scrutinized the menus, as if committing them to memory. "I have to go now," Olivia said for her benefit. "One of the parents has requested a meeting."

"Where's that gonna happen?" asked Janis.

"In the student parking lot at nine o'clock." Olivia looked at her phone. "I have ten minutes to get there. See you later." Then she called out, "Thanks, Cookie, for breakfast and the coffee."

"Anytime," he answered.

As she left the kitchen through the back door, Olivia's heart began to pound. *I don't want to be late,* she thought, jogging toward the pathway into the grove.

Once she caught sight of the parking lot she slowed to a walk, now aware of sounds overhead. *Clap, clap, whir* caused her to look up.

A helicopter hovered over the parking lot as if looking for a place to land. With a dip and a pause, the wasp-like rotorcraft drifted forward then back, finally settling on the ground below.

Good thing there's still room, what with all the vehicles.

Standing in the pathway, Olivia's heart beat faster. She watched the blades whir as a man appeared in the open door. Simon Court stepped down, ducking from the fast-moving blades.

He looked in her direction, motioning with his hand for her to come closer. When she didn't advance, he broke into a trot. "Good, you're on time. Come on then, we're going to have this talk where we can't be overheard." He smiled and took her by the elbow toward the craft.

Olivia wanted to pull away from his grasp, but she remembered her assignment. *I may get important information from this conversation.*

She followed Court, her heart racing as they approached the whirling blades overhead. Ducking her head, she stepped up the stairs right behind him.

Even in the cockpit, the noise continued.

How will we ever have a conversation with all this racket?

Court pointed to the back seat. She slid into the space behind the pilot, sitting down as Court slid in beside her.

The copter immediately lifted, drifting forward and back and then upward with a jolt. Olivia held her hands in front of her stomach. She looked out the open doors.

I could fall out so easily!

She gulped back the sour taste in her throat.

"Put the belt on," hollered Court. He pulled his own seat belt over his lap and clicking it closed. Then he looked to Olivia to indicate she should do the same. She shortened the belt and clicked it closed, inhaling deeply to soothe her anxiety.

As the helicopter made its way over the academy admissions office, Court handed her a pair of headphones.

He put his on first and then pointed to her. "Your turn," he shouted. She followed his directions, scrunching the headset over her hair, twisting the ear cushions for a snug fit.

"Can you hear me?" asked Court, the sound coming from her headphones.

She nodded.

"You can talk now," he explained. "We're connected on the same channel. No one else can hear, just the two of us."

Olivia gulped as her stomach flipped and then flopped, the nausea coming in waves as the helicopter adjusted its flight pattern. She looked out the side, watching the uneven terrain of the mountain come closer.

One burst of wind and we'll crash into the mountain.

Her eyes drifted downward as she gasped.

That's the Lily Rock trail where Dave went over.

Her hands began to shake. As soon as she turned away from the open door she looked at Simon Court, who held a small smile on his lips as if enjoying her panic.

She clutched her stomach with both hands, sitting farther back in the leather seat. The pilot directed the helicopter toward the canyon, and it took a sudden lurch before rising again. Olivia jumped as Court's voice came up in her earphones.

"I see you aren't familiar with this mode of transportation, Miss Greer. This will be one to write home about." He chuckled as if he'd made a funny joke.

She knew it was at her expense.

"I'll make this quick so that you can get back to whatever you're doing at the school. I want you to know that your sister is in grave danger, even more danger than you are right now. If she continues to interfere with my plan for the future of the academy, she'll be fired and replaced within a day. I have a candidate all lined up, ready to move right into her office." He smirked,

"You mean Rydell Cox?" she asked, aware of the fear in her voice.

"He'd be an excellent choice," Court said, a ruthless smile on his face. "Of course, she could step down of her own accord and avoid all the messiness. It would give me the chance to appoint Cox without parents objecting. Not that many would. Your sister has gotten herself into quite a predicament with a dead tutor on her hands."

Olivia gulped. "Have you spoken to my sister about any of this?"

Court's raspy voice replied, "That's what you're for. You talk sense to her, and that way no one sees me as involved. Of course, she could put up a fuss and then..." He looked toward the open door on his side, his eyes lingering as if to deliberately show Olivia what might happen to anyone who resisted his plan. "As I was saying, another terrible accident might happen, and then Rydell Cox would be right there to pick up the pieces."

He's threatening me and Sage, and not even subtly. What a bully.

"I'd like to return to campus now," Olivia said in a firm voice. "Officer Janis Jets wants to interview me about Dave Franco's death. You don't want to make Jets wait." When he didn't respond, Olivia continued, "You've made your point. Just get me back on the ground."

She watched Court's jaw tighten at the mention of Janis Jets. He nodded. "It's good that you see reason. Sure, we'll take you back. Hasn't this been wonderful? A sightseeing trip in the San Jacinto Mountains at no cost?" He leaned forward to tap the pilot's shoulder.

In a sudden motion the helicopter ducked, then turned.

Olivia's stomach lurched, as she frantically swallowed to stop from losing her breakfast down the back of the pilot's neck.

Simon Court didn't speak for the rest of the flight.

By the time the helicopter landed in the middle of the student parking lot, Olivia had already removed her headphones. She watched Court leisurely taking off his headset. He took hers and then looked out the window before handing both sets to the pilot. "You don't need to be in such a hurry," he said to Olivia, noting with a side glance how she huddled in the corner.

"I have to talk to Sage," she reminded him.

"That's right," he nodded, a quizzical look coming over his face. "I'll go first then." He unbuckled his seat belt, then bounded out of the doorway, ducking his head as he moved down the steps to the ground.

Olivia followed. Once her feet hit the pavement, she lost no time walking past Court. She didn't look back or say goodbye.

When she came out of the woods, she stood next to a tree outside the Curated Cuisine to check in on her stomach.

I'm feeling nauseous.

Only then did Olivia finally take a deep breath—immediately followed by rolling nausea. She ducked back behind a tree, bending over her knees. Her stomach heaved as she vomited the remains of her breakfast.

I'll never eat bacon again.

CHAPTER ELEVEN

When Olivia could stomach being around food again, she leaned against a tree trunk to take a breath. Students and parents filled every nook and cranny of the Curated Cuisine. Olivia could not find a table with an available seat. She looked past the piled plates in the corner.

Standing room only near the wall.

Cookie Kravitz stood in his usual place, watching the room with arms folded. When he saw Olivia a slight smile came to the corner of his mouth. He walked closer. "You look like you could use some more coffee," he commented dryly.

Her stomach dipped. "Actually, some tea would be good right now." She ran her hand through her hair, the back of her neck feeling sticky since the helicopter adventure and the resulting stomach upset.

She could feel Cookie watching her as she made her way toward the hot beverage bar.

What tea would Meadow pick in such a circumstance?

She imagined herself telling the older woman, "I was threatened by a man while trapped in a helicopter over the

Lily Rock trail, where a dead body was found. Is there a tea for such a situation?"

She reached for chamomile and lavender. Pots of hot water simmered, steam rising from each spout. She grabbed one handle and poured the scalding water over her tea bag. As soon as she placed the pot back, a student helper swooped down to take the container to the kitchen for a refill.

"I'm the refill guy," he said to Olivia over his shoulder, his back disappearing through the kitchen doors.

Olivia held the hot mug in her hand as she looked over the room. Cookie, in his customary pose, surveyed the dining room like a hunter looking for prey.

Olivia walked toward Cookie, still holding the hot mug of tea. She turned to stand beside him, taking in his perspective. "So what do you see that I don't?" she asked.

He didn't answer at first as his neck shifted from left to right.

The man is begging for a metaphor. Now he reminds me of an owl who looks for prey, neck shifting without moving his body.

"If you'll excuse me," Cookie muttered, ignoring Olivia's question. Striding across the room, he lifted an empty plate from the bakery table. With the other hand he gestured to a student helper to take the plate away. He spoke into the server's ear. The student turned beet red and fled toward the kitchen.

"No plate goes unfilled on his watch," Olivia mumbled under her breath.

Each sip of tea calmed her stomach. She kept observing the diners until she heard a familiar voice from across the room.

"Just stop it, I don't want to talk about your pathetic

ideas anymore," exclaimed Abbey Court. Legend hovered over her, dressed in a long flowered skirt, with a peasant top exposing a bit of hair on her chest. Her dangly hoop earrings bounced against her unshaven cheeks.

"There's never a good time to talk about an idea that isn't yours," Legend rebutted, flouncing away before Abbey could reply.

Olivia took her last sip of tea; she felt the residue of leaves on her tongue. She placed the empty mug on the table marked for dirty dishes, then made her way across the room toward Raleigh, who stood with a plate held high over their head so as not to get jostled in the crowd.

They're looking for somewhere to sit.

Olivia waved, pointing to an empty chair next to her corner of the room.

Raleigh smiled, maneuvering through the crowd toward the chair. Once they settled, Olivia came closer for a conversation.

"Hey, Raleigh. This place is a madhouse."

They smiled, carefully cutting the cinnamon roll into equal-sized pieces, beginning in the center and working methodically to the outside. With each piece arranged in a circle, they plunged a fork into one delicious bite, then the next.

Olivia watched Raleigh eat. When finished with the roll, they moved on to the bacon, finished that, then started on a bagel. Using the knife, Raleigh carefully spread a thin layer of butter over both halves. They reached for the cream cheese and spread a layer over the butter, precisely covering every open space.

They are quite particular in every action they take. Not that I think they would, but if Raleigh wanted to kill some-

one, they would meticulously plan and then execute without flinching. Just ask that bagel.

Olivia pointed. "I'm fascinated by your style. The more butter and cream cheese the better, for me. I tend to be a mounder, not a spreader."

"I never heard that word before...mounder." They took a bite of the bagel.

"That's because I just made it up."

Olivia leaned toward Raleigh to ask, "Could you round up the rest of the Tone Rangers for a meeting, let's say right before dinner? I'd like to talk about last-minute details before tomorrow's parent recital."

They nodded, taking another bite of bagel. "I'll get them together, what time?"

"Let's say 4:00." *That will give me time to find Janis.*

Olivia patted Raleigh on the shoulder, making her way across the room toward the main entrance. She walked around the students and parents lined up outside, waiting for their chance to enter the dining room.

Dave Franco dies a day ago and still, life goes on. Look who's in line...

"Hey, Anais," she called out.

Anais had been staring at her boots, half listening to a woman who stood next to her dressed in shorts and a Lily Rock Music Academy T-shirt. The shirt looked new, the words *Parent Weekend at the Lily Rock Music Academy* silk-screened on the front with a logo of Lily Rock over the left breast.

The woman turned to speak to Anais, who was still staring at her boots.

Olivia glanced at the balding man who stood on the other side of Anais. He looked upward toward the trees, his hands in his pockets.

"Hey, Anais," Olivia called again, walking closer this time.

The woman must have heard Olivia call out. "Someone is talking to you," she told Anais, pulling on her sleeve. "Maybe one of your teachers?"

Anais looked over. She stared at Olivia and tentatively smiled, walking away from the line toward her. "Hi," she said quietly.

"How are you this morning?" asked Olivia.

"Kind of bummed about Dave jumping off the cliff."

"I was there for the rescue." Olivia observed Anais carefully.

Does she assume that he jumped or is that what's being said around campus?

She cleared her throat. "The police have not determined what happened to cause his fall," Olivia instantly realized that she sounded too close to the facts. *You're undercover, you idiot. Stop sounding like you work for the constabulary.*

"I think that's how it works; I watch a lot of police procedures on Netflix," she added, hoping to cover her tracks.

Anais nodded. "See those people?" The girl pointed to the woman and man who held her place in line.

"Are those your parents?"

"Those are my grands," said Anais.

"Grands, like the big biscuits?"

Anais giggled. "No, grands like I used to be a little, and so I started calling them the grands."

"I thought the grandparents called the grandchild a 'grand'," Olivia said.

"Not in my case," Anais smiled. "I named them first. They are the grands."

"Want to introduce me?" offered Olivia.

"Yeah, come on."

Both of the grands smiled eagerly as Olivia and Anais approached. "I'm Carl Butler, Anais's grandfather," the man said. "This is my wife, Jean." The woman reached for Olivia's hand and gave it a vigorous shake.

"We're delighted to meet you. You're the Tone Rangers's coach, right? We are so looking forward to hearing them sing tomorrow."

"Have I met you before?" asked Olivia.

"Oh no, not in person. Anais's college counselor told us who you were when we arrived yesterday. He has your photo on his desk, from a newspaper clipping about your band."

Olivia felt her neck tingle.

That's very odd. I don't even know Cox.

Carl Butler changed the subject. "The campus looks like it's improved this past year, at least the cafeteria part. Maybe my son's money is being put to good use."

"Now stop, honey. This isn't the time to talk business," chided Jean Butler. "It's time to fuss over Anais. Don't you think she's spectacular?" asked the woman, giving no room for anything other than agreement.

"Oh, I do," said Olivia with conviction. "She's an excellent alto with musical sensitivity."

"Of course she's good at music," agreed Carl. "It's the college admission test she needs help with. Now that the tutor—what's his name?—has turned up dead, we'll need to find someone else."

Jean tapped her husband's elbow. "Don't worry. Abbey's dad will have someone for Anais by this weekend. He hasn't let us down yet."

Olivia must have looked confused because Carl quickly added, "Rydell Cox has been our college admissions counselor for years. We pay him out of the trust fund and he gets things done. Rydell introduced us to Simon Court, and that's how Anais got to the Lily Rock Music Academy."

Obviously from LA with all that talk about money.

"And that's how the Lily Rock Music Academy got a new cafeteria and dining room?" added Olivia, keeping her voice light.

The couple didn't flinch. Jean spoke up first. "That's one of the ways the school benefitted. We also donated an equal amount to an orphanage in Tijuana. Simon handled everything. Such a good thing to do, invest in the lives of underprivileged children."

And a good tax deduction.

Olivia turned toward Anais. "Did Raleigh text you? We're rehearsing this afternoon at four o'clock?"

"I'll be there," she said quietly, staring at the dirt once again.

Pulling on the girl's hand, Olivia separated Anais from her grandparents to speak privately. "Why don't you come to the rehearsal a little early, say around 3:30? We can talk more about Dave—and the music, of course."

Anais glanced back at her grandparents. "Okay, I'll be there." Then she whispered in Olivia's ear, "It would be good to get some space from the grands. They're a bit... oppressive."

Olivia chuckled and murmured back. "It must be challenging to be everyone's center of attention."

Anais sighed. "See you soon."

That's two Tone Rangers. If Raleigh texts Abbey and Legend about the rehearsal this afternoon, then we'll have a rehearsal and an interview all rolled into one.

. . .

In the administrative office, Olivia rubbed her nose, aware of a musty smell emanating from the curtains. Since the last time, artwork had been hung on the walls with pushpins.

Probably trying to impress the parents.

A desk had been shoved into a corner, with a computer and printer stacked on top. No one sat in the available chairs.

Three inner doors were closed to the center room. They looked identical except for a plaque indicating the occupant. "Sage McCloud, Academy Director" was on the one to the far right, and "Rydell Cox, Academy Guidance Counselor" was on the middle door.

And behind door number three?

Olivia reached out and knocked.

"Come in," came Janis Jets's voice. As soon as she stepped inside, Jets looked up from her computer. She motioned for Olivia to sit down across from her desk.

"I'm almost done with my notes. Keep yourself busy for a minute," Jets told her.

As she sat down her phone buzzed. Michael's name showed up on her screen.

She tapped the green button to answer and asked, "How are you?"

"Fine, tried your place for coffee and then realized you're staying at the academy."

"Cookie made me coffee and breakfast this morning," she said playfully.

"That better be all he did for you," mumbled Michael.

When I tell him about Court's threat, he'll be furious.

"About our dinner tonight..." he started.

Olivia had been dreading this moment since she'd agreed to meet with Janis instead of going out with Michael.

She blurted out her news. "I can't make it this time. I am so sorry. Janis wants to see me to talk about the case."

She exhaled slowly, waiting for Michael's reply. She watched Jets, still focused on her computer, seemingly oblivious to the conversation. "I bet I'll be getting double pay too, since it's working on the weekend," she added, making an attempt to sound more professional.

Jets turned in her chair, giving Olivia a double thumbs-down.

"Or maybe not," said Olivia. "But seriously, I want our dinner to be special. We've waited so long to go on a real date. Let's try for next week?"

"One more delay," muttered Michael. "I told you I wouldn't wait forever."

Fearful she'd gone too far, her brain began to search frantically for a way to salvage the situation.

"I'm not going to keep doing this. You're either in or you're out. I'm done scrambling."

Olivia's face froze. *I don't want him to give up on us.*

"I am a victim of my own lack of time management, that's all. I want to have our dinner, but how about this? Do you want to come to the academy instead? I'm sure Janis would appreciate your perspective."

"Do you think so?" Michael's voice shifted.

Olivia looked at Janis. She shook her head vigorously, giving another thumbs-down.

Olivia made a sad face.

Janis relented. "Go ahead and invite him," turning back to the work on her computer.

"I just got confirmation. Dinner for three in this office, right after my coaching session with the Tone Rangers."

"I'll bring the food," Michael added, his voice sounding lighter.

By the time they disconnected, Janis Jets had shut down her computer. She focused her blue eyes on Olivia. "I saw you go on that helicopter ride right after breakfast. Bet you weren't so happy with your decision to eat all that bacon."

Olivia felt a rumble in her stomach at the mention of bacon. "Please don't name any food related to pork again," she begged.

Janis chuckled. Before she could say more, the door behind Olivia opened, revealing a man dressed in a three-piece suit. He stepped inside without invitation, closing the door behind him.

"Hello, Rydell," Janis said, her voice dropping.

Ignoring Janis, he stopped in from of Olivia. Would you leave us for a minute? I have important business to discuss with the police officer."

Olivia felt the hair on her neck raise.

Now here's a man who wears his superiority like another skin-tight suit.

She didn't object but rose from her seat to step out of the open door.

No one here to observe me eavesdropping.

She closed the door behind her and stepped closer to it, leaning almost against it.

"Hey, baby, want to get a bite to eat later?" came Rydell's voice. He'd turned from demanding official to smooth-talking Don Juan in the time it took for the door to close.

Before Janis could answer, Cox added, "You can wear those sexy leather pants for me, just like last time. Come on. Say yes."

"I can't have dinner, but I could forget my pants on our next date." Janis responded dryly. "I could go all Winnie the Pooh just for you."

Janis and Rydell laughed, making Olivia's skin crawl. She leaned even closer to the door.

So she's dating that guy? I can't believe Janis would stoop so low.

The doorknob began to turn, giving Olivia barely enough time to scoot across the room before it fully opened. She pretended to scrutinize the bulletin board as Cox walked past without a greeting. Avoiding his own office, he headed toward the exit.

Olivia waited for Cox to leave before she stuck her head back through Janis's doorway. "Is your private moment over?"

For a second Janis didn't seem to register the meaning of her question, and then her face flamed bright red. "You heard us, right?" She fumbled with a pencil on her desk. "I guess you know we're dating."

"I guess I do," admitted Olivia, keeping her voice light. "Do you want to talk about the case now?"

Janis frowned. "I sure as hell don't want to talk about my feelings. Sit down and tell me what you've got."

Olivia did as told, searching her mind for what she'd learned that morning. "I have a rehearsal with the Tone Rangers," she glanced at her cell phone, "in twenty minutes."

"About time you take this assignment seriously."

"I've got a feeling about one of the kids—Anais."

"Don't tell me you sang her a tune and she started blabbing all her secrets to you like the last time."

"I didn't sing to her." Olivia felt the sting of Janis's words. "But she's acting oddly and she's really upset by Dave's death."

"He was her tutor." Jets nodded. "Kids get attracted to tutors. Was there something going on with the two of them?"

Olivia's stomach clenched. "I hope not. She's just seventeen and he was at least in his late twenties. Plus as you know, he had a wife with a baby on the way."

"So what's your take on Dave Franco? Was he a good guy, is that what you're saying?"

Olivia took a moment to remember the percussionist. His serious attitude, wanting to help the students. Plus he played music with nuance. "He didn't overpower his bandmates," she said as if that would explain. "That's saying a lot for a guy who could make the loudest sound in a folk group."

"Oh sure, like I know what that means," said Janis.

"It means he wasn't a showboat. He played underneath other musicians to back them up and only took a solo when it seemed right for the music, not just for his ego."

Jets stared at Olivia. Her eyes widened as if taking in the information.

"That's probably the most insightful thing I've heard about the guy since I started this investigation."

Olivia leaned over the desk toward Janis, sensing their old connection. But before she could smile, Janis shut down the moment.

"Time for you to interview the suspects. Time for me to check on the guy next door."

"He left the building," commented Olivia dryly.

"Is that so?"

Janis doesn't look disappointed, just curious. Maybe she's wondering where she left the leather pants...

CHAPTER TWELVE

It wasn't until Olivia walked away from the admissions office that she admitted to herself, *The sooner I interview the Tone Rangers the better. I need to get on this before Janis gets mad.*

Taking the path through the woods felt calming to her nerves. The clumps of dirt stuck to her worn cowboy boots, a sting from a mosquito assaulting her ear...

Smack went her hand. "Stop nagging me," she said aloud, looking at the remains of the insect's body in her palm.

Olivia inhaled. The scent of pine filled her nostrils. She inhaled again, more deeply feeling her abdomen expand, then she exhaled from her nose.

I can taste the trees on my tongue. No matter how late or distracted, this breathing thing works.

Inhale, exhale.

A blur of motion a distance away caught her eye. Mayor Maguire trotted on nimble paws toward her, his tongue hanging out the side of his mouth.

"Where have you been, doggo?" Olivia greeted him.

He came up to her and sat in front of her feet. She bent over to scratch behind his ears. The dog kept his eyes on hers, as if he had something on his mind.

"I know that look, M&M. You want me to come with you." She fluffed his ears again. When she didn't make a move, he stood on his back feet, then raised his front paws to place one on each of her shoulders. Before she could admonish him, he licked her closed mouth.

Olivia laughed. "Okay, Mayor, what's your deal?" She took one paw in each hand to direct him back to the ground.

Mayor Maguire turned in three circles and then barked playfully.

Olivia laughed again, watching the dog circle one more time before coming to his place by her right foot.

I have no idea what he's trying to tell me right now, but I know it must be important.

"Let's go," she told him.

This time she followed the dog farther into the woods, his excited tail encouraging her to walk faster. Olivia broke into a trot to keep up, but he suddenly stopped in his tracks. Olivia stopped right behind him, holding her breath so that she could hear. Muffled sobs came from a short distance.

Someone's crying.

Mayor Maguire stepped forward as Olivia followed. The dog skulked around three pine trees clumped together, giving Olivia a chance to move ahead without him. Her heart thudded in her chest.

"Sage," Olivia called in a quiet voice.

Sage lifted her head from a picnic bench, her face swollen and red from crying.

As soon as Olivia greeted her, the mayor came closer. He inched his way to nudge her thigh with his black nose, his tongue reaching to lick a tear.

Olivia approached the dog and her sister gingerly, sitting close by on the bench.

Sage turned and patted M&M, her eyes eventually finding Olivia.

"What's wrong, honey?" Olivia asked.

Sage sniffed, pulling out a wad of napkins from her pocket. Dabbing at her face, she spread out one napkin and blew into it. Two nose wipes later she looked over at Olivia again, attempting a smile.

"A small breakdown, if you must know."

"This has to be a difficult for you," Olivia said. "Parent weekend and Dave's death."

Sage nodded. "It was hard telling the families about Dave. Then Janis told me I had to keep everyone on campus, maybe into next week. She doesn't know when the police reports will come back and it's all up in the air."

"That's what she told me."

A puzzled look came over Sage's face. "How are things working out in the dorm? Have you learned anything from the students about Dave?"

"Kind of," said Olivia. "I'm actually on my way to a rehearsal with the Tone Rangers now. Janis wants me to keep asking questions. Anais has already spoken to me and I've seen Abbey. Raleigh and Legend are more elusive, but I hope to get them to open up eventually."

"Does Janis think one of my students actually killed Dave? They all loved him and said he was a lifesaver when it came to helping with their college admission prep."

"Lifesaver or not, Janis Jets leaves no stone nor suspect unturned."

"Of course, it's possible that a teen could kill someone, I just don't see it happening here at the academy. I mean, we have student meetings about killing bugs and if it's the ethical thing to do." Sage sighed. "Actually the parents have been so supportive over all of this. They like the time with the students. It's kind of sweet how even grandparents shadow their grandchild through the day."

"You mean Anais and the grands?" asked Olivia.

"And others," said Sage.

"I spoke to Anais and her grandparents while they were in line for lunch. They seemed nice enough. I did get a bit nervous when they told me about their connection with Rydell Cox and Simon Court."

At the mention of Rydell Cox, Sage's lips made a straight line. "I think Cox wants my job. Every time I turn around in that office, he's popping out of his door to see what I'm doing, like he's waiting for me to make a wrong move so that he can report to Court and the advisory board."

I'm not going to mention my helicopter ride, at least not yet. Sage doesn't need to worry about me.

"So you think there's an actual plan to fire you and put Cox in your job?"

Sage nodded. "I do, in fact. I know that's the plan. I feel it in my gut."

"Will you push back?"

"I will stand my ground. It will probably make them come on stronger, but I don't care. It's not just about me. The students need someone to show them the bigger picture. High school isn't just a path to getting into college with an early admission.

"Kids are young and need time to get to know themselves while they're learning. Look at the Tone Rangers. All they think about is that audition coming up. They have no idea how to listen to each other and work as a group. That's a necessary life skill, don't you think? That's what's important to me, and I seem to be the only person who cares about what lies beyond the next year."

Olivia nodded. "More bands break up because of communication obstacles than anything else. If they can't talk to each other, there's no chance for consensus. I didn't go to college, but I would have appreciated that lesson in group dynamics."

"Plus many of the adults live through their kids, thinking a prestigious college makes up for what they didn't have. They're the ones who are the most vulnerable to guys like Rydell Cox and Simon Court who promise early admission to Harvard or Yale."

"So you're not going to resign over the pressure," said Olivia, certain in her observation.

"I am not!" stated Sage. "I'm not leaving the position until I get a notice that I'm fired. Like I said, it's not just about me."

Olivia slid closer to Sage, placing her arm around her shoulders. "Then I'm not going to say otherwise. But I am going to keep my eye on you and I'll tell Janis about the pressure you feel."

I hope Janis will pay attention and not dismiss Sage's concerns...

During their conversation Mayor Maguire had circled the bench, alternating his stare from one face to the other. Now he stopped to look up at Olivia.

"Oh drat, I have my rehearsal with the Tone Rangers. I have to go. I'm late already." Olivia patted Sage's knee. "We've got this, honey. You're not alone." She stood up from the bench.

Sage sniffed. "I'm feeling better. Now if I can just stay away from that jerk of a guidance counselor. He gives me the creeps."

Olivia reached out a hand, and Sage took it, pulling herself up to stand. "I don't think you have to worry too much. Rydell seems to be focused on other people right now." Olivia hesitated but then blurted, "He and Janis are having a thing, if you know what I mean."

"No!" exclaimed Sage. "I thought Janis had better taste than the likes of Rydell Cox. He's so sleazy."

"Apparently he likes Janis dressed in leather pants. What can I say?"

"*Ick* is the only word for that," Sage said, a slight smile on her lips.

"I agree, but we can talk more later. I'd better be on my way before the kids give up and I don't get my 'interview'." She used air quotes around the word interview to make Sage smile.

"I'll head back with you," said Sage.

Mayor Maguire walked between them, his tail wagging happily.

By the time Olivia arrived in the auditorium, the Tone Rangers had formed a semicircle of chairs. Legend sat on the end, her head bent over a cell phone.

Clumps of dirt beneath the chair had fallen from her hiking boots. Then when Legend crossed her legs, the sole of one boot showed leaves and dirt crushed into the crevices.

Raleigh sat next to Legend, also looking at a cell phone. Distressed jeans exposed large patches of skin underneath the fraying. They also wore a Lily Rock Music Academy T-shirt hanging loosely over their thin torso, along with the same style hiking boots.

Anais sat next to Legend. She'd arranged her blond

curls in a high ponytail and wore shorts and a T-shirt. Olivia noted the addition of expensive leather cowboy boots.

What happened to her other pair of matching boots? Maybe she's already individuating from the Tone Rangers. Wait a minute. Those look just like mine!

Olivia looked down at her scuffed cowboy boots. *She's wearing shorts like mine as well. Maybe I'm the new role model...that would be a first.*

Abbey Court sat as far away from her nemesis, Legend Watner, as she could. No phone in her hand, she stared straight ahead. At the sound of Olivia's voice, Abbey looked up.

"Hey guys, sorry I'm late," Olivia said. "Oops," she corrected herself. "I know you aren't all guys. I really have to be more careful of how I address people."

Legend and Raleigh shrugged. Anais and Abbey said nothing.

Olivia pulled a chair from behind the piano to sit in front of the Tone Rangers. She took a long look at each student, giving each one a thorough once-over. Only Anais met her gaze.

When no one acknowledged her, she spoke, "I wanted to say how sorry I am about the loss of your tutor and my friend Dave Franco. This has been a shocking time. How are you holding up?"

"We're okay," said Abbey primly. "The school isn't dealing very well with this catastrophe. My father is very upset."

Olivia looked around to invite anyone else to speak. The other three paid no attention to Abbey or Olivia.

"Is your dad here this weekend?" asked Olivia.

"He'll be here tomorrow. He's detained by important

business in Los Angeles," responded Abbey, as if she'd been asked to memorize the answer to that very question.

"How about you, Anais?" Olivia addressed the shy girl. "You and the grands having some fun this weekend? Have you been able to put aside thoughts of Dave's death?"

Anais nodded, but kept her eyes on her cell phone.

"I think Dave was pushed off the cliff," said Legend abruptly. She smoothed her skirt with a brushing motion. "I think someone at the school didn't want him helping us. They knew we'd score higher on the SATs, and they pushed him off to keep us down."

Olivia felt confused. *Somehow the Tone Rangers have put themselves in the middle of Dave's death.*

"Say more, Legend, about the other students."

"We get extra help because we're going somewhere. A top-ranking college is only the beginning. Our parents pay for us to get the best education, which means they have to hire a tutor. Abbey's dad made sure Dave was here for us weeks before fall semester. Everyone knows Simon Court has a ninety-nine percent college acceptance rate for all of his clients."

Abbey nodded, words pouring from her mouth. "My father is the premier counselor in Los Angeles. He also works across the country to help families with their gifted and talented kids."

"I see," commented Olivia.

For once Abbey and Legend agree. She shifted her glance to Raleigh.

"What do you think, Raleigh? How are you holding up since the death of Dave?"

Raleigh clicked the cell phone off. Looking over at Legend, they spoke in a quiet voice. "The thing is, me and

Legend may have been the last people to see Dave before he, you know, toppled off the cliff."

Legend glared at Raleigh. "Now is not the time. You don't need to confess to our tutor."

I wondered if I was good enough for this elite group of self-promoters, and I think I just got my answer.

Olivia pushed back her indignation, keeping her voice neutral. "What makes you think you were the last ones to see Dave?"

"We were hiking the Lily Rock trail and saw him standing near the cliff. He wasn't alone. He was smoking a cigar with Cookie. They didn't notice us, so we just hiked deeper into the forest to avoid any small talk." Raleigh turned their head to avoid Legend's dirty look.

Abbey fidgeted in her seat, as if she too were uncomfortable with Raleigh's confession. "I am personally exhausted from adults asking me where I'm going to college and what my scores are on the PSAT. It's like all they think about is my potential as an adult." She folded her hands in her lap.

Anais looked up from her cell phone. "My grandparents bought me a new pair of boots today," she said, completely off topic.

Abbey patted her knee. "That's nice, sweetie, but we aren't talking about your choice of footwear."

Olivia took a moment to process what she'd heard.

The boys saw Dave before his fall. They claim to have continued hiking in the other direction. More importantly, Cookie was with Dave. I'd better tell Janis.

"What time did you see Cookie and Dave?" Olivia asked.

Both Legend and Raleigh stared Olivia down.

"And that's your business because?" asked Legend.

"I'm just trying to understand what happened," Olivia

tried. "It's all been such a shock. Dave was a friend of mine, you know."

Raleigh took out his phone and handed it to Olivia. "I took a selfie of us in front of that old oak tree and here's the time stamp. It was 3:54 exactly."

Raleigh, dressed in a T-shirt and baseball cap, could be seen in the photo, one hand giving a thumbs-up, the other hand out of the frame, most likely holding the cell phone. Legend wore a similar faded baseball cap, smiling next to Raleigh in the photo. They looked like two students enjoying each other's company, hiking on the Lily Rock trail.

At least that's what the timely snapshot implies.

By now Legend grew restless, squirming in her chair. Anais stared distractedly over Olivia's head. Abbey scrolled on her cell phone. Only Raleigh looked ready.

Maybe we'd better start our rehearsal. I don't want to get their defenses up any more than I already have.

Armed with her new information, Olivia said, "Let's run through your set one time and then we'll work on the details for tomorrow's concert."

"Olivia," said Anais, "will we ever get to hear you sing?"

Being admired by an impressionable teen feels good.

"Sweet Four O'Clock plays the weekend after next at the outdoor amphitheater. I'll make sure to have a ticket for each of you at the box office."

"Don't bother for me," snarled Abbey. "I'll be taken out of this antiquated place and living at another prep school by then. Goodbye Tone Rangers," she said, waving her hand as if to brush off a fly.

"Good riddance," Legend fired back. "Sopranos are a dime a dozen, and now I can sing most of the high parts."

Olivia sighed. "That may well be, but we still have a

concert tomorrow. So let's make it your best. Stand now and let's sing 'Closer to Fine' as a warm-up."

After an hour's rehearsal Olivia felt her stomach growl. *I'm hungry. Time for a break so I can refuel.* "Good rehearsal, everyone. I'll see you tomorrow an hour before the concert. Wear black."

Rather than chat with the students, she folded her chair, stacked it behind the upright piano, and made her way to the stage exit. As soon as she had one foot out the door she heard her name called.

"Olivia, how was my singing today?"

She turned to face Anais. "Your intonation is spot-on as always."

Anais's face glowed with the compliment.

"Did you have a good voice coach growing up?" she asked.

"I did," Anais said, nodding, "but I'm sure I'm not as good as you."

Not again. I think this girl has a crush on me.

Easing her purse over her shoulder, Olivia looked longingly toward the Curated Cuisine. "Do you want to walk with me?"

"Oh, I do," said the girl.

Side by side they made their way along the footpath, along with Mayor Maguire, who joined them midway.

"Is that your dog?" asked Anais.

Olivia chuckled. "Now that you've asked, let me introduce you to the mayor of Lily Rock." She stopped in front of M&M, who moved ahead, blocking their path.

"Mayor Maguire, meet Anais Butler. Anais, meet Mayor

Maguire." The dog lifted his right paw for Anais to take, and she giggled, extending her hand.

"He's the mayor?"

"Yes, he is, and you can call him M&M—that's "my nickname for him." The dog dropped his paw and then wagged his tail.

Anais shook her head. "Lily Rock is a funny place. But I like it here."

"I do too. It took some time to realize I belonged, but now I call Lily Rock my home." Olivia felt her spirit lighten as she spoke those words.

That admission was a long time coming.

Anais cleared her throat. "Before we get a snack, there's something I want to tell you about Dave and his death."

Olivia made every effort to look relaxed.

Maybe I'm going to get some pertinent information for Janis right now.

"Of course," she said immediately.

"I think I overheard Abbey telling her father that we're all better off now that Dave was, you know, dead."

"You heard her say that?"

"On her cell right before you got to rehearsal. I'm sure she was talking to her father, I saw his name come up on her screen before she answered. I pretended not to listen. Most people ignore me anyway, so she didn't think I'd understand what she was saying."

Olivia felt confused. "What I don't get is why she thought she could talk right in front of you."

"Oh, Abbey does that all the time. She's not the only one. Just because I'm quiet, people think I can't hear and don't have any opinions."

"But you do hear things. Thanks for letting me know."

They walked a few more steps before Anais spoke

again. "So do you think that Abbey's father pushed him over the cliff?"

"That might be possible, but don't forget, Anais, we have no proof that Simon Court was even here when Dave died. He has an alibi for Los Angeles—at least I think he does."

Stop talking, Olivia. You'll be giving up your cover with too much information.

"That's what I heard from the Lily Rock police officer, Janis Jets," Olivia hastily added. "She told me in passing, you know, one grownup to another...over coffee."

Could I make a bigger mess of this?

"You know the police in Lily Rock?" Anais asked, eyes wide with admiration.

Olivia squirmed and then changed the subject. "I sure do miss Dave, but right now I'm hungry. Let's find a snack, maybe Cookie has some of his home-baked chocolate chip cookies straight from the oven."

"I hope he remembered the pecans this time," sighed Anais.

With Mayor Maguire between them, they walked toward the Curated Cuisine.

CHAPTER THIRTEEN

Later that afternoon Olivia had a few minutes before meeting up with Anais. On her way to the auditorium, she spotted the grands, who spoke animatedly to the very person she wanted to talk to.

Rather than join them, she ducked aside to keep out of sight, wanting to observe the three in line. She focused on Anais, checking for any clues in her behavior.

What would guilt look like on a seventeen-year-old girl?

Anais didn't pay attention to her grandparents. Instead she looked down at her feet, lifting one boot then the other, seeming to admire them. By keeping silent and disinterested, she deflected all efforts from her grandparents to engage in conversation.

Anais looks like a normal teen to me. I'm just like her. If it weren't for Janis's assignment I'd be by myself on the back deck looking at the woods, perfectly content to be on my own.

Maybe if I go around the side of the building I can slip in the back door and grab some cold bubbly water. Ol' blue eyes won't mind, so long as I stay out of his way.

As nonchalantly as possible, Olivia slowly circled to the

left, taking a page from Anais's playbook. She stared at her feet, walking with slow deliberate steps, until she was out of earshot.

The gentle sway of leaves in the grove caught her attention. Kicking the toe of her boot into a pile of decomposing leaves brought the ever-present odor of pine up to her nose. She sniffed and sneezed, then inhaled deeply.

Pausing a few moments to appreciate the quiet, she circled again, arriving at the back door of the kitchen uninterrupted. She ducked inside, stopping at the threshold.

"Sit pretty, Mayor," came Cookie's voice.

Mayor Maguire stood on his back legs in front of Cookie, eyeing a piece of meat in his hand.

"Good doggie. Okay!" Cookie gave the universal release command of dog trainers. Mayor Maguire leapt from his pose to snatch the meat right out of his hand.

Cookie likes the mayor.

Olivia smiled at them. Cookie came right over. "To what do I owe this pleasure?" he asked.

She retied her hair into an informal ponytail and then spoke. "I'd like to walk in the front entrance, but I'm so tired of making small talk. If you point me in the right direction, I'll find a bottle of sparkling water on my own and then get out of your way."

"Do you want lemon or lime with that?" he asked with a grin.

"Lemon would be wonderful," she said. She watched him open the industrial-sized refrigerator and pull out a sparkling water. He poured it into a glass and then reached for a lemon stored on the carving island. With three quick slices he created wedges, one of which he slipped over the edge of her glass. "Here you go," he said, handing the glass to Olivia.

"Thank you so much," she squeezing lemon juice into the water and taking a quick sip, appreciating the cool water sliding down her parched throat.

Cookie watched her with a smile. "You're pretty thirsty. It's hot in these parts. Don't forget to hydrate."

The aftertaste of lemon tingled her lips as Olivia took another drink. She finished the entire contents of the glass. "When I drink water my thoughts clear up," she commented. "Ever happen to you?"

Cookie laughed. "Not with water, it doesn't. I have had some pretty big insights over a neat glass of Scotch though."

"I remember that feeling," she told him. "Scotch was my drink of choice a few years ago. But now I stick to water with bubbles." She placed the glass on the counter, watching Cookie.

"I understand," he said softly. "A lot of guys I served with in Afghanistan are the same. Clean and sober, water only."

"Are you enjoying parent weekend?" she asked, adroitly changing the subject.

"Twice as much food to prepare, but not a problem. I have lots of help in the kitchen and with serving. Plus I've been fending off complaints with a certain amount of...if I say so myself...finesse." He pretended to polish the nails of his right hand on his immaculate white apron. "How about this? I'll put several bottles of cold sparkling water into an ice chest and I'll send Brad up to your room to deliver them. He should be about done at the front door."

"Oh, that would be wonderful," Olivia smiled. "I can't thank you enough."

"Do you want any food with that?" asked Cookie. "Any food preferences or allergies I should know about?"

"I am an omnivore, full-on dairy-product-consuming,

embrace-the-sugar kind of woman," announced Olivia with pride. "But I do appreciate how you take all of the food requirements of every person into consideration."

"It's part of my job," he commented, pointing toward the pantry in the back. "If my food safety isn't enough, I keep medications for the students in the back, just in case someone needs an antacid or something to soothe their stomachs. Everything's checked with the nurse, of course. That makes the parents very happy." Cookie nodded.

"Thanks for the offer of extra water. I would appreciate a small cooler in my room. Hopefully I can return home in a couple more days."

"Jets mentioned that to me, how she's holding people in place until they can decide if Dave's death was an accident or deliberate."

Sensing that Cookie might connect her with Janis's investigation, Olivia quickly interjected. "I'm just here for the kids. Sage wanted me to step in. The old resident advisor left last week before Dave died. She needed a temp until they vetted another person."

"I see," said Cookie, staring her straight in the eye.

I don't think he believes a word I'm saying. I wonder if he'll report back to Simon Court.

"I better go now," Olivia hastily added. "I want to put together a set list for tomorrow's recital."

"Your water should arrive within the hour. See you later, Olivia."

By the time she reached her room, exhaustion had traveled from her head to her shoulders and back. Stretching out on her narrow bed, she tightened her shoulders and released them, repeating the same pattern with her chest, back, then legs and feet. Tense, hold, then release. After scanning her entire body she inhaled and then exhaled three times, when a knock at the door disrupted her concentration.

It must be Brad. I almost forgot about him.

She stood, stepping over to open the door, revealing Brad holding a small cooler.

"Here's your water," he said with his usual lazy smile.

Olivia reached for the cooler, gesturing for Brad to enter the room. She gasped as someone slipped behind to follow.

"Cayenne!" she cried. Setting the cooler at her feet, Olivia reached up to hug her tall friend.

"It's wonderful to see you," Olivia added, dropping her arms.

Brad laughed, spinning the desk chair around to sit down. "I called her and she came right away," he explained.

"Why did you call Cay? Not that I mind." She turned back to smile at the tall woman who seated herself on the edge of the bed.

"I saw you doing that weird thing in the woods—you know, skittering toward the cafeteria and then changing your mind...and then you thought no one could see you and you walked to the back entrance? Anyway that looked suspicious to me, so I called Cay. I knew she'd talk to you woman to woman." Brad grinned as if he'd figured out a really difficult math problem even though no one thought he could.

Olivia sat on the bed, bringing her legs up to her chest as she propped her back against the wall.

"Anyone like a water?" she asked.

"I'll take one," Cayenne said. Then she stood and walked to the window. Since she didn't say any more, Olivia turned to Brad.

"So how are things going with parent weekend?"

He frowned. "Okay except for Dave." Brad glanced over

to Cayenne, who continued to look out the window, her hands clasped behind her back.

"Were you and Dave friends?" asked Olivia. "I didn't realize."

"I knew him from high school," explained Brad. "Everyone who lived in Lily Rock was bused down and we'd sit next to each other on the ride. I knew him before he played drums, if you can believe it."

"Then do you know his wife?"

"Linnea? Sure, I know her. I haven't talked to her for a while though, and now it's just too hard." Brad's face softened.

"It's very hard to talk about death," admitted Olivia.

Cayenne turned abruptly from the window. "Death is the only important topic to discuss. Everything else has little to no significance."

Not knowing what to do with Cayenne's assessment, Olivia nodded. Before she could comment, Brad spoke.

"So let me tell you about my last conversation with Dave. He was worried, you know." Brad's voice grew insistent.

"About the baby?" Olivia asked.

"Not the baby, about his job of tutoring and teaching test taking."

"He didn't say a lot about the tutoring gig to me," Olivia admitted.

"That's just it, tutoring wasn't his whole job, at least as he explained it," Brad said. "Dave was prepping the students for their college admission tests. And get this, he wasn't just prepping the kids. He took the tests for them."

Olivia pushed her back harder against the wall, feeling her gut clench. She glared at Brad. "What do you mean he 'took' the tests?"

"Abbey's dad would pay for plane tickets and he'd go to other parts of the country where he'd pretend to proctor. Each student took the test in a different location, prearranged by that Court guy.

Parents took the kids to Dave and then he'd watch the kids mark the answer sheets, making sure they used a certain number two pencil. Afterward he'd mark another test himself with the same pencil, putting in enough correct answers, forge their signature, and turn it in as their work. A guaranteed high if not perfect score."

Olivia stared at Brad, momentarily shocked.

What a diabolical plan. I can understand why Dave was so upset. I wonder if his conscience finally got to him—a motive for suicide, if that's actually what happened.

"So tell me, what are those parents thinking, using their money to subvert the system and get their kids admitted into college? I feel sorry for the regular students who play by the rules." Olivia couldn't keep the indignation from her voice.

"College isn't like that anymore," said Brad. "According to Dave, as long as you have the money, anything goes."

"I have trouble believing things have gone that far." Olivia shook her head.

She glanced at Cayenne, who stood quietly in the corner, her hands still clasped behind her back.

Is she planning on joining this conversation?

"I had an idea I wanted to run past you..." Olivia spoke directly to Brad. "Let's take up a special collection for Linnea and the baby at the student recital tomorrow. The parents can afford to donate. And then maybe you could deliver the money to her since you're old friends from school."

"I would do that for sure," Brad nodded. "Just don't forget, you always think the best of people. The parents may not like it when we ask for money. All they care about is getting their kids into college. Anything that distracts from study, exams, and practice for their next competition is considered unnecessary."

"They're parents. They have the best interest of their children at heart. Surely they want the town and the teachers to support the students as we all process this death."

Brad's eyes narrowed. Then his face relaxed. "I think it's a good idea. Count me in. I'm just hoping you're right."

Olivia nodded and then turned to Cayenne. "You're awfully quiet over there by the window."

Cayenne unclasped her hands, bringing them to her sides. "I'm just taking things in. Your voice and Brad's," she said, "and the atmosphere, especially in this room. Even the view out the window gives me pause for thought."

Knowing better than to interrupt when Cayenne intuited her surroundings, Olivia bit her lower lip. *What's she seeing and hearing that I don't?*

"You two can talk. I have to get back to work." Brad rose and made his way to the door. "See you later." He closed the door behind him.

At the click of the door, Cayenne sat down in his chair. She spun it so that she faced Olivia. "Why are you here?"

"I'm a temporary resident assistant—"

Before she could finish her undercover explanation, Cay shook her head. "Don't give me that. You're here to help Officer Jets and her investigation. I feel the tension emanating from you, it's thick and filled with fear. Why are you afraid, Olivia?"

Olivia knew better than to lie to Cayenne. This wasn't the first time her friend had shared her inner wisdom.

"I'm undercover," she admitted to Cayenne. "Janis put

me here to eavesdrop on the Tone Rangers. Plus..." Olivia took a deep breath and continued to explain, "I got my first helicopter ride today. It wasn't anything I expected..."

Cayenne leaned forward as Olivia told the story about her ride with Simon Court.

By the time Olivia finished the story, Cayenne had raised her hands to her chin, holding them together as if in prayer.

She wants to tell me something, maybe a sensation or feeling she's gotten from my story. But I've forgotten a detail... In that moment the image of the key she'd made a copy of came to Olivia's mind.

She turned and pulled out the drawer next to her bedside table.

"There's another thing I want you to know." She held up the key. "Cookie Kravitz, the cafeteria manager, dropped a small key under a bench in the park. He was talking to Simon Court about the students. After they left, I grabbed the key and then had a copy made, which I kept. I gave the original back to Cookie."

Cayenne nodded. Her fingers intertwined as her face grew serious. "May I hold the key for just a moment?"

Without hesitation Olivia handed it to Cayenne. Palm open, she closed her dark eyes. Her face relaxed as she inhaled deeply. On the exhale Cayenne closed each of her fingers around the key, beginning with her thumb. Eyes still closed, she took another breath, and on the exhale she released her fingers one at a time in the opposite order.

Finally Cayenne opened both of her eyes, handing the key back to Olivia.

Olivia sighed. "What do you think? Are you getting messages from the key or something?"

Cayenne sat on the edge of the worn chair. "I'm not a psychic. I can't tell your future, but I can help you pay attention to who you are and your situation. The key, as you already concluded, is very important to your work. You instinctively had a copy made, indicating you'd need the key in the future. Put it back in your drawer and wait. You'll know when the time comes.

"I feel danger in your path for yourself and Sage," continued Cayenne. "That was evident in the helicopter ride, when Court threatened you and warned about Sage. I suggest you tell Janis Jets all the details, everything you can remember about the helicopter ride as soon as possible, so that she can provide protection and know where to look when the time comes."

In an instant Olivia's mind cleared. Fatigue fell away from her body like a snake shedding its skin. She felt tingling in her fingers and at the back of her neck. "I think you're right. I must pay attention to potential danger and not put the helicopter incident aside just because I felt uncomfortable." Olivia dropped the key back into the drawer, sliding it shut.

She felt afraid but confident. She just had one more question for Cayenne.

"Do you know how Dave Franco ended up at the bottom of the cliff?"

The Two-Spirit shook her head. A look of calm came over her face. She closed her eyes, pausing. When she opened her eyes again, she stood up as if to leave. "I'm not a mind reader, but I do feel a shadow here on campus that could turn destructive. Just keep that in mind as you move forward with Officer Jets...and Michael," she added. "He will serve as your protector and guide as he always has."

As if released from a trance, Cay's eyes sparkled and a

smile came to her lips. She bent over to give Olivia a goodbye hug. Olivia's cell phone buzzed from the nightstand as Cayenne prepared to leave.

"Go ahead and answer that," Cayenne said with a smile. "It's probably Michael. I'll see you later." She closed the door behind her as Olivia grabbed her cell phone. Michael Bellemare's name appeared on her screen.

"Hello."

"Hey there. You sound sleepy, taking a nap?"

"Just talking to Cay," she answered softly.

"She's in your dorm?"

"Just left. Good to see her. What's up?"

"I'm ready to order burgers and fries for dinner."

"I haven't seen Janis in the last few hours. I guess we're still on."

"I'll call her before I order. Then I'll text you the time and the three of us can meet in her office. Afterward I'll walk you back to your dorm," he said hopefully.

"Is that what you college kids did? Walked each other back and forth to the dorms?"

"Yep. I forgot you didn't go to university. You're so smart. It would have been a natural fit for you. Would we have dated, do you think, if we'd known each other then?"

"You're a bit older, and chances are we wouldn't have run into each other, even if we did go to the same school, which is most unlikely."

"I was imagining a more romantic scenario in my head with less detail, but I get what you're saying."

Olivia sighed. "I hope Janis wants to eat now. I'm starving. I lost my breakfast and didn't eat much for lunch."

"You mean you skipped a meal?"

"No. I actually lost my breakfast behind a tree. I'll tell you later. Bye." Olivia disconnected the call.

She lay her head down on her pillow to go over in her mind what she would say to Janis and Michael about the helicopter ride when the time came.

"Olivia, over here," came Michael's voice. He'd parked at the far corner, in a shadow near the pine trees.

She waved and made her way toward him, her heart skipping a beat.

He stood with one hand resting on the driver's side door, wearing a soft blue T-shirt against worn jeans. Black sneakers and a broad smile completed his confident look.

She walked toward him, aware that his eyes lingered on her smile.

"Hi," she said shyly. "Thanks for bringing the food." She placed both hands on his chest, leaning close to whisper in his ear, "Where is it?"

He pointed toward the back seat of the truck where three bags sat, one filled to the top with french fries peeking out. His arms wrapped around her back to pull her closer.

"Better get moving or the fries will get cold," she said teasingly.

"We could get going or...we could step right under the trees and I could tell you how much I've missed you."

Olivia nodded. "We could do that. And I want to do that, I really do."

"But..." He smiled at her, his eyes bright with anticipation.

Looking over her shoulder, Olivia grinned mischievously as an invitation for him to follow as she walked into the woods. A few feet into the shady grove she turned to face him, placing both hands on his chest. He reached over to push a strand of hair from her face.

"You're so beautiful," he said quietly. "I've wanted to kiss you for over a year. Do you think we could do that now, just once?"

Olivia didn't need another invitation. She reached her hands up the side of his face, staring at his mouth. He ducked his head and caught her lips with his. She felt his tongue caress the inside of her bottom lip gently as he pulled her closer.

"That was more than once," she gasped, pulling away with a laugh.

"I believe it was." He grinned, his arms dropping to his sides. "But now we know one thing."

"What's that?"

"We click just as I've always suspected. In every way, we're meant to be together." His eyes opened wide, daring her to disagree.

"I'm going to change the subject now, not because I disagree, but because Janis expects us," she explained as if to a child.

To her delight, Michael took no offense.

"Of course, we've got a job to do. More about us later, but Olivia?"

She stepped back, still looking at him.

"Not much later."

Olivia chuckled, reaching out for his hand. "Don't you think I want it too?"

A look of surprise came over Michael's face. "You admit that you're attracted to me?"

"Oh please, I've been thinking about you since the first time I saw you, when I got in that accident and you pulled me off that cliff."

"But you ran away."

"My feelings scare me, always have. But now it's time to find Janis and solve this murder."

They walked side by side toward the admissions building. "Whose car is that?" Michael pointed to a BMW convertible parked in the lot. "It doesn't look familiar."

"Probably the new admissions counselor. His name is Rydell Cox and I think he's the reason Janis wears leather pants to work."

"He doesn't fit in with the rest of the staff. That car belongs in student parking."

Olivia laughed. "You can tell a lot about people by their car choice."

"Like my truck, for example," added Michael with a smile. "Dependable, dusty, and a bouncy ride," he added, watching her laugh.

"Uh-huh, like your truck and every other truck in Lily Rock."

They bantered their way to the entrance door, which Michael opened, letting Olivia step ahead of him. "You look good in shorts," he commented under his breath.

"No more flirting, we have work to do," she insisted, pointing to Janis's closed door.

Michael took a moment to inspect the admissions front office. "Sage in there, Rydell in there, and this is Janis?"

Olivia knocked on Janis's door.

"Come in," came the voice.

Michael stepped in front of Olivia, holding up the brown bags. "I've got your dinner, Officer Jets. Plus I brought your assistant. I know you'll be glad to see her."

Janis Jets scowled. "Get in here. Put those bags down.

You pull in another chair. We have to talk. I've got the information from the coroner."

"Yes, ma'am," they said in unison. Michael scuttled a chair to the desk from the other room. Olivia took another chair from the corner. He closed the door and they both sat across from Janis, waiting for her to tell them the next move.

CHAPTER FOURTEEN

Michael slid burgers from the sack, plopping the paper bag with the fries in the middle of the desk. "Have at it," he commented, selecting a fry for himself. He moved his chair closer to Olivia so that their knees touched.

Jets, on the opposite side of the desk, stared at them both. "Let me cut to the chase. We don't have a lot of time to figure out Franco's death, what with the anxious parents breathing down my neck. We could keep them a couple more days after the big concert, but then I'm afraid Simon Court will file a lawsuit."

"Litigious," added Michael, grabbing a second fry from the bag.

"I have some information for you," Olivia quickly added.

Janis held up her hand." I know you do, but not until I've told you about the report from down the hill. The coroner and the forensic detectives looked for certain indicators. We have three assumptions here. Our victim may have accidentally tripped. He may have jumped, or he may have been pushed."

"I have information from first-hand witnesses just before the murder," Olivia said.

"It's not your turn yet, Nancy Drew. Didn't you learn to raise your hand in kindergarten like the rest of us?"

Olivia raised her hand with a smirk.

"Put your hand down. That was an example, not a request."

Jets reached for a fry. She turned to Michael. "These are soggy. Do better next time."

Michael nodded and then grabbed the whole bag. "No problem, more for me. You were saying?"

Jets frowned as Olivia turned to Michael. "Be careful," she said in a loud whisper. "Janis is crabby and is afraid of losing control of her investigation."

Michael nodded, his face looking serious. "I see. Thanks for telling me. Want a fry?" He offered her the soggy sack.

Olivia took one, looking back at Janis, who glared at them both.

"As I was saying, the first thing we look for when considering a suicide is previous attempts. Since we found Franco lying on his side, we were pretty sure he didn't jump. But pretty sure isn't enough in my line of work." Janis gave them a direct look.

"Detectives down the hill took a deep dive into Dave Franco's past and found absolutely nothing that would indicate he was suicidal. He has no history of hospitalizations for injuries or psychiatric issues. Never even saw a therapist or called one. In fact, his tutoring work with the teens leaned into life coach more than tutor, and he was taking classes for a certificate.

"Plus Linnea, his wife, says he seemed concerned but perfectly fine with the news of having a baby. I did suggest that she look for any notes Dave might have left, just in case he considered taking his own life and wasn't telling anyone his plan. Linnea looked high and low and did not find a suicide note. Nor did we find any emails on his computer or phone. No texts. Nothing. So we ruled out suicide."

"He was a little concerned about being a good dad," Olivia added. "In one of our last conversations, he mentioned his own difficult upbringing and that he hoped he could do a better job than his father. He said his dad wasn't a great role model. That's what he mentioned."

A thoughtful expression came over Janis's face. "That's good evidence but not what you might think. He was concerned but hopeful. Do you hear that? He wanted to do better than his father, which means he planned on being a great dad."

"He was just working through his new life," added Michael. "Women aren't the only ones who worry about having babies."

Olivia felt relief. Until this moment, she didn't realize she'd been condemning herself for not picking up on Dave's concerns and inquiring more at the time.

Janis looked at Olivia, her face softening. "Just so you know, most people who take their lives by jumping off a steep cliff leave stuff at the top before they leap. We found a wallet and a cell phone at the bottom of the cliff...near the body."

"So you don't think it was a suicide?"

"I feel ninety-nine percent certain he did not take his own life," said Jets. "Unless we can find an actual witness who saw him jump, then we can rule out suicide."

Michael crumpled the bag in his hand, tossing it over Janis's shoulder toward the trash can. "So what about an accident?"

Jets flipped open her laptop. She clicked a few tabs,

stopping on one. "We have to eliminate other possibilities as well as an accident. According to the coroner's report, if he jumped or if he was pushed then we have a physics problem."

"I was terrible at physics," said Olivia under her breath.

"I know a little," Michael said. "It's all about gravity."

"Well thank you, Mr. Smarty Pants," Janis commented dryly. "Forensic science can give us a bit more than that."

Olivia held up her hand. "Could you spare all the details and just tell us—was he pushed or did he accidentally trip?"

"Let's just say I don't think he tripped." Janis's face looked grim. "Dave was a young guy, in good shape, a frequent hiker of the Lily Rock trail. He knew the territory and he knew the potential dangers. Linnea said they hiked the trail nearly every week and that Dave often took the kids he tutored for a hike when they were working through difficult issues. Plus there were no rocks or bushes at the top of the cliff that would cause a person to trip and fall. Only a steep drop-off."

"He did wear those hiking boots all the time," Olivia agreed.

Maybe that's why all of the Tone Rangers have identical hiking boots. Dave encouraged them to get outside in nature. He probably did less formal tutoring while they hiked together.

"The coroner found no trace of drugs or alcohol in his system," Jets said, looking over her computer screen.

"Did you look for footprints?" asked Michael.

"We did. We found Dave's bootprints, size 11 hiking boots, and another pair of size 8½ hiking bootprints. The dirt had been kicked about, it took my guys some effort to distinguish all the footprints, but those two stood out as the most distinct and recent.

"We're looking into the prints, but I don't think it will help. Lots of people stand in that area to gaze at the view, including students and faculty. The footprints could be from anyone.

"They did find bruising on Dave's neck but no blood under his nails or skin or anything like that." Her voice died off, causing Olivia to look up.

"Are you telling us everything?"

A flush brightened Janis's cheeks. "What do you mean, everything? This is an ongoing investigation and I'm keeping you in the loop." Her voice sounded indignant.

"You didn't answer my question," said Olivia. "I have this sense that you're holding back some information."

"All in good time, Nancy Drew. Now tell me what you've got," Jets said smoothly.

"Just so you know," Olivia said, "I do have eye witnesses. Two of them. Oh, and one person who overheard a phone call between Abbey and her father."

Janis Jets sat up straight in her chair. "Did someone actually see Dave pushed over the cliff?"

It was Olivia's turn to sit back and take her time. "Not exactly." She pulled a small notebook from her back pocket. "I took down some details right after our rehearsal so that I could tell you what I learned from the Tone Rangers."

When Olivia finished explaining, Jets began typing furiously on her computer. "Let's back this up, so we can get the timing right."

"Abbey Court called the constabulary around four

thirty last Friday afternoon." Jets looked to Olivia for confirmation. "That's when we first learned about the body."

Olivia nodded.

"Then a couple of your Tone Rangers, Legend and Raleigh, told you they saw Dave smoking a cigar with Cookie at around 3:54 p.m. Rather specific, isn't it?"

"He took a selfie and had a time stamp," Olivia explained.

"But those two claim to have scampered away into the forest like Hansel and Gretel, so they didn't see anyone push Franco," Jets said dryly. "And then you got a report from Anais that she overheard Abbey Court and her father discussing Dave's death."

"They didn't sound very sorry either," said Olivia. "If we can believe Anais, they thought they would be better off with Dave dead." Olivia swallowed a lump in her throat. "Plus I'm not sure Cookie is telling us everything he knows. He's the guy you need to interview because he may have been the last one to see Dave alive."

Do I tell Janis about the key business with Cookie? I think that's more about Sage and her job. Plus Janis is worried about getting this wrapped up before the parents rebel. That would be worse for Sage, so I don't need to complicate the investigation any more than it is.

"It's not Cookie," exclaimed Janis Jets, her face flushed. Then she corrected herself. "I guess it could be Cookie, but he feels so controlled. I can't imagine him pushing someone over a cliff impulsively, and this act, it just feels like a knee-jerk reaction."

Olivia wanted to object but stopped herself. *Just 'cause a guy has a secret ingredient for pea soup, it doesn't mean he isn't a killer.*

Michael turned to Olivia, his eyebrow raised.

He caught it too. Janis is very defensive of the Curated Cuisine chef. Interesting.

Jets closed her laptop, sliding it to the end of the desk. She looked across at Olivia and Michael. "Good work. You brought me some interesting clues."

"All you got from me was a burger," commented Michael.

Jets nodded. "Don't forget your vast knowledge of physics."

Michael grinned. "Ah shucks, Janis, happy to help."

Olivia sat back, enjoying the return of the easy banter between Janis and Michael, but stood just a moment later, looking toward the window. "Do you hear that?"

"A car alarm?" asked Janis, standing behind her desk.

"I bet it's the Beemer in the lot," Michael said, sprinting to the door.

"How do you know which car?" asked Olivia, following quickly behind.

"The man is a fountain of knowledge, from physics to car alarms," remarked Jets. She grabbed her keys, the last to follow.

In the parking lot Rydell Cox stood near his BMW holding his key fob up, his thumb pushing repeatedly. *Beeeeep.* The horn kept sounding.

"Someone try to break into your car?" Michael could barely be heard over the blaring alarm.

"Must have been one of those kids," hollered Cox. He pushed the button on the key fob again. "Stupid idiot probably tried to open the car door, looking for money on the floor."

"Give it a minute," Michael pointed to the fob. "Your battery may be low."

Cox stopped clicking and the incessant alarm stopped.

"I don't believe we've met. I'm Michael Bellemare, a Lily Rock resident." He held his hand out.

"I'm Rydell Cox. Are you a supporter of the arts?" He reached for Michael's hand.

Michael shook his hand vigorously. "Sure am. I've heard that you're the new admissions counselor for the Lily Rock Music Academy?"

"I am. I've been here since the fall." Cox slid his hand back from Michael's grip, wiping it against his pant leg.

"Nice car you got there," Olivia commented, standing just a foot away.

Cox nodded and then his glance went beyond her, stopping at Janis Jets. "Yes, it is a nice car, one of my favorites. I have a couple more in the garage at home. Beverly Hills, that's where I live."

He's rich. He has more than one car. He probably lives in a big house in an expensive neighborhood. He knows how to wheel and deal, and if I wait I'll hear a name drop.

"My neighbor, Magic Johnson, told me about Lily Rock. He sent one of his kids here for summer camp a few years ago."

And there it is. That about completes the introduction. He's local, from Los Angeles, like the Tone Rangers. Very interesting.

Olivia glanced at Michael, who maintained a disinterested pose, his hands in his jeans back pockets, his face immobile. "Say, I've met Magic. We have friends in common."

Rydell looked surprised. "You have? Well I haven't seen him in a while, you understand."

"I know we can't call him right now, but why don't we have a drink at the pub anyway and share our stories?" Michael suggested.

Cox looked sheepish. He stammered, "Sure, b-but—"

Michael jumped right in. "How about right now. You don't have anything planned, right? Let's meet at the pub. You know the place, you've been here long enough."

Cox rocked back and forth on his expensive loafers. Olivia found herself looking down at them and then looking up at Janis.

I wonder if those are some of the footprints they found near the cliff.

Janis stood nonchalantly to the side, watching Michael and Rydell circle each other. To Olivia's amazement, Cox turned to Janis, a huge grin coming over his face. "Hey, honey, why don't you join us for a drink at the pub? You and..." He pointed to Olivia. "Do I know your name?"

"Olivia Greer," she said calmly, trying not to look surprised.

In an instant Cox took charge of the situation by grabbing Janis by the arm as he pulled her closer to his side. "The four of us then, in half an hour at the pub."

"See you soon." Michael grabbed Olivia's hand before she could blurt out an excuse.

"I'm coming," she hissed at him, trying to shake her hand away from his.

Michael kept hold of her hand in his firm grip. He walked briskly, slightly dragging Olivia by his side. They didn't speak until they reached his truck. He helped Olivia with her door, holding his finger to his lips. Then he let himself in behind the steering wheel.

Michael made sure all the windows were closed before he began the conversation. "So that's Rydell Cox," he said, laying his arms on the steering wheel.

"Yes, it is."

"Thinks he's really important," said Michael. "Do you think he really knows Magic Johnson?"

"Doesn't really matter if he does or doesn't. What we know is that he needs to impress people."

"Were you...impressed?" Michael's left eyebrow lifted.

"Not at all," answered Olivia.

"Me either. In fact, the guy makes me just a little nervous, especially the way he acts around Janis."

"He is not the type of person I thought she'd hook up with," admitted Olivia. "At first it was kind of funny, but now it feels slightly sinister. What's his game anyway?"

Michael looked over at Olivia and smiled. "We'd better keep our eyes open. I think our friend Janis may be in a bit of trouble with this guy."

Olivia felt her stomach drop.

He's right. I think Rydell has motives for getting close to Janis. Maybe he wants to know what she knows, to use the information to support his case that Sage is in over her head. I don't like that man, that's for certain.

Michael patted Olivia's thigh before starting up the engine. Backing out of the parking space, he shifted, directing the truck toward the main road. "To the pub we go," he told Olivia. "I'm concerned about their budding relationship. Let's see if we can find out more over a beer and a sparkling water."

Michael gave Olivia a side-eye and she filled in, "I know Cox likes her leather pants."

"Right," said Michael, "but what else does he want from our Lily Rock police officer?"

"If they're busy giggling on the phone, then she's less focused on figuring out who killed Dave Franco."

Olivia reached over to take Michael's hand. She curled

her fingers inside of his. "I'm worried about Janis. Plus I wanted to tell you sooner..."

Before she could broach the subject of Janis's job interview, Michael jammed his foot on the brake. The truck came to a sudden halt. "What the..."

Lights flashed overhead, as the sound of slapping filled the air.

"Is that what I think it is?" asked Olivia, dropping Michael's hand to open the passenger window. She stuck her head outside and then pulled it back in. "It's a helicopter. Looks like it's doing surveillance."

Michael shifted the truck into drive, making a left turn into the Lily Rock Brew Pub parking lot. "Not just looking, it's trying to land in the middle of the pub parking lot. I'll pull up on the street. We can walk from there."

Michael made a U-turn, edging to the side of the road. Olivia hopped out of the truck as He pulled his keys out of the ignition.

"I don't know what's happening to Lily Rock. First we got Magic Johnson's best friend working at the music academy and now a helicopter parked at the pub."

Olivia nodded. "Just hearing the helicopter made my stomach turn."

Michael took her hand, looking both ways before walking across the road. "Let's see who needs a beer so bad he's parked his helicopter in front of the brew pub."

They walked side by side down the driveway. He kept a firm hold of her hand. When they reached the bottom of the incline, the helicopter had already landed. A man in a tracksuit ducked under the blades, making his way toward the front of the pub.

"I think that's Abbey's dad," observed Olivia.

"He's wearing white sneakers," Michael commented.

"Yes, he is," confirmed Olivia.

"I'm thinking footwear is important," Michael said with a smile.

"Because Janis has lots of footprints at the crime scene," Olivia said.

They stopped walking and watched from a distance.

Cox pulled in, parking his BMW at the far end of the lot. Olivia saw Janis let herself out of the passenger side. She ran her hand over her uniform and then sauntered around the BMW to meet him. He grabbed her by the shoulder and she came willingly.

"Did you hear that?" Olivia asked Michael.

He nodded, his face grim. "Janis giggled. I heard it with my own ears. Gave me chills, not in a good way."

Cox gestured at Simon Court, who waited for the couple at the foot of the stairs. Court was the first to stretch his hand out in greeting. When Court dropped Cox's hand he turned to Janis Jets, enveloping her in a big hug.

"I guess they're all friends," commented Michael dryly.

Olivia bit her tongue to keep silent, an escaping sigh giving away her dismay.

CHAPTER FIFTEEN

Before Michael could go greet Rydell and Janis, Olivia yanked his hand. "Follow me," she led him toward the pub stairway.

Dank earth met her nostrils. She stepped underneath the steps and closer to the building so as not to be seen. Michael leaned next to her.

"Why are we hiding?" he asked, his hot breath on her ear.

She turned to whisper back. "I want to observe how they interact together without us. Did you see that hug Court gave Janis? Gave me the creeps!" Olivia held her finger to her lips. Rydell and Janis made their way up the slatted stairs and stopped right above Michael and Olivia's hiding spot beneath.

Olivia looked up, pointing to what she saw. The space between the steps revealed Cox's and Jets's legs, stepping close together. Her stomach lurched.

He's got his arm around Janis.

Olivia caught her breath as Janis Jets stumbled on the stairway. "Watch out, you big lug. I nearly fell," came Jets's voice.

Cox grunted, giving Janis a little shove. "We haven't even started drinking yet. You're a little off balance tonight, sweet cakes."

Ugh. Sweet cakes. Why does Janis put up with that nonsense?

Olivia inhaled sharply as Janis stumbled again, her knee landing on the stair ahead.

"Ouch," she cried. "I'm sure clumsy."

For just a moment, as Janis leaned into her knee, her stark gaze darted between the slats of the stairs, staring straight at Olivia and Michael. She winked at them before Cox jerked her back to her feet.

"I've got it now," Janis assured her companion, her voice slightly slurred. The couple continued toward the pub entrance.

Court came next. Right behind Janis and Rydell, he waited for Janis to catch her balance and then let out an exasperated sigh. "I wish you two would stop making a spectacle of yourselves. Get going. We have to talk inside."

After all three had made it up the stairway and through the pub entrance, Olivia drew a deep breath.

"That was a close one," Michael muttered. "Did you see the wink? I guess Janis knew we were hiding here."

"I'm going to text Janis so she knows we're not coming. I don't want to be seen in the pub with that group," admitted Olivia. Her fingers tapped the phone and then she pressed Send.

"We're putting her in a difficult situation, alone with Cox and Rydell."

"She's not alone in a crowded pub, plus she's a cop. She can handle this. Plus her behavior is confusing me. I don't trust her right now, and I'm worried she's gotten mixed up with the wrong crowd. Maybe she's been lonely and she just fell for the first guy—"

When Michael didn't say anything, Olivia continued, "I wanted to tell you earlier, Janis is interviewing for a new job."

Michael's body grew very still. "Say what?"

"She's interviewing with the Riverside Police Department. She told me she doesn't fit in Lily Rock anymore."

"I don't believe it. Janis wouldn't do that to us. She's been the officer in charge for years now. The small town job wasn't the first choice on anyone's list except for Janis."

"I saw the interview letter. It's for real," insisted Olivia.

"I take your word for it. But I have trouble wrapping my mind around her applying for another job anywhere except Lily Rock."

"It's not for sure yet," Olivia said, "but until it's definite one way or the other, I want to steer clear of drinks at the pub and the rest. I don't want to be the one to spill the beans by accident."

"So you want to turn around and go home?"

"When I saw the helicopter and Simon Court, I wanted to run. He's another one who gets under my skin. The first time I saw him was at the constabulary when he tried to bully Janis into filing a complaint against one of the Tone Rangers. And then he trapped me in his helicopter and threatened to hurt Sage. He made it quite clear that I could be silenced with a slight shove into the abyss."

Michael's body tensed. "I didn't realize until now that was more than a scenic ride. Did you tell Janis?"

"No, but I did tell Cayenne."

Michael pulled Olivia closer. "I'm not just alarmed, I'm plenty angry. If you have to keep temping, why not somewhere, anywhere other than the constabulary?" She heard the harshness in his voice. "Tell me more about the complaint incident. Maybe there's something in that first encounter that will pin down Court's motive. I think he pushed Dave over the cliff. He's my number one suspect."

"Simon Court is certainly the most menacing. Even that first time, he demanded justice for his daughter, but it felt like he had another agenda for wanting to file a complaint. It felt like a test to see if Janis would cooperate. She didn't, by the way. She delayed him long enough there's been no more mention of the slapping incident, especially since Dave's death."

Olivia took a deep breath. "I want to go home, at least for a few hours. I want to check in with Sage most of all. Then I can go back to the dorm for another night. Just one more look to make sure they're off the stairway and then we can go."

Olivia ducked her head, making her way out from under the stairway. Standing up straight, she heard laughter pouring from the outdoor patio, the voices of people enjoying each other's company, along with the occasional clank of silverware against dishes. The smell of barbecue on the grill from the back of the pub kitchen made her smile. She inhaled deeply before reaching for Michael's hand.

Michael didn't need any more encouragement. He planted a swift kiss on her upturned lips. "Done and done. Let's get out from under here and then I'll drive us to your house. I'll hang around for as long as you want."

They walked silently to the truck, Olivia glancing back over her shoulder once when laughter from the pub caught her attention. When they reached his vehicle, she pulled him closer.

Olivia wrapped her arms around Michael's middle, giving herself to his warm embrace. He held her for several minutes, bending his face toward her soft hair. "You smell good," he told her, inhaling deeply. "What kind of shampoo are you using?"

Olivia pulled back with a laugh.

"I want to know everything about you," he explained. "I find you infinitely fascinating."

Olivia leaned away to ruffle the back of her hair, fluffing it off her neck with one hand. "That's me, a never-ending source of fasc-in-ation." She fluffed her hair again and then patted her head.

Michael unlocked the passenger side of the car and helped her in. He walked behind the truck to unlock the driver's side, lifting himself into the seat with ease. "Okay then, we're heading home."

"I'm going to give Sage a call," said Olivia, reaching for her cell.

Michael nodded his agreement, starting up the truck.

"Hello?" came her sister's voice.

"Hey, honey. Are you home?"

"I'm still in my office," Sage sighed. "But I've been getting some paperwork done and answering questions from parents about Dave's death. Hopefully Janis will find her killer soon so that we can get back to our academic schedule."

"You are my she-roe," Olivia said, trying to be encouraging. "Michael is here with me and we wondered if you would like to hang out for a bit. It's been over a week since the three of us got together, what with you working so hard."

"I would love that. Let me wrap this up at the office and I'll be home in fifteen."

"See you there." Olivia smiled as she clicked off her cell.

"Feel better now that you've connected with Sage?" Michael asked.

"I really do. It's just so odd and I worry about her. That admission office gives me the creeps since Rydell Cox moved in. Then when he won Janis over and she set up her office next to his, I felt like Sage got pushed out of her own space."

"I see." Michael navigated the winding roads back to Olivia and Sage's house. "We can ask her how she feels and check out her impression of Janis and Rydell."

As they drove down the gravel driveway toward the house, Michael reached over to hold Olivia's hand.

This is gonna be a thing, the hand holding. I kind of like it.

He only dropped her hand when she got out of the truck. Together they made their way to the front door, where Olivia pulled out her key. Once inside the house, she punched in the alarm code, and the incessant beep stopped.

"I'm going to look for a beer, want anything?" Michael offered.

He feels at home here.

"Sparkling water with a squeeze of lime," Olivia called out. Then she shouted, "Sage is driving up. Better make that two beers."

When Sage walked in the front door, Michael handed her a cold bottle right from the refrigerator. "Want to sit outside?" he suggested.

Sage dropped her briefcase and took the beer. Then she gave Olivia a sideways hug. "Give me a minute to change clothes and I'll meet you guys on the deck." After a long sip she walked toward her bedroom, the bottle held by her side in one hand.

Once outside Michael adjusted the deck chairs and

turned on the heater. "It's getting a little chilly in the evenings," he commented. "You got that sweater wardrobe all ready?"

"I've got sweaters galore," Olivia said, dragging a table in front of the chair so that everyone could put their feet up and look out at Lily Rock.

Sitting down, she viewed the forest of pine trees, stately and quiet. One lone caw from a crow echoed in the twilight. Michael walked back inside the house.

Closing her eyes, Olivia listened. She heard Sage step through the doorway onto the deck. Rising up in her chair she called out, "Hey, sis. What a beautiful evening."

Sage gave Olivia's cheek a peck and then sat down in an empty chair with a fresh bottle of beer in her hand.

In a minute Michael arrived with crackers and sliced cheese. He'd arranged them in circles on a worn cutting board. Nudging the remaining chair with his foot, he sat down and placed the board on the table so that everyone could reach. Sage sat up to be the first to grab a snack.

"You two are the best. I so needed to get away from that hullabaloo at the academy."

"We met the new admissions director," Michael said as he settled back into the chair next to Olivia.

"Apparently he's besties with Magic Johnson," Olivia added.

Sage made a face and then took another sip of beer. "I still can't believe he's dating Janis."

Both Michael and Olivia nodded.

"I think Rydell rented a house over in the Pine Creek area, where Janis lives. A lot of our faculty live there, a bit away from the campus but an easy commute."

"That makes sense," Olivia added. "I can see why faculty doesn't live on the campus, except for the dorm supervisor."

Olivia looked over at Sage. "But what I really want to know is, how are things going with Rydell Cox?"

Sage took another sip of beer. "He's hard to figure. I had that immediate dislike of him the first time we met."

"I did too," agreed Olivia. "He doesn't fit with the Lily Rock Music Academy tradition of being laid back. He doesn't even dress the part. Plus he's busy trying to impress people with his car and name dropping. I just feel uneasy around him. Maybe he pushed Dave after a heated discussion. Do we know his alibi for the time of death?"

She continued, her voice growing more heated. "I'm thinking Simon Court either helped or did the job himself. Those two meeting at the pub gave me the creeps."

"Gave you the creeps?" Sage said. "How about you work with Cox right next door? He's the worst, always lingering in my office, leaning over my shoulder at the copy machine. When Janis's door is partially closed, he touches me on the back for no reason and then looks to see if she's watching."

"Very creepy," said Olivia.

"The creepiest," added Michael.

All three stared into the woods, sighing collectively.

Olivia swirled the ice cubes in her glass, flicking the lime wedge off the side into the remaining sparkling water. "So now that we've agreed on Cox, I'm back to thinking it may be Court. He is more than creepy. He's diabolical the way he shows up in that helicopter."

Oops, I didn't tell Sage about Court's threats.

"What's going on with the helicopter?" asked Sage.

By the time Olivia told her the whole story, Sage had finished her second beer. Even in the dark Olivia could see tears forming in her eyes.

Sage spoke in a low voice. "Court wants me out, Olivia.

He's so menacing and I don't want to put you in danger just because of my stubborn refusal to quit a job."

"That's just what he wants!" Olivia said firmly. "He'll win if you resign, and then what will happen to all of those kids who aren't Tone Rangers? The students who want to get a fine arts education and attend good enough colleges?"

Sage inhaled deeply. "I feel like my job is being stolen right out from under me. Court acts like he's in charge of the whole school. He pops in and out whenever he wants, not like the other parents. Plus he's always talking with Cookie in the kitchen. That worries me. He's got Rydell Cox in his pocket and now Cookie."

"Do you think Cookie is part of Court's plan to take over the Lily Rock academy?" asked Michael.

Olivia paused to consider her next words. "I like Cookie. I do. But he hangs out with the wrong people. I saw him and Cox in the park a couple of days ago. Two of the Tone Rangers saw Cookie and Dave talking at the very spot Dave was pushed over the cliff."

"He was pushed over?" Sage's eyes grew wide. "That's been established?"

"That's why we wanted to talk to you," Michael said, setting down his empty beer bottle next to his chair. "Before Cox interrupted our dinner with Janis, she shared information from the coroner's report. And then before we could talk about our next moves, Cox's car alarm went off and interrupted our plan of action. It was as if he were listening in somehow and deliberately made a scene. After that Janis seemed totally distracted and blind to the investigation."

Remembering Janis falling on the stairway, Olivia added, "And she's hanging all over Cox, stumbling around as if she's been day drinking."

"What are you saying?" exclaimed Sage. "That is not the Janis Jets I know."

"So finding Dave's killer is up to us then," Michael said.

Olivia glanced toward Sage. "The three of us can work together."

Michael looked at both women, then away. His words came out slowly. "Let Janis do what she does with the police department while the three of us figure out why anyone would want to kill a good guy like Dave Franco."

Now we're talking. We don't need Janis. Sage is our third. She's a good observer and she has the most to lose if we don't find the killer before the parents revolt.

"Hey, we're the newly revised three musketeers." Olivia raised her glass for a toast. Michael and Sage raised their empty beer bottles in agreement.

Michael stood up and turned to Sage. "If we're going to be a team, then another beer is in order. You want one?" he asked Sage.

"I've had enough," Sage said. "I need to have a clear head for work." She sat back in her seat, lifting her feet to the low side table.

Michael gathered Olivia's empty glass before heading to the kitchen.

When he returned with his second beer and a sparkling water, he paused before closing the glass door. M&M trotted right past to sit in front of Sage's feet.

"Look who I found," Michael said, handing Olivia her drink.

"He's been shadowing me everywhere," said Sage, reaching down to pat M&M's head.

The dog walked behind Sage's chair, past Olivia's, to sit next to Michael.

"Hey, buddy," Michael said, running his hand into the curly dog fur on Mayor Maguire's chest.

"M&M is our D'Artagnan, the fourth musketeer," said Olivia.

The dog smiled at Olivia. He then stood to make three turns, flopping down on the warm wood. He closed his eyes, his tongue hanging out the side of his mouth.

It was Sage, not Michael, who drove Olivia back to the Lily Rock Music Academy. They left him in the kitchen putting away glasses and dishes.

"I'm not sure I can handle the pressure of this job anymore," Sage admitted to Olivia. "I want to stay because of the students, but maybe the music academy is changing and it would be best for me to go gracefully."

"I think you should talk to the school board first. They're the ones who hire and fire people. As far as I know your job description hasn't changed for the past five years. You've built up the school and provided funding for the new performance center. Don't forget the renovated dormitory and cafeteria. How could they just dump you after all of that?"

Sage shook her head. "Don't forget Court had himself placed on the advisory board just this past summer. He's got clout and he doesn't care about me or anyone else except his daughter."

"I know he claims to care about Abbey, but why wouldn't he just go away as soon as she goes to college? She'd be at her fancy university and then he could leave us alone."

"We can always hope," Sage said, pulling into the student housing parking lot. "Here you go." Sage stopped in front of the dormitory. "I'm going to park by the admissions office and work a couple more hours before heading home. Thanks for getting me out of my rut. I loved chatting with you and Michael."

Olivia leaned over to give Sage a peck on the cheek. "Love you."

She closed the passenger side door of the old truck, waving goodbye.

That night Olivia lay on the bed in her dorm room. Unable to sleep, she considered what she knew and what she did not.

What is the connection between Rydell Cox and Simon Court? Did they know each other before? And even though I like Cookie, is he somehow involved with the other two?

Olivia closed her eyes. In order to fall asleep she thought about her breathing. *Inhale, exhale.* For a moment she felt her thoughts let go but then she became aware of voices in the hallway.

A door banged shut. Someone called out, "Goodnight." Opening one eye she saw the hallway sensor light flick off.

CHAPTER SIXTEEN

On Sunday the Curated Cuisine hummed with activity. More parents had arrived early that morning, taking time to catch up with their children over a cup of coffee and a finely baked tidbit from the sweet table. The chocolate croissants were a particular favorite.

Olivia slid in the back door, her hair still wet from a shower. "Hey, Cookie, any of your dark roast ready to go?"

Apron freshly laundered and tied around his barrel chest, Cookie looked the epitome of calm and in control. He smiled at Olivia. "Come to the back room, you can have a cup of my special blend." Olivia followed him. A smaller coffeepot sat on a table with two mugs waiting.

"This feels like a deluxe walk-in pantry," Olivia observed, looking around the room. "I'm going to call it the curated pantry. You take organization to a whole new level."

Cookie poured a mug of coffee and handed it to Olivia. "Watch out you don't spill." He poured another mug for himself. "I worked closely with the supply officers on board ships. They taught me a few tricks. One thing I learned was to have coffee for everybody, then a big brew of better-than-average blend for friends, and in the back have a small pot of the best coffee, the expensive kind, like Kona. This morning I share my best blend with you, a true aficionado of the roasted bean." He smiled at Olivia.

She turned around to look more closely at the shelves, lined with baking tools.

"Strictly for my baking," Cookie explained, nodding proudly at the array of cake accessories, cookie sheets, and Bundt pans. "No one else is allowed to touch them so that I can keep everything in its place."

Olivia inhaled the aroma of the dark blend. "So good," she said after her first sip. "I didn't really appreciate coffee until the last couple of years."

"Part of your sobriety?" he asked.

Did I just see a look of approval on his face?

Basking in his appraisal and companionship, Olivia looked toward the opposite wall from the baking shelves.

I wonder if my duplicate key fits in one of those lockers...

Refurbished with fresh paint, each one had been stripped and sprayed with a pastel color. "They remind me of Easter eggs."

"Most like the colors of *The Great British Baking Show*," Cookie suggested.

"Are you a fan?" Olivia asked. "I've never seen the show."

"That's right," Cookie grinned. "I love that Paul Holly-wood. I only wish I had mixers to match the lockers."

"Were they always here?" Olivia asked.

"I had them installed when I got here. I saw them lined up in front of a dumpster, asking to be repurposed. I guess parents objected to such old-fashioned decor for their newly minted offspring."

Olivia burst with laughter, coffee snorting out of her nose. "Those are special teens you're talking about."

Newly minted offspring...very funny.

She looked for a cloth to dab at her jeans. "Over by the sink," Cookie advised.

"The flexibility of denim never surprises," mumbled Olivia, staring down at the wet spots on her pants. "Do you like working with teens?" She asked Cookie as he topped off her mug of coffee.

"I like working with teens most of the time. On the one hand, these kids are just a couple of years younger than the enlisted sailors I fed on ships. On the other hand, I worked the White House for a few years, and if you think the parents are snooty here, just try being polite to a senator who sends back her pea soup because she doesn't think it looks green enough."

On the one hand...on the other hand. Reminds me of Janis—the old Janis, that is.

"You remind me of Officer Jets. She's always talking about one hand or the other."

A blank look came over Cookie's face. He scratched the back of his neck. "I've talked to her a little, just a few days ago, and then I ran into her on campus, just passing by."

"I've been working as her temporary assistant at the constabulary office. Now I'm also filling in at the dorm as a temporary assistant."

His eyes narrowed. "I've heard that you assist all over the place, don't you?"

I'm gonna let that go.

Olivia pointed to the lockers again. "So that key you accidentally lost that I returned? Does it open one of those?"

"It does. I use the lockers and so do the students. They put phones and in some cases music instruments inside for safe keeping while they help me with serving and cleaning up. We got the locks to keep people from accidentally borrowing a phone or a trombone." Kravitz smirked at Olivia.

"I remember having lockers like that in high school. They had those combination locks. People would look over your shoulder to get your numbers when you weren't paying attention."

"That's why we have the lockers keyed," said Cookie. "I run a tight ship here. No hanky-panky on my watch."

Olivia took her empty mug to the sink. "I'd better get going. Thanks for inviting me to the special coffee club. A long day ahead of us with all of these parents milling around."

"Take a paper cup for the road," he offered. "Will you be performing with the staff at the recital? I've heard you are really good. 'The voice of an angel', someone said to me."

Her cheeks grew hot. Olivia ducked her head. "I take no credit for my voice. Got it from my mom." She took the cup with the lid from Cookie's hand. "Most people don't like the old-time tunes, but I'll be singing one tonight. I'll be the last faculty member before the Tone Rangers, my student group."

She left Cookie, making her way out of the pantry. *So twice Cookie admitted he'd heard about me from someone else. The Lily Rock grapevine grows with wild abandon, especially at the music academy.* Holding her to-go cup aloft, she exited from the back door, making her way on the footpath to the auditorium.

Olivia walked through the double doors of the auditorium, lingering as her eyes adjusted to the light. She inhaled deeply, smelling the combination of wood and wax used over the past fifty years, since the auditorium was first built.

She walked down the center aisle, admiring the old wooden seats with the red upholstery, worn thin with use.

I wonder if people will miss this old place when they start using the new performing stage. Maybe it's time to let the old ways die. Thank you, Bradley Cooper.

Stepping up on the stage, Olivia turned around to look at the empty seats.

By tonight, every one will be filled with students and parents waiting to be entertained. The Tone Rangers will debut a new set, judged by parents before they begin their auditions in another month.

If they sound and look good, then there's a chance the academy board will ignore the other complaints about Sage. If not...

She found the stacked chairs. One by one she unfolded four in a semicircle before placing her chair in front of the others. She sat down to wait for the arrival of the Tone Rangers.

The last rehearsal before a performance is so crucial, it could make or break their confidence.

Olivia took a moment to close her eyes and center herself. Like flies flitting over a tidbit of food, her thoughts raced in her head.

Not now, not now, not now, she told each annoying idea. Finally she connected with her place of silence underneath the wordy confusion.

Still no sign of the Tone Rangers.

Olivia listened to the room, imagining all the voices and music that had filled the space for the past forty years. The hair on her arms prickled, but she ignored the feeling, drifting more deeply into her meditation.

Hands grasped around her neck, Olivia gasped, shock leaving her mind blank. A voice spoke harshly in her ear.

"I know what you're up to. Stay away from the music academy or you'll be sorry."

She yanked at the vice-like grip around her neck, desperate for breath. Pulling away one finger, she tried to loosen the grip.

Air leaving her lungs, she made a last effort to push her legs underneath her, but her attacker shoved her back into the chair.

"Help," she gasped, feeling her windpipe constrict. The fingers tightened again, just enough to stop her breath.

As soon as the grip loosened, she gasped for air through her mouth. With a quick twist, she turned her body slightly in the chair. Her heart pounding in her chest, she tried another breath, but the fingers tightened again.

Her hands dropped to her lap, her head dizzy. And then, the hands were gone. She gasped for breath as she leaned over, holding her head in her lap.

She rose to her feet to look around for the assailant.

The stage curtain rustled as if someone had hurried past to use the side exit. "Stop," she yelled hoarsely.

Then someone said her name.

"I'm here, Olivia." Legend stood at the foot of the stage steps. Her hair, pulled back in a ponytail, revealed a huge smile and recently applied makeup. Even her eyes shone, black liner emphasizing their round shape.

"Legend, did you see anyone in the parking lot by the side exit?" Olivia asked, her voice straining and weak.

"Didn't see anybody. The rest should be here soon. We talked at the cafeteria." Legend went to sit in her usual chair, paying no attention to Olivia.

Before she could explain what had just happened, the other three Tone Rangers came through the back.

"What's the matter with your neck?" Raleigh asked.

Olivia's hand raised to cover her throat. She decided quickly, *I'm not going to tell them. They need to rehearse. I'll deal with my problems later.*

"No time for chitchat," Abbey interrupted. "We'd better run through our set before the next group gets here and pushes us out."

The three singers sat down right away. Abbey tucked her sneakers under the chair, her bottom lip pouting.

Olivia glanced at Abbey, waiting for someone to explain.

"She's upset because the group voted her out. I'm the new lead of the Tone Rangers," Legend said.

"It's not fair," cried Abbey. "You waited until my back was turned and then conspired against me without giving me any warning."

"We warned you," Raleigh spoke up. "We told you over and over that we wanted to go with Legend's idea and get some fresh arrangements for new songs. You just didn't listen." They folded their arms across their chest.

Olivia looked at each face.

I wonder if the admission pressure and looming auditions have finally taken their toll.

"Let's talk about how to handle the new group dynamic later. Right now it's the recital details that need to be finalized. Before we warm up, I want to ask your opinion about another matter entirely."

She waited a second before continuing. "I would like to take up a collection for Dave's family, Linnea and the new baby. We could work an explanation into

our introduction of our last song. Then you four could collect money from people in the back, on their way to the reception."

"I like the idea," said Raleigh immediately.

"Oh, me too," agreed Anais.

Legend tugged at her skirt to cover her knees. She didn't speak.

"Well I think it's a stupid idea and a big waste of time," said Abbey. "My dad didn't send me to the Lily Rock Music Academy to shake down parents for extra donations. We're supposed to be working and getting early admission to college."

Olivia watched the other Tone Rangers. No one else spoke up.

"You surprise me," said Olivia quietly, looking directly at Abbey. "You'd think someone of your privilege would welcome the opportunity to support a family in need."

Now the other three Tone Rangers stared at Olivia as if she'd spoken a foreign language. Finally Legend said, "Abbey is all work, work, work. That's why they voted me to be the lead of the Tone Rangers. We're all exhausted, right guys?" She turned to Raleigh and Anais, who both nodded in agreement.

"I'm exhausted and sad," added Anais in a quiet voice. "I really liked Dave and I'm so sorry he died."

Olivia turned to Abbey who, for the first time, looked human. Her bottom lip trembled. Then as quickly as she'd shown her feelings, she turned on the voice of authority.

"A new tutor has already been hired," Abbey said in a prim voice. "My father arranged for our first sessions on Monday. There will be no time to collect money. We need to get to bed early and start the next day. The new tutor will have much higher standards and expect a lot more results than Dave."

"I don't care about another tutor," Anais wailed. "I didn't know Dave was having a baby." Tears filled her eyes. "He never mentioned that to me."

"Or me either," said Raleigh. "We hiked together, me and Legend and Dave. He never said a word."

"I didn't know," Legend chimed in. "That's going to be tough. I'll talk to my parents. They're not here for the weekend, but they'll write a check, I know they will."

"The grands would be happy to donate," added Anais.

Olivia nodded at the group. "Okay, then let's get singing. I assume we'll do the set we've been practicing, and then after the recital, we can work on some new arrangements with your new song leader." She smiled at Legend, who stared at her hiking boots, lost in thought. "You've got your Indigo Girl song, and then we have the finale of the concert."

"The song you taught us...from the '70s, right?" said Anais with a smile. "I like that one."

"I'll sing the first section," said Olivia, "and then you come in for the last part like we practiced."

"What about your autoharp?" asked Legend. "If you use it for accompaniment, it won't be a cappella."

Olivia nodded. "I can sing without accompaniment since I'm part of your group."

"You'd do that for us?" Raleigh looked surprised. "You're kind of known for the autoharp thing."

"I can be part of the Tone Rangers and change my style. I'm here to support you."

Abbey glared at Olivia. "That's what you say now. There must be something in it for you."

She's so cynical for such a young person.

The Tone Rangers began their first song, and Olivia waited until the end to critique.

"You need to come in a bit sooner on the chorus," Olivia cautioned Abbey. "Other than that, you all sound spectacular, and you're going to be amazing! I'm proud to be a part of your finale. Thanks for including me." In her most enthusiastic voice, Olivia added, "I can't think of anything to say other than, have fun!"

Ending on that piece of encouragement, Olivia folded her chair, stacking it behind the piano. The students followed her example. By the time Olivia shuffled music into her bag, only Legend remained.

"Could I talk to you for a minute?" she asked Olivia. "I didn't tell you earlier, but I'm worried."

"What is it, Legend?"

"Remember I said that Raleigh and I saw Dave talking to Cookie that day he died? How we didn't stop and ran into the woods."

Olivia nodded. "I remember. You took a selfie by the oak tree and it said 3:54."

"That's right, but I didn't tell you everything. When we got to the end of the trail, I said goodbye to Raleigh and I circled back to catch Dave. I wanted to check in with him."

"Did you have anything special you wanted to bring up?"

"I wanted to end our tutoring sessions. I wanted to tell him that I didn't need anyone to take my tests for me."

Olivia felt confused. "Maybe you had it wrong, Legend. Dave wasn't supposed to take the test. His job was to prepare you to take the test."

Legend shook her head vehemently. "You don't understand. My dad arranged for Mr. Court to get me a tutor. I liked Dave, but I didn't know he was supposed to take my test for me. I thought he was preparing me to do better on the exam. So when he said I'd have to get on a plane and meet him in Tucson for the test, I got suspicious.

"I called my dad and we had it out. It turns out that he paid Dave to take the test for me!" Tears of indignation welled in Legend's eyes, her mascara running down her cheeks in black streaks.

"But I never got to talk to say anything to that day. When I arrived, Cookie had left. Dave had his arm around Anais because she was crying. I didn't want to get in the middle of all that, so I turned and ran back toward the woods. I decided to talk to him later."

"How much later was it when you saw Dave and Anais?"

"Only a few minutes, fifteen at most. In fact I know it was then because I looked at my cell phone and there was a call from my dad. He probably wanted to keep yelling at me to change my mind about the test. My phone said 4:15."

So Anais also saw Dave right before his death.

"You did the right thing telling me. I have connections with the constabulary and I'll make sure Officer Jets knows. But for now I'd like you to get some rest before your performance."

And then if you want to change your story and admit you pushed Dave, you can...assuming you did it...which I'm not sure about.

Legend ducked her head. "I'm just tired, you know? Dave died, now I'm the head of the Tone Rangers, and I'm supposed to get good grades with all this going on. I haven't had time to volunteer anywhere, which I'd better get to before I apply for early admissions in six weeks. It's a lot."

Olivia reached up and patted her shoulder.

"Things are going to get better, and I think being the lead Tone Ranger will look very good on your college application. But for now, go back to the dorm and see if you can rest. Drink lots of water too."

"You sound like my mom."

"I'm sure she'd say the same." Olivia nodded, removing her hand from Legend's shoulder.

Once Legend left, Olivia made her way toward the exit. Her neck still stung where the hands had gripped her skin. Olivia ran her fingers over the sore area.

The singing made me forget about the attacker.

She shoved the curtain back, where she assumed the intruder had escaped.

I'm going to look around a bit and see if there are any clues.

Eyes on the ground, Olivia walked slowly toward the curtain, pulling it aside again to check the floor for any evidence the assailant may have left behind.

Except for some dust, I can't see anything unusual.

Stepping from the darkened back door exit out of the auditorium, the sun blinded her view. She pulled sunglasses out of her pocket and then looked around. The dirt path leading to the student parking area looked clear. Then she sighted a red BMW at the farthest point in the student lot.

Why would Rydell Cox be parking here?

By the time she reached the BMW she grew worried.

I won't touch his car because he has that sensitive alarm. But if I'm careful, I can look inside.

The windows, tinted dark gray, made it difficult to see, unless she held her hands to the sides of her face to block out the glare.

First the back seat. There's his briefcase. Oh, and there's one of those lanyard key rings. Maybe he has his own locker in the curated pantry...

"Can I help you?" a voice inquired. Rydell Cox stood behind Olivia, his hands on his hips. "Why were you staring into my car?"

Olivia felt a wave of nausea rise from her throat. *Lie, Olivia. Lie as if your life depends on it!*

"I was wondering what a BMW looks like inside. I'm in the market for a new car and yours was so convenient."

Look at his eyes narrow. He's not buying my whopper for a minute.

"Come on, you can't afford a Beemer. Nice try. Leave me and my car alone." He turned on his heel.

Olivia walked away from the car toward the dormitory, quickening her pace. *I swear that key ring in the back of his car is the same or identical to the one Cookie dropped. I need to get a look in those lockers.*

CHAPTER SEVENTEEN

Right after lunch Olivia slipped into the Curated Cuisine for a cup of coffee. She took a to-go cup and walked back toward her room. She felt her cell phone buzz in her back pocket. Stopping, she reached with her free hand, noting Janis Jets's name on the screen. "Hey, Officer Jets, how are you today?"

"I'm working and it's Sunday, how do you think I'm doing?" came a grumbly voice.

"Coming to the student teacher recital this evening?" asked Olivia.

"Wouldn't miss it for the world. You know how I love a bunch of kids making music while besotted parents look on."

"Do I hear sarcasm dripping from your voice?" inquired Olivia.

"Why don't you come see for yourself? Meet me in my campus office in an hour. I've got some news from the coroner."

"Really? I also have news for you. Remind me to tell you about the lanyard and the key. I think they matter."

"What lanyard and what key?"

"Like I said, later. Oh, and I need to tell you about the guy who threatened me. At least I think he was a guy. And I have this bruise on my neck to show you too. Looks like we have lots to share with each other."

Janis's voice shifted. "Olivia, are you okay? I'm not kidding around."

The old Janis, the one I knew before...it's the tone of her voice.

"I'm just fine. A little bruise, not a big deal."

"Bring your stories and your bruises to the admissions office in an hour. Until then stay out of trouble."

"Will do," chimed Olivia, clicking off the cell phone.

By the time she reached her dormitory, she'd finished her coffee. Tossing the paper cup into the receptacle in the lobby, she walked up the stairway to her room on the second floor. Only the whir of the hallway fan could be heard.

She leaned over to pick up a plastic baggie that lay in front of the room next to the showers. She sniffed.

Smells like a chocolate chip cookie.

Olivia walked past the showers to her room, unlocking the door. When she stepped inside, she gasped.

The top of her suitcase had been unzipped; someone had left her clothes strewn across the floor. Olivia felt her stomach tighten. She turned, noticing her closet had been left open.

She pushed the door open further to find her recital dress and two T-shirts pulled from the hangers, left in a pile. She checked the corners, making certain no one was hiding.

I don't understand. Why would someone rummage through my clothes? I've only been here a couple of nights.

Her eyes grew wide.

The key.

She rushed to her bedside table, tugging on the drawer. Once open it revealed a small container of tissues and... no key.

Olivia sat on the edge of her bed, knees shaking. She took her cell phone, about to hit the Call button, but then changed her mind. She texted Michael instead.

> Any chance you could come over to the dormitory? My room's been vandalized.

Within a minute Michael's name appeared on her phone screen. With a shaking hand she accepted his call.

"Are you okay?" he asked immediately.

She told him about coming back to her room and the missing key.

Michael's voice lowered, his sense of calm steadying her nerves. "I'm supposed to meet Janis in her office in half an hour. I'll come by and—"

"I'm supposed to meet with her too," said Olivia.

"I'll come right over to your room and we can go together. Lock your door and don't answer unless it's me," he cautioned.

"What good will locking my door do? It's obvious someone had a key to break in."

"It's a precaution," he explained. "Try shoving a desk chair under the knob. You could raise a ruckus loud enough for students to get curious, should someone try again."

She gulped. "You dead Janis are scaring me."

"If someone is threatening you and bothering to turn your room upside down, then you must know something that you don't realize you know. It's making someone very nervous. Maybe they think you saw the killer..."

"But I don't know who it was!" protested Olivia. "I have

a few people who make me suspicious, but I have no idea who killed Dave."

After saying goodbye, Olivia clicked off her phone. She stood on shaky legs to look at herself in the small mirror over the dresser near the doorway. Touching her neck with one finger, she examined it more closely.

I do have a bruise. Evidence for Janis. And for the record? Ouch!

Michael and Olivia found Janis in her new makeshift office, sitting behind the conference table she'd made into a desk. The two chairs across the table remained where they'd left them the evening before.

Michael gestured with his head. "Is Cox in his office on a Sunday?"

Janis looked over and back at Michael. "He's not there, but why don't we close the door just in case he comes in."

"What about Sage, is she in her office?" asked Olivia.

"She's down at the auditorium getting ready for the concert this evening," said Jets, still staring at her laptop in front of her.

Olivia asked, "How did your evening go last night with Cox and Court at the pub?"

Janis looked up and then shut her computer down. "I saw you two canoodling under the stairway."

"We weren't exactly canoodling," argued Olivia. "We were avoiding your company. That whole helicopter landing in the parking lot was a bit much."

Jets sighed. "It was over the top, but I had to play along. Rydell and Simon Court are old buddies."

"So Rydell is your new squeeze?" asked Michael.

Jets's eyes narrowed. "You could say that. We've been spending some time together of late."

"He's the one you've been on the phone with all week?" asked Olivia.

Jets's face went blank, then she nodded. "Oh, you mean back at the constabulary, when I was on the phone, before the death? It must have been Rydell. Let's leave it at that." Janis leaned over the table toward Olivia. "Before I fill you in on what I've learned, tell me more about how you got that bruise." Janis pointed to Olivia's neck.

"Like I said on the phone, I closed my eyes for a few minutes to center myself before the Tone Rangers arrived for their rehearsal. Then I felt hands around my neck, choking me. I could barely breathe. Before I could turn around, someone said, 'I know what you're up to. Stay away from the music academy or you'll be sorry.' I wanted to chase the culprit, but the kids showed up for their rehearsal. I didn't want to alarm them, so I just sat down and put the whole thing aside until afterward."

Jets placed her elbows on the table, resting her chin in her palms. "So who do you think it was?"

"I'm not sure," Olivia answered quickly. "The voice sounded low and gravelly and unfamiliar."

"Did you see anything, like arms or even footwear? Did you look down?"

Olivia shook her head. Glancing at Michael's stricken face, she reached for his hand. "Tell Janis about your room now. I think all of this is connected," he prompted.

She explained about her room being tossed. "I think they wanted the key," she said. "That's the only thing missing from my room, not that I had anything valuable there for such a short stay."

Jets's eyes narrowed. "Am I supposed to know something about this key? I don't remember you telling me."

"The one Cookie dropped under his bench when I saw him and Cox having lunch together. I told you a few days ago, at the constabulary!" Olivia felt exasperated.

What happened to the Janis Jets who never forgot a detail?

"Oh right, I remember now. I told you to hide it in your bottom drawer. It seems you didn't follow my directions as usual."

"Plus somebody tried to strangle me in the auditorium. At first I thought somebody may be after my duplicate key, thinking I had it on me. By then the Tone Rangers arrived and I didn't want to alarm them so we just rehearsed as usual. By the time I rushed outside, I found Cox's car with a key in the back."

"Not your key?"

"No." She shook her head, touching her throat.

Janis lifted her chin and dropped her elbows underneath the table. "So we have a break-in, a missing key, and a threat by a man who strangled you from behind. Oh, and let's not forget the helicopter ride. Maybe this is all about getting Sage out of the way. I need to make a call." Jets reached for her cell phone. "You two can go now," she said dismissively.

"I think Olivia needs a bodyguard," Michael insisted.

Jets looked at him, surprise showing on her face. "Isn't that how you two met in the first place? You were her bodyguard, even though she didn't know it? Get outta my office, both of you, and guard each other's bodies, I don't care. Just let me continue my investigation.

"And you," Jets pointed to Olivia, "take your bodyguard and go home. No more snooping for right now. I thought you'd be more discreet, but somebody has figured out that you're my mole and working for the police."

"I *am* working for the police?" Olivia felt somehow pleased.

"Not that way," mumbled Janis. "You were helping me out in an unofficial capacity, and now you'll get out of my hair. I suggest you take a day or two off—without pay, of course—for recuperation." Jets glanced at Michael, a sly look in her eye. "Or for body-guarding, if that's what you're calling it."

Olivia frowned. "No can do," she told Jets. "I have a gig tonight with the Tone Rangers. After that I can go home but not before."

"And I," added Michael, "will be your bodyguard until Janis arrests the killer. Any chance of that happening in the near future?"

"Not sure," mumbled Jets.

"I'm not leaving yet. I told you my information, now it's your turn to tell us about the coroner."

Janis Jets placed her cell back on the table. She looked at the closed door behind Michael's back, then spoke. "There's more to tell about all of this but on a need-to-know basis. This death is not the extent of the inquiry. My guys actually found this on Dave's body, when they first discovered him at the bottom of the cliff."

She reached under the table into her briefcase, bringing up a small round disc with a wire attached.

"What is that?" asked Olivia.

Michael bit his bottom lip.

"It seems Dave was an informant," answered Jets. "Someone used him to get recordings of Cookie, Court, and Cox."

Michael stared at Janis. "Their names are an alliteration. Did you notice?"

"I have no time for grammar lessons. Anyway...Franco was an informant, that's all I'm saying."

"Did Dave record any of the Tone Rangers?" Olivia asked.

"I haven't heard all the tapes, but I think the kids were left out. But Cox, Court, and Kravitz are our main suspects. That's why we're interested in everyone Dave spoke to those few hours before his death."

Olivia watched Michael's jaw tighten. He leaned forward to ask, "Are you telling us that the cops weren't the ones wiring Dave?"

Jets shook her head. "Not us. Somebody else. That's what I'm saying. This need-to-know conundrum is out of your pay grade. You two don't need to know just yet."

Olivia sat in stunned silence.

Michael squeezed her hand.

Jets continued to stare at them both, her mouth in a grim line. "Now get going, you two. There's the concert and the body-guarding. That should keep you both busy for the rest of the day."

Janis picked up her phone once again, before Michael and Olivia left together, closing the door behind them.

Michael put his arm around Olivia. "This isn't as simple as it once seemed."

"You can say that again," agreed Olivia. "I was going to tell Janis about Anais and what she told me earlier. Until she played that need-to-know card. Then I got irritated."

"So tell me," Michael urged. "What did Anais say about Dave?"

"She saw him on the cliff, right around the time he fell to his death."

"That may be important to Janis's timeline. But Jets gave us an assignment, so let's get going on that. What's our next move?" asked Michael.

"I want to pick up my clothes and go home. It would feel so good to sleep in my own bed tonight."

"Not without my company," Michael responded. "I don't have to sleep in the same bed, but I do have my bodyguard assignment from Janis. Maybe on the sofa?"

Olivia shared a smile. "The sleeping together will hopefully happen very soon, just not tonight."

His dark eyes lit up, accompanied by a big smile. "As soon as I'm done being your bodyguard, I'll turn in my badge and sign up as your boyfriend."

She reached out for his hand, holding it close to her side as they walked toward the parking lot.

"Testing one, two, three," came the voice of the academy sound engineer. "Would you move that mic to the right about three inches?" he directed Olivia.

"Will do. Is that okay?" She tapped the mic.

The sound engineer nodded.

"I have to go," she told him. "My group needs some last-minute instructions before the recital."

"I can help," volunteered Michael. He jumped onto the stage, relieving Olivia of the microphone.

"Thanks," she muttered. "I wonder where the Tone Rangers have gone?" She jumped from the stage to look around the auditorium.

A short search revealed the group in the green room backstage. They sat together, each in a folding chair, all four heads bent over cell phones.

"Heads-up, everyone, it's time for a check-in before the recital begins," she told them in her most cheerful voice.

Abbey's chin rose first. "My dad will be in any minute. He wants to talk to us."

Olivia shuddered.

I don't remember inviting Simon Court to deliver a pep talk.

Her index finger inched up her neck where the attacker had left his mark.

He could have been the person who assaulted me.

Her stomach lurched and she inhaled deeply.

Speak of the devil...

Wearing his usual black and white tracksuit, Simon Court strode through the green room door. He held a briefcase in one hand and a look of impatience on his face. Abbey leapt to her feet, reaching her arms out. "Hello, Daddy, I'm so happy to see you."

"Not now, Abigail. I'll see you after the concert. We can talk then." Court shoved Abbey aside with his shoulder, making his way across the room toward Olivia.

Olivia took the initiative to speak first. "Take your time with your daughter. She's been working so hard on this performance and she wants your attention in the worst way. Can't you see that?"

He leaned in, his face an inch from hers. "The kid is too needy," he hissed. "Stop playing into her weaknesses and work on her strength. It's your fault she's no longer the lead and I want you to change that before tomorrow."

Instead of backing away, Olivia insisted, "Not my decision. The Tone Rangers choose their own leader, plus Abbey might need a break. She's looking a bit fatigued lately."

Court glanced over his shoulder, spinning around just

as Abbey resumed looking at her phone. The other three Tone Rangers stared back at him. It was Legend who finally shook her head, her eyes dropping back to her cell.

"Abbey looks okay to me," muttered Court. "She's always got her face in that phone, so I can't tell."

She always has her face in her phone because you won't talk to her.

Olivia looked directly into Simon Court's eyes. "I'm going to rehearse with the group right here in the green room. You are not invited. Abbey will talk to you after the recital."

Before he could refuse, Olivia used a hand gesture to get the attention of the group. "We're going to sing now," she announced, using her voice of authority. Immediately Legend looked up. She elbowed Raleigh. They all stood, phones put aside, eyes on Olivia.

Outnumbered, Court left.

"I have a few words to say to you," Olivia told the group. She looked into each pair of eyes, taking her time before moving to the next. When she stared at Abbey, the girl looked away.

"I want to talk to you about the recital." Olivia reached for a piece of chalk. She stood next to the old green board to write their two-song set list. All of the singers nodded their agreement.

"Any questions?" Olivia asked.

"Will this be our last recital in the old auditorium?" asked Anais.

"When will the new amphitheater be ready?" added Raleigh, rubbing their hand under their nose.

"It won't be the very last recital. The new amphitheater won't be ready until next spring," answered Olivia. "I know the architect and that is his estimation."

"I hope it's ready for our graduation," Abbey said quietly.

I think she actually likes the academy for all of her complaining. She sounds sad.

Then Legend spoke up. "I think Abbey should lead for this performance. She has the perfect voice. I can start up when this is over."

Does she feel sorry for Abbey now that the group picked her as their new leader?

Abbey's eyes grew wide. "How come you're so nice all of a sudden?"

Olivia watched Legend nervously shift her feet under the chair. "I'm just saying, you are a good singer," muttered Legend.

Olivia cleared her throat. "Okay then, we can talk about the rest of the school year later. Now I want to address how we'll collect money for Dave's family. Don't forget, even Broadway actors do this on occasion. They pass the hat amongst their patrons for any number of causes.

"Here's how it will work. Ms. McCloud will introduce me and the Tone Rangers as the closing act of the recital. She'll talk about Dave Franco and ask the audience to donate some money to his wife and her baby. After we exit the stage each of you will grab one of these." Olivia pulled out a stack of black top hats, holding one up. "You'll meander through the crowd holding out the hats."

"Posters with photos of Dave and Linnea have already been staged in the Curated Cuisine," added Anais. "Cookie and I put them up on tricornered easels last night."

Olivia nodded. "Good thinking. With all of the recital energy, people may need to be reminded while they eat afterward.

"Now then," Olivia said, facing her group. She felt her

eyes unexpectedly tear up. "So here's my speech, the one I make before every gig, to myself and to the rest of the band." She brushed hair from her face to gain composure.

"The music is not about us, it's about the listeners. We're performing for their pleasure the best we can. The message of your last song will hit people differently. But trust me, some will be moved. Your voices and those lyrics are the perfect match."

Legend nodded, as the other three circled their arms around each other's shoulders.

Abbey said, "Just for clarification, we are to exit right after the song."

"That's right," added Olivia. "Don't wait for, nor expect, applause. The best thing you can receive is that utterly foreign sound that comes from the audience when they are deeply moved."

"Silence," said Legend. "We've never ended on silence before."

"You may not this time, but I can assure you, in this instance the silence will be far more satisfying than any applause. Trust me."

"I do," said Anais. Olivia looked into her shiny eyes filled with tears. The others nodded in agreement.

They're open now, all the way. We've found the right emotional tone, that's not predictable.

"One last thing," she added. "Let's sit together in the front row of the auditorium. I'll give a thumbs-up when it's time to move backstage."

Olivia opened the door as the Tone Rangers filed out.

CHAPTER EIGHTEEN

A single spotlight beam, center stage, illuminated Sage McCloud. She held the microphone in her hand, raising it to her mouth. "Hasn't this been the most amazing concert so far?" she asked the audience.

Applause erupted with an occasional "bravo" thrown in for good measure. Sage waited for the applause to die down, a small smile on her lips. "Before we hear the final song from the Tone Rangers and my bandmate Olivia Greer, I have an announcement."

Olivia looked down the row at her singers. They stared ahead, as if frozen to their seats.

Abbey's wringing her hands and Legend's twisting the collar of her shirt.

Olivia caught Abbey's eye, giving her a thumbs-up.

Abbey nodded, leaning into Anais for support. As soon as Sage put the microphone back, the four singers slid from their seats toward stage right. Olivia followed, the last in line.

Stopping behind the curtain, the Tone Rangers huddled together.

"We've got this," said Olivia, sharing a bright grin. "Now it's time to have some fun."

"Money will be collected after the finale. If you see a Tone Ranger with a top hat, just drop your contribution in the basket." Sage finished her speech which was followed by mild applause.

As soon as the clapping stopped, Olivia poked her head out from the curtain. The single spotlight from above began to dim. She gathered her confidence around her like a warm coat, striding center stage, hearing instead of seeing the audience.

She felt the heat of the spotlight covering her head then shoulders. Once the light reached her feet, an illumination formed on the stage floor around her feet. Then and only then did Olivia inhale.

Her voice filled the auditorium.

In one phrase she felt a shift in the room, the audience listening, bringing their full attention. She held the last note, feeling it drop into her chest before she began the next phrase.

She became aware of her singing voice and her thinking voice, communicating silently at the same time.

Like the words in this song, that's what I want for all of you. Become yourselves, Tone Rangers, no matter what your parents say.

Olivia took a deep breath as she launched into the chorus, "Teach your children well."

The audience, mesmerized by her voice, held a collective breath.

Most of you know this song. Go ahead then, her inner voice nearly shouted.

As if they heard the unspoken invitation, voices in the front row began to hum along with the chorus. Soon other voices joined in, then people from the middle and the back of the auditorium began to sway.

She'd known all along, because Olivia was born knowing, that the entire audience would join in singing. If they knew the words they'd add their voices, and if they didn't, they'd hum along.

But then, she dropped her voice back to a near whisper of a song, and the audience knew to drop back with her. As she continued to sing Olivia heard the soft scuffling feet behind her. The Tone Rangers slid silently into place, just as they'd rehearsed. She finished her verse and they stepped forward.

Anais and Abbey to her left, with Legend and Raleigh to the right. She felt a hand on her shoulder and then a pat.

That must be Anais.

Tingles came up her spine as she inhaled deeply. "And you of tender years..." The Tone Rangers now joined her, echoing in a close harmony, supporting Olivia's solo. "Can you hear and do you care."

An electric current ran up her spine.

We found the groove.

And as soon as the teens took over the harmonies, Olivia dropped out, leaving them on their own. She slipped away to stand off stage.

Now the audience fell quiet, listening to the interweaving harmonies interpret the Graham Nash "Teach Your Children" song. As the singers increased their volume, the audience collectively leaned forward, anticipating the traditional Tone Ranger finale, where they gradually grew louder and louder, ending with a big sound.

The singers rounded toward the final chorus, the one that really mattered. The one Olivia had rehearsed with them over and over. Abbey took a step forward. She stood directly in the spotlight.

In the clearest of sopranos, Abbey sang, her voice soaring above the audience, Then Legend stood next to Abbey and took her hand as they sang together. Anais and Raleigh joined them then the light beamed down on the four teens, holding hands, singing in tight, exuberant harmony.

When the Tone Rangers reached the last chord in full volume, they dropped hands and the spotlight went out. They didn't wait to take their well-earned bow, nor did they wait for the applause. They filed off the stage, passing by Olivia through the side stage exit.

No one in the audience spoke or made a sound. As Olivia had predicted, silence filled the auditorium, a sound so big it felt louder than any applause.

"Teach your parents well," muttered Olivia to the kids. "And so you did."

Later on at the reception, Raleigh Ulrich spoke to Olivia. "I'd like you to meet my parents."

"Sure, Raleigh, I'll follow you."

They sidled up to a couple in their mid fifties. Olivia held out her hand. "It's a pleasure to meet you," she said.

"I've heard so much about you this week," commented the tall man with graying hair.

Raleigh's eyes.

He shook her hand firmly. "I'm Robert Ulrich and this is my wife."

She stood as tall as her husband, sharing a huge smile. "Raleigh says you really care about your students."

Raleigh's smile and sensitive chin.

Olivia shook Lucy's hand. "I had no idea Raleigh felt that way. They keep their feelings to themselves."

Mr. Ulrich nodded in agreement. "I can now see what Raleigh meant. You don't flinch at the pronouns."

Olivia modestly ducked her chin. "I have some slip-ups, especially in my thinking. But my spoken words are getting better."

"It took us a while too." Mrs. Ulrich patted Olivia's arm.

"Mom," interrupted Raleigh, "have a bite to eat; these cookies are amazing."

"Thank you, dear," she replied, selecting one from the top.

"I'll introduce you to our cook." They offered Olivia a cookie before sliding away to return the plate to the buffet table.

Robert Ulrich's eyes narrowed. He looked around the room. "Do you know the chef?" he asked Olivia.

"I do. He's over by the donation table talking to Simon Court."

Swallowing the last bite of cookie, he wiped a crumb from his lip and then turned to Olivia. "What do you think of the academic program here? Is it up to elite college standards? We're thinking about Harvard for Raleigh, though studying isn't their favorite."

"Does Raleigh have any academic challenges?" Olivia asked.

"Not since Simon Court took over. Raleigh's improved in every subject. I'm concerned that without a tutor they may lose ground. And as delicious as those cookies might be, I didn't send them here to eat baked goods."

"Honestly, Olivia—may I call you Olivia? Raleigh has no time to lose. Every minute counts to prepare for college admissions."

"I think you might want to talk to Sage McCloud, the principal, about your concerns." Olivia smiled, breaking eye contact with the concerned father.

I'd better end this conversation before I blab about any school politics.

"I have to go," she said, smiling apologetically. "Lots of parents to meet."

"I see Court over there and I'd like to have a word," Raleigh's father added, moving away.

"Don't forget to write a check for that poor man's wife and baby," Mrs. Ulrich called after him. "A big check, dear. She'll need lots of help."

Instead of heading straight toward Anais and her grands, Olivia followed closely behind Robert. Then she veered right as he approached the donation table. Instead of engaging in another conversation, she leaned against the wall to eavesdrop.

Simon Court and Cookie Kravitz were deep in conversation. Robert Ulrich stood close by. Olivia snagged a cookie from a student server, holding it in her hand as a decoy.

Court spoke the loudest. "Stop worrying, Ulrich. I'll get you a locker key before you leave this weekend. Raleigh can pick up the paperwork. I only need a couple of signatures. He can sign for you if you want. It's no big deal."

"Why not send it electronically?" asked Cookie.

"Because papers can't be traced," said Court. "I'm surprised you haven't figured that out."

"What's to trace?" asked Cookie.

Court faced him, a snarl on his lips. "Don't play dumb with me, Kravitz. This isn't your first rodeo."

Maybe Raleigh's father isn't as innocent as he seems.

Before she could pull out her cell phone, Anais and the grands made their way toward Olivia.

"What did you think?" the girl asked, her face all smiles. "Were we a hit?"

Olivia opened her arms to give Anais a quick hug. "You were amazing. The Tone Rangers never sounded better." Anais leaned into Olivia's shoulder.

Her grandfather spoke first. "An unconventional performance." He cleared his throat. "Not quite the thing for auditions. I'm sure you'll coach them differently by then."

"Just a few weeks away," added Jean Butler. "Anais will be traveling to take her SAT next weekend. Is there a way she can practice while she's gone?"

Olivia glanced over at Anais, who stared at the buffet table.

Is she listening to what they're saying?

"From my perspective, the song 'Teach Your Children' would make an excellent audition piece."

Carl's head jerked back. "You know colleges aren't looking for a cappella groups who are trying to teach a message to their parents. The competition is as bad as sports. Each student has to be well behaved with no incidents of drug use or poor academic attendance. They want quality harmony and attractive dress. Like those boots, for example." He pointed to Anais's feet. "Not for judges of Ivy League colleges."

Jean pulled Anais by the hand. "When Anais lost her old hiking boots, she made us buy new ones just like yours. She admires you so much. But now it's time to get her hair styled and to build a performance wardrobe for auditions. She requires heels, not boots."

Anais looked beseechingly at Olivia.

"Appearance is a consideration," Olivia said hesitantly.

"All the other a cappella groups have elaborate stage costumes and more conventional show choir costumes," explained Anais's grandmother. "They dress up for their interviews as well. Anais has to look young and vibrant and of course sexy. That will get her the early bid."

A grandmother wanting her granddaughter to turn on the sex appeal. Now that's not something I'd considered.

Carl Butler turned to look across the room. "You girls chat while I go talk to Simon Court. I hope he has a replacement for the other guy. What's his name again?"

"Dave, Dave Franco," said Anais in a loud voice. "He was not just 'the other guy,' he played in Olivia's band."

Anais looks ready to burst into tears.

Feeling the girl's discomfort, Olivia said, "Come with me, Anais, there are some amazing chocolate chip cookies that have your name on them." Olivia took the girl by the hand, eyeing Simon Court, who had moved across the room. He stood overseeing the crowd, like a gladiator ready for battle.

Circling behind a group of students, Olivia pointed to the cookies as Anais smiled gratefully.

"Can I help you ladies?" asked Cookie. He stood behind the refreshment table, refilling a plate with savory nibbles.

"What are those?" asked Olivia.

Cookie ran his fingers through his goatee. "I'm dropping these off at another table. Cheese, bacon, and chili bites. They're very popular with the parents, I hope I made enough."

"I'll have a cookie." Anais pointed to the plate at the other end of the table.

"Is there something no one likes?" asked Olivia. "I'll try one."

"You're an odd duck. No one wants what other people don't want."

"I always want what other people don't want. Just call me oppositional."

A clear voice came from behind Cookie. "Or you can call her a pain in the behind like the rest of the town."

"Officer Jets," Olivia mumbled, holding a chili bite to her mouth. "These are amazing!" she exclaimed. "I'll take two more."

Cookie laughed, reaching for the platter. "Add some dipping sauce and you'll be a complete convert," he pointed to a small table by the kitchen door.

Olivia took her plate, heading toward the condiment table. She was waylaid by Abbey Court.

"Olivia," she said, "could we talk, just the two of us?"

"Let's duck into the kitchen and chat. Want a chili bite?"

"Oh no," said Abbey. "I'm too upset to eat." Abbey held the door for Olivia as she walked into the kitchen.

"We could talk in the pantry." Olivia gestured with her head.

"Where the lockers are?"

"Yes. There's a small table with two chairs."

Once in the door, they sat down at the small round table. Abbey cleared her throat.

"I know I was supposed to tell someone a lot sooner than this, but I didn't know who. That police officer is kind of mean."

"Officer Jets?"

Abbey nodded. "I didn't want to tell Rydell either. He'd go right to my father."

"You don't confide in your father?"

Abbey shook her head. "I have to be very careful what I say to Daddy. He's easily upset and he's overworked. I don't want to be the cause of any problem for him, he's done so much for me and the Tone Rangers."

Olivia wanted to disagree. "But *you've* done the work, right? You're the one who gets the grades and goes to rehearsals. You're the one who organizes all of the auditions and takes care of the group, or least you were the one until recently."

"I do what I can. That's why I want to tell you something. Something about Dave and the day he died. This investigation is going to mess up our schedules if it continues into the week, so I'm hoping that Jets woman will arrest someone so that we can get back to a normal routine." Abbey leaned forward. "I saw Dave fall off the cliff."

Olivia's eyes narrowed. "You saw him fall?"

Abbey nodded. "That's right. He stood on the edge and looked down. Then he fell face forward and disappeared from my sight."

"So you weren't standing close to him?"

"I was running and saw him from the forest, a few feet away."

Abbey's face remained composed.

Olivia felt a tingle up her spine. "Did you call out or try to stop him?"

"It was too late. I ran as fast as I could to get help."

"When you say fall, do you mean he tripped and lost his balance? That kind of fall?"

"I don't know." Abbey ducked her chin toward her chest. Other than hiding her face, Olivia detected no emotions coming from the girl.

"Why tell me now?" asked Olivia.

"Because my dad is upset. The police are threatening to cancel classes this week. Daddy talked to Raleigh's parents and Anais's grands. They all agree. We can't afford to lose the time with early admission coming up so soon."

"That would make your dad happy?"

"It would help," said Abbey, moving her hand from her chin, revealing her entire face.

Now I'm really confused. Abbey tells me that Dave fell off the cliff, yet Janis's report confirmed that Dave was pushed. So Abbey is lying.

Olivia chewed the last bite, taking time to respond. "You need to talk to Officer Jets about what you saw. She's the official lead of the investigation."

Abbey blinked. "That's all you can say?" Pushing her chair away, she abruptly stood. "I'll talk to Officer Jets. Thanks for not helping." She stomped away, leaving the door to the pantry open.

Olivia tossed her paper plate into the trash. She looked around the small room, her eyes stopping at the row of lockers. *I wish I still had my key.* Turning around she made her way into the main kitchen. The sound of scratching came from the back door.

Opening the door carefully, she smiled at Mayor Maguire.

M&M trotted past Olivia, holding something in his mouth. He walked around the kitchen prep table sniffing the floor. When he made a full circle, he returned to Olivia.

Olivia gestured to him, bending down as he sat at her feet. "What do you have there, M&M? Is that a shoe?" She tickled his chin. When he didn't drop what was in his mouth, she tugged at the end.

Mayor Maguire crouched down on his front legs, growling as an invitation to play tug-of-war.

"Drop it," Olivia said in her commanding voice.

The dog looked up, considering his options, the toe of what looked like a boot still clamped in his mouth.

"Leave it," Olivia tried, unsure what command he'd been taught.

Jaws loosened as the entire boot fell to the floor.

"A hiking boot," Olivia said aloud. She picked it up and held it in her hand.

A size 8½ medium-width right-footed hiking boot. I wonder what happened to the left?

The one in her hand had been imprinted with tooth marks. She looked inside."

This looks like a woman's boot, or a very small man's.

Mayor Maguire pushed against her knee with his nose.

"Okay, M&M, I'm sorry, but I have to keep the boot. This may be important evidence for Janis Jets's case. You are a good doggie." Olivia patted the mayor, scanning the kitchen.

She walked toward the sink, looking into the cupboard beneath. Sure enough, paper bags had been neatly folded and stacked. She took one, opened it, and dropped the boot inside.

"If anyone asks, I can call this a doggie bag. Not exactly a lie, is it, Mayor?"

Olivia made her way into the dining room, the dog at her heels. She scanned the room and found Michael standing in the corner talking to Janis.

Just the two people I need to see.

"Olivia?"

Sage stood in front of her, eyes swollen from crying.

"Hey, are you okay?"

Sage covered her face with her hand, her shoulders shaking.

"Oh honey, what's wrong?" asked Olivia.

Sage shook her head back and forth without speaking.

"Let's get away from this crowd. Come on, head back through the kitchen. We can sit in the grove and talk."

The room grew quiet as people began to stare.

Olivia gripped Sage's shoulder, pulling her close. "Nothing to see here, folks. My sister gets very emotional after recitals." Olivia walked backward toward the kitchen door, M&M close to her side. She bent closer to whisper, "Don't worry. Everything will be okay."

Through the kitchen and then outside the back door, Sage and Olivia walked toward the woods. "I just want to get away from this place," Sage muttered.

"That's just what we're doing," Olivia said, her arm still wrapped around Sage's shoulders. By the time they sat side by side on the bench, Olivia couldn't hear the voices from the Curated Cuisine. Even Sage's shoulders had stopped shaking.

"I'm so sorry. I've made a fool of myself in front of the very people I wanted to impress." Sage sniffed into her sleeve.

"But the recital went so well, what's the matter?" asked Olivia.

"I thought the recital was a big hit. That is until Simon Court accosted me afterward."

"He's just a bully," Olivia said soothingly.

"A bully who fired me ten minutes ago." Sage burst into tears again, her hands forming fists. "He smiled when he did it too, as if he enjoyed my pain. I hate him!"

Olivia felt her stomach knot. "I don't think one person, even the board president, can fire you. There is a process which requires warnings and paperwork and counseling. I know you're angry right now, but there must be a way to fight back. We'll figure this out, don't worry. We're sisters and we'll find a way, even if we have to hire an attorney."

She felt her arm nudged by Mayor Maguire. He leaned past Olivia's knee, laying his head on Sage's lap.

CHAPTER NINETEEN

Back at their house, Olivia put on a kettle for tea. Mayor Maguire sniffed at the door. "You want to go out?"

His short bark said, "Yes."

She watched him trot outside into the dark.

Sage appeared wearing red eyes and pajamas. "I feel like a kid who got bullied at school. Are you making tea? Meadow would always do that when I came home crying." She smiled at Olivia.

"I am happy to be your Meadow. What a difficult day, and then to end with being booted out of your job." Shaking her head, Olivia looked into the cupboard. "What will you have? Herbal, I presume?"

Sage pointed to her usual licorice blend, while Olivia opted for chamomile and mint. Sitting across from each other at the kitchen table, they clinked mugs together. "Cheers," Olivia said.

"Back at ya," replied Sage.

"I'm still curious," Olivia began. "Did he act like he could fire you to humiliate you in front of the parents and students...or did the entire board vote to get rid of you?"

Before Sage could answer, a scratch came from the back door.

Olivia's eyes lit up. "He decided to come back." When she opened the door, the mayor trotted into the kitchen, bringing a smiling Michael Bellemare right behind.

"I've been looking for you both. Any of that for me?" He pointed to the tea mugs.

"Help yourself," offered Olivia.

Michael selected Earl Grey. He dropped the bag in his Carpe Diem mug. The pot of hot water had just enough left.

"Caffeine this late?" Olivia commented. "We are in for a long night... Sage got fired, you know."

"I heard. She doesn't deserve to be treated this way, especially with all the pressure of parent weekend." Michael frowned. "That was all anyone could talk about after the reception."

"Yep," answered Sage.

"Not sure Court can summarily decide to fire any academy employee without going through due process with board approval," added Michael.

"That's what I tried to tell her, though I'm not sure she heard me." Olivia nodded at Michael, glancing back at Sage.

"Not sure I care," said Sage. "The parents? They seem to want something I can't deliver."

Michael pulled a third chair from the corner of the room and sat down at the table. "Assuming the academy does terminate your contract, I just want to say that change doesn't have to be bad." He smiled at Olivia over his mug of tea. "I have news about the investigation. Is this a good time?"

Sage brushed tears aside. "That would be therapeutic for me. Enough about my woes, tell us everything."

He cleared his throat. "So I spoke to Janis tonight. She's ready to call in the three main suspects."

"That would be Cookie, Cox, and Court," said Olivia.

"The three C's, that's what I'm calling them."

"Does Janis want us in on the interviews?" asked Sage.

"She wants Olivia but did not mention you. Probably figures you have enough on your plate right now with the students and parents."

"At least until I'm given my termination notice," Sage muttered.

Michael picked up his mug, taking a sip. "I do have a message for you. Janis sent all the parents home after the reception. In fact, if I may quote Officer Jets, 'Tell Sage to tell those overzealous helicopter parents and grandparents to wave goodbye.'"

"That sounds like Janis." Sage yawned.

"You must be so tired," Olivia said, looking at her half-closed eyes.

"I am officially beat. So if you two sleuths don't mind, I'd like to try to get some sleep. Tomorrow will most likely bring a lot of phone calls and questions. I want to be prepared, especially if I have to announce my firing to the student body and staff."

Sage left her mug in the sink, and Mayor Maguire rose to follow her as she walked out of the kitchen.

Michael and Olivia, left alone, stared into each other's eyes.

"I have a lot to tell you," whispered Michael.

"Do we have to talk now?" she murmured, leaning to press her lips against his ear. "Can't we, you know, kiss first?"

"Great minds think alike," Michael pulled Olivia closer." Let's just warm up a bit before we talk about suspects and arrests."

She nuzzled his neck, feeling the stubble of beard. "I'm pretty sure Janis would not encourage any of this, but then who made her the boss of us?" Her lips pressed against the side of his mouth, and he turned his head to kiss her fully on the mouth.

She gasped as his tongue explored her lips.

"Too soon?"

"Don't stop," she said, leaning in closer.

After a while he pulled away, running his finger over her jaw. "Stopping is the last thing on my mind, but we have to get ready for tomorrow."

Olivia sat back in her chair. "On the one hand, I think getting ready for a police interview may be the last thing on my mind."

Michael grinned. "But on the other hand? Since you're no longer playing hard to get, I can wait one more day."

Olivia rose to her feet. "Then let me put the kettle back on for more tea. You can fill me in on what Janis expects. Plus, I have some news for you. Mayor Maguire may have cracked this case wide open."

Olivia refilled the kettle. She felt Michael's eyes watching her from behind. He tapped his fingers on the table, waiting for her to return. "I want to hold your hand," he hummed under his breath. When she sat down he reached across the table.

"Kind of hard to concentrate, but the tea will help. Okay, you go first. What did you learn from the mayor?"

"I have actual evidence," Olivia remarked. "Just give me a minute." She returned with the brown bag containing the worn hiking boot. "The mayor brought me this item during the recital reception. He walked right into the kitchen with the thing in his mouth."

She held the bag open for Michael to look inside. He

immediately reached in." Not what I expected," he held the boot a loft, surprise written on his face.

Olivia continued to explain. "If I remember correctly, Janis said there were hiking bootprints at the top of the cliff. She distinctly mentioned a size 8½. The mayor's piece of evidence fits her description."

Michael inspected the boot carefully, looking on the inside and closely at the sole. "Will you hand it over to Janis for forensics to have a look?"

"Tomorrow morning."

"And do you know if it belongs to anyone in particular?"

"That's the hard part." Before she could finish explaining, the kettle wailed. "Let me get the water. Do you want another Earl Grey?"

"Don't worry, I'll get the kettle. You stay right there."

Michael freshened both of their mugs with new tea bags, pouring water to the brim. Olivia wrapped her fingers around the handle, waiting for the contents to cool before taking a small sip. Only then did she pick up the conversation.

"I think this boot belongs to Anais. I'm not sure how the mayor got it or where the other one is, but I do know that Anais got new boots a couple of days ago." She explained about the grands and how they took Anais on a shopping trip before parent weekend.

Michael looked inside the boot again. "I don't see blood or anything."

"No one said Dave was bleeding before he went over the cliff."

Michael paused to remember. "But Janis did say there were lots of shoe and bootprints on that bit of dirt."

"Janis mentioned bootprints. I'm more interested in how Mayor Maguire brought me this boot when Anais's grandparents went out of their way to tell me how they bought a new pair for Anais."

"I do find the grands' conversation odd. Along with Mayor Maguire's discovery, it may point to our killer. I put my confidence in the mayor."

Olivia grinned. "Me too, because he's psychic and all."

"I'm a believer," he insisted, as if Olivia might doubt. "So are you thinking what I'm thinking? That Anais may have pushed Dave over the cliff?"

"She's not immune to impulsive behavior. No one is. Plus she told me she talked to Dave right before his death."

"Okay, that's interesting. I'm not sure what their relationship was about other than tutoring."

"It's not that. They weren't, you know, having a fling. At least that's not the vibe I get from her."

He didn't argue. "So they weren't together, but he did tutor her. Could something have come up regarding that relationship?"

Olivia considered in silence. "It may be about the Tone Ranger tutoring. I know Dave was hired by Simon Court." She took her mug to the sink and rinsed it out. Then she sat back down at the table with Michael. "So I showed you mine. What do you have from Janis?"

"She answered a lot of my questions, including why she's dating Rydell Cox. But I told her she'd be the one to give you the details. So let's just say everything about Janis makes more sense now."

"Is that your way of saying we're done here until tomorrow?" asked Olivia.

"Oh, not by a long shot," he insisted, standing up from the table. He reached for her hand to bring her to her feet. "I think we've talked way too much. It's time for a little action. Your place or mine?"

Olivia felt her cheeks flush. When she raised her chin, she smiled. "My place is closest. Lead the way."

Michael led her through the great room, down the stairs, into her suite. He shoved the door closed behind them before pulling her into his arms.

Olivia's heart beat wildly in her chest as she reached down to pull off her top in one move.

The next morning her eyes opened to sunshine streaming from the window. Stretching her legs, she patted her hand across the bed. *Look who's here.*

A lazy smile came over her lips.

Michael stirred, rolling over on his back. His arm reached over to pull her closer.

"Last night was not my imagination," he commented.

"So it was good for you?" she asked lightly, crossing her fingers under the covers.

"Well worth the wait." His head moved next to hers as he nuzzled her ear.

"Again?" she asked.

"Why not? Unless you have something else to do..."

She rolled to face him and then lightly kissed his lips.

By the time they showered and dressed, Mayor Maguire stood in the kitchen hovering over his food bowl. He looked up at her, tail wagging in anticipation.

She measured two level cups of kibble in his bowl. Then she reached into a metal container, pulling out a cookie shaped like a dog bone. She dropped it on top of his breakfast.

"Dry food this morning, but I promise something more

flavorful tonight. Bone appetite."

Michael smiled. "Those look homemade," he commented.

"I bake them myself," admitted Olivia, stooping to pet Mayor Maguire's furry head.

"Of course you do. How about a cup of coffee for the road and then off to the constabulary. Janis pinged me three times."

Olivia picked up a cup. "I forgot to check my phone."

"Obviously you had other concerns on your mind this morning," he said with a sheepish grin.

She faced him, inching the fingers of one hand up his chest. "I've got a bit of baggage from another relationship. I admit that. It's like my emotions are on hold and I don't want to let go. But then you smile and we laugh and I know we're right together."

"It took you a while," Michael eyes brightened, "but just so you know, our first date still needs to happen. Saturday night, dinner for two."

"I think that will work for me." She took a step back to stare into his eyes. "I'm going to call you boyfriend if you don't mind. Now that we know we're compatible, I think it's only reasonable."

"Okay, girlfriend. So why don't we move along and go solve a murder."

They reached the constabulary with one parking place to spare. Michael navigated the truck to the curb. He leaned over to give Olivia a peck on the cheek before removing his car keys and stepping down to the pavement.

She released her seat belt and then opened the passenger door.

"All safe and secure," Michael said as the truck beeped. They walked together toward the entrance of the constabulary.

To Olivia's surprise, Janis Jets sat behind the receptionist's desk. She was too busy staring at the computer to even say hello.

"Hey, boss," Olivia commented. "Get outta my chair."

"Be quiet," mumbled Jets. "I'm reading something important. I'll get to you in a minute. It's Monday morning. You're late."

"My fault," Michael said.

Jets looked up. She stared at Michael and then Olivia and then back at Michael. "I don't believe it. You two have finally sealed the deal. Geez, took you long enough."

"You don't know that for sure," objected Olivia, fluffing the hair on the back of her neck to distract Janis from commenting on her pink cheeks.

"Come on, I'm a detective. Your glow, his swagger. It's obvious to me." Jets hid her smile by turning back to the computer.

"How about we make a pot of coffee and meet you back in your office?" Michael offered.

"Good idea. By the way, stop swaggering. You look ridiculous."

With a deliberate shift of his shoulders, Michael walked through the sliding doors. "How's that?" he asked Olivia. "Do I look like a guy who just got lucky with the love of his life?"

"I don't have to be a detective to see that," laughed Olivia.

On the way down the hall Olivia glanced at the empty cells. "Do you think she'll have an arrest by the end of the day?"

"I think she thinks so," he commented.

By the time Olivia rinsed the glass carafe, Michael had ground fresh beans. She measured twelve spoonfuls into the basket with the paper filter. "I'm adding the water to the reservoir," she called to Michael, who had already taken a seat at a table close by.

Olivia selected two clean mugs, setting them on the counter, and waited for the coffee to finish brewing.

"I wish I still had that key to one of those lockers at the academy," she mused. Michael was reading a paper copy of the *Lily Rock Gazette*.

He dropped his paper. "Someone stole that key for a reason. I wonder how long Janis is going to take to get back here."

"She doesn't seem in any big hurry."

"Are you still her assistant? And if you are, why is she sitting at your desk?"

Olivia's eyes narrowed. "I'm not sure if I'm still employed by the constabulary. My job got murky when she moved me into the dorm."

Sputtering its last bit of water, the coffeepot finished brewing. Olivia picked it up and poured hot coffee into two mugs, then brought them to the table.

"I forgot the cream and sugar."

He stood up to pull out her chair. "I'll check the refrigerator, you go ahead."

Janis Jets walked into the room. She looked over Olivia's head toward Michael. "Bring the pot," she ordered. "I need a refill and to catch you two up on our morning activities."

Jets sat down. She reached into her back pocket for her cell phone, laying it on the table in front of her.

"I scheduled three interviews, which will start in twenty minutes. I'm putting the suspects in three different rooms, recording each one, sticking to the details and hoping for a confession."

Olivia's eyes widened. "You've got a plan for the suspects in place already?"

"Notified them last night. If one fails to show, then we know whodunit. If all three show up, which I think they will, we'll play one off the other. I don't think anyone will miss the opportunity to prove themselves innocent during an interview."

With an extra mug in one hand and the pot in the other, Michael returned to the table. He set the items down and then shoved his hand into his pocket. "Here are the sugar and creamer packets." He tossed them down. "I'm assuming we're talking about Cookie, Cox, and Court?"

"That's what I told you last night," Janis confirmed. She picked up the carafe to pour more coffee into her mug.

"Who do you think is our killer?" asked Olivia, intrigued by Janis's calm.

"I don't know who the killer is, but I do know who it isn't. One of those men is not like the others."

With that cryptic statement, Jets took a long sip.

Olivia looked at her, curiosity written all over her face.

"I'm only telling you what you need to know. That's our motto, Ms. Amateur Sleuth."

Olivia sighed.

You may think it's one of those men, but I'm not so sure. Anais may be a prime suspect.

Janis looked over at her cell phone. It lit up immediately. She glanced at her texts. "Yep, Simon Court is on his way."

"Is he coming by helicopter?" Michael asked with a sly grin.

"I sure as hell hope not. I don't need any early morning

commotion. I got a number of phone calls the last time he landed in the pub parking lot. One guy thought aliens were landing from Mars. He demanded that I arrest everyone."

Olivia's eyebrows shot up. "Aliens, huh? An interesting assumption, not that Court doesn't fit the description. He's not a Lily Rock kind of guy."

"I'm done being professional," Janis said flatly. "I'm just gonna tell it like it is. He's a jerk. That doesn't mean he's a criminal, but we can always hope."

"Comeuppance," muttered Olivia.

"Exactly," agreed Jets. "I love it when a jerk gets his comeuppance. An old-fashioned word for *you reap what you sow*."

"Do I hear an amen?" asked Michael.

Janis's cell phone buzzed again. "He's here," she said, standing up. "Meet me in interview room three. You," she pointed to Olivia, "at the table beside me, and you," she pointed to Michael, "behind the two-way mirror."

Janis looked at them, one then the other. "Most of the time you two get in my way, but I have to admit you see and hear what I don't. Keep notes, Mike. And Olivia, just sit there and feel stuff. Your intuition may pay off when we get back to talk about the interviews."

"When will that be?" asked Olivia.

"When I say so." Janis's jaw clenched. "You have your assignments."

Feels like old times. The three of us together, using our unique skill sets for good. Olivia felt a brief moment of excitement. But then a sense of foreboding came over her. She nervously rubbed her neck, taking a deep breath.

What if it turns out Simon Court did kill Dave Franco? Abbey will be crushed. She loves her daddy so.

CHAPTER TWENTY

Looking casual in his tracksuit, Simon Court sat on the opposite side of the interview table. He wore a calm smile.

Olivia entered the room and sat next to Janis. They both faced Court.

The police officer spoke first. "Mr. Court, I'd like your verbal consent to record our interview."

"Yeah, not a problem; not my first legal rodeo. I'm quite familiar with the legal system. Of course I rarely make a personal appearance, that's the job of my attorneys." He leaned forward. "I won't need to be there this time either. You have no case."

Jets kept her face immobile. She pulled out a folder, opening it on the table. "We have a photo of you talking to Charles Kravitz in the Lily Rock park the day before Dave Franco's death." Jets turned the photo around so that Court could see.

Olivia gulped.

That's a picture from the day I ate lunch in the park. Does Janis realize the camera also caught me two benches over?

Court glanced at the photo, shoving it back at Janis Jets. "So far as I know, there's no crime in talking to the cook at my daughter's school. She has special nutritional needs and I just wanted to make sure he was aware."

"I see," said Jets, pulling out another photo. "Then perhaps you can explain this photo of you and Dave Franco talking on the very cliff where he took his fatal fall."

With tightly drawn lips, he looked at the new photo Janis pushed in front of him.

"Dave and I were pals, you know. We'd smoke a cigar and shoot the breeze at that spot every time I visited Abbey. He was an interesting character, a good percussionist too. I wanted him to teach me how to play the snare drum." He pretended to hold sticks and air-play, his face relaxed, a slight smile on his lips.

He reminds me of a hockey player who turns a shoulder to avoid a body check.

Olivia held her calm pose as her stomach did a loop-the-loop.

I wonder who took that photo of Dave and Court? Probably won't matter unless she has a recording of their conversation. Court can make up anything he wants to about these photos. He seems to be enjoying himself.

Jets took back the second photo, placing it carefully into her folder. She stood and motioned for Olivia to follow.

"I'm done here?" demanded Court.

Janis slowly turned to face him. "Oh no, Mr. Court, you're not done here. Just sit tight while we interview Charles Kravitz. He'll most likely tell us more about your conversation in the park."

Janis paused as if something just occurred to her. "By the way, where were you between four and four thirty in the afternoon on the day Dave Franco died?"

Court paused briefly before answering. "I was with my daughter. Took her out for coffee for parent weekend. We're very close, Abbey and I. She'll be happy to tell you we were together and the exact details of our father-daughter conversation."

Janis nodded. "We will speak to Abbey to confirm your memory of time and place. What coffee shop was that?"

In an instant Simon Court stood up from his chair, shoving it away from the table with a kick of his shoe. "Are you implying my daughter and I would lie?"

Janis ignored Court's display of temper. She shifted her phone and notebook to her other arm. Without looking back, Janis stepped out of the interview room as Olivia followed.

"Close the door?" Olivia's eyebrows raised.

Jets nodded an affirmation.

Court's shouting could still be heard through the closed door as they made their way down the hall. "You're going to regret this. I warn you. I'll have a lawsuit slapped on you and this entire town by the end of the day."

"He's still yelling," Olivia said.

"Music to my ears," said Janis, smiling. "He's on the defensive now, right where I want him. Guys like that don't like it when you question anything they say. He doesn't even care if he's lying or telling the truth. All he wants is my obedience. Once he gets off his indignation high-horse, he'll realize the bigger problem. Maybe I have a witness who overheard the conversation."

"Did you see me in that first photo?" asked Olivia.

"I knew you were there. Did you overhear anything I need to know?"

Olivia thought for a moment. "Not really. I was shocked that he and Cookie seemed like such close buddies. You know the rest, about the dropped key. What I'm wondering is if you actually think someone overheard their conversation on the cliff?"

"I might have been overly optimistic. But he doesn't have to know that. Let him stew and think someone did overhear. Now it's time to interview Kravitz."

"Before we do the next interview, I have a question."

Jets faced Olivia. "What's that?"

"Why would Simon Court want to kill Dave? I am still confused about how a small-town musician and part-time academic tutor would pose any threat to such a wealthy and influential man."

"I know what you mean, but when you've been at this as long as I have, you know that it's the small guys like Dave Franco who get trapped in the bigger picture."

Jets's eyes grew dark. "Why don't you check in on Mike and give me a moment to think?"

"Will do," Olivia said, opening the door to step in. She found Michael staring at three oversized computer monitors.

One for each suspect.

He looked up to give Olivia a grin.

"Janis is going to grill Kravitz in interview room two. Just wanted you to know," said Olivia.

"That woman is the master of deceit. She looks so innocent and tells people just enough so they'll think she knows more than they do. I've got to hand it to her."

Olivia sighed. "I'm gonna miss her when she leaves."

Michael gave her a noncommittal look, as if he didn't understand. When Olivia raised her eyebrows, he added, "Just keep watching Jets. Don't worry about anything else."

Olivia gave a small one-handed wave and then closed

the door. She walked a few feet, stepping into interview room two.

Facing the entry door, Charles Kravitz tapped a large gold ring on the table. He looked directly at Janis Jets, who smiled back.

He's not one bit afraid of Janis. It's like he's saying... bring it.

When he didn't remove his eyes from Janis's face, Olivia sat down first.

Janis sat next to her.

Olivia coughed to break the tension. "Excuse me," she mumbled quietly.

"Mr. Kravitz," Janis began. "I have a photo to show you." She shoved the same picture she first showed Court toward Kravitz. "According to Simon Court, you two have a personal relationship outside of the Lily Rock Music Academy."

Kravitz sat back in his chair, not looking at the evidence. "Actually Simon and I knew each other in the Navy. We both served together before he got out. I stayed in and retired from the service. We didn't reconnect until this year."

"So you had plenty to catch up on, talking at the park in this photo?" Janis tapped the picture to bring his attention to it.

When he didn't comment, she continued. "A reliable witness tells me you dropped a key under the bench that day."

Kravitz nodded toward Olivia. "She returned the key a few hours later."

Janis pressed on with her inquiry. "What does the key unlock?"

Kravitz shrugged. "Court claimed Abbey was lactose

intolerant and needed special dairy tablets before certain meals. He thought she'd forget the pills, so he left the key and the medication with me in the pantry. I know the nurse had that covered, but overprotective fathers can't be underestimated. I went along with his idea just to look cooperative. I guess the key just slipped right out of my pocket that day."

"So there's nothing other than the tablets in that locker?" Jets's dubious expression conveyed a lack of belief in Kravitz's story.

"There are various uses for the pantry lockers, but Abbey Court's locker just contains what her father gave me...so far as I know," he said carefully.

Now Jets stared him down. She looked right into his eyes, taking her time. Then she inched her fingers over to remove the photograph. "We'll check into the lockers after this interview to make sure." She pulled a key out of her pocket and dangled it in front of Kravitz. "This is the master to all of the lockers."

"You don't say." He smirked at Janis.

"One more question. Where were you between four o'clock and four thirty the day Dave Franco died?"

Cookie chuckled. "Serving my pea soup to all who wandered into the Curated Cuisine. Lots of people saw me. Ever tried my soup?" he asked with raised eyebrows. He gestured with his thumb toward Olivia. "This one is a huge fan."

Janis didn't rise to his bait. "Never mind your soup. You will stay a little longer. I need a few words with another suspect who may or may not corroborate your testimony."

Kravitz laced his fingers behind his head, expanding his barrel chest like a gorilla in the zoo. "No problem. I'll take a snooze while you're gone. I learned how to sleep anywhere during my time in the Navy, even standing up. Actually, any chance I could get some coffee?"

Jets pointed to Olivia. "My assistant will bring a mug."

"Cream or sugar?" she asked like a waitress in a donut shop.

"Both," he said, closing his eyes.

Once in the hallway, Janis sighed. "Okay, we got two down, one to go."

"Do you think Cookie is the guy?" asked Olivia.

"My favorite suspect is the last one we'll question," stated Janis. "Rydell Cox in interview room one. Tell Michael."

"So favorite means the one you like to go out with or the one who murdered our victim?"

"Maybe both. Just 'cause we dated, doesn't mean he's not the killer. I've dated many a criminal in my time. Any more questions, Nancy Drew?"

"Where did you get that second key to the lockers?" Olivia felt her cheeks flush because she thought she knew the answer.

Jets grinned. "Oh, that old thing? When I went into the drawer at the constabulary to get the key, it wasn't there. I had the feeling you were hiding something. Don't know why, call it my investigation instincts. Anyway I had a younger cop toss your room and he brought the key to me. I didn't know at the time you made a duplicate."

"When I told you about the key being dropped, you didn't seem one bit interested."

"I got interested later. No harm in that. I just didn't want to go through the song and dance to question you, so I took matters into my own hands. That's why they pay me the big bucks. No more questions. Time for the next interview."

"Don't you want to know what Kravitz is doing all alone in the interview room?" Olivia asked.

"He can be knitting a new chef's apron for all I care. You just want an excuse to see Mike. Go ahead. But don't be long!"

Olivia opened the door. She found Michael watching Cookie Kravitz on the oversized computer screen. Kravitz, for all intents and purposes, looked fast asleep.

Michael grinned at Olivia, pointing to a large computer screen. She stepped closer to look over his shoulder. Interview room one was occupied by Rydell Cox. He turned toward the mirror on the right to take a long look at himself. He smoothed back his hair, checked his smile, and then adjusted the necktie on his crisp white shirt.

"He likes looking at himself," remarked Michael. "He doesn't realize I also have him on camera."

Michael scanned at all three screens.

"We're heading to interview room one. I'll leave you to it." Olivia told him. She closed the door behind her.

Walking past Janis, she moved briskly toward the break room, returning minutes later with a mug of coffee. She left the mug in the room with Cookie Kravitz, who looked up and smiled before he closed his eyes again.

"Thanks," Kravitz said. "I'll be sure to leave perfect fingerprints if you're looking for mine, right here on the handle." She heard him chuckle as she closed the door.

Janis Jets waited at the corner for her to catch up. They entered the next interview room together and sat down opposite Rydell Cox.

Cox spoke first. "I agree to be recorded. Let's get on with this. I have a Lily Rock academy principal whose job I intend to take over as soon as it's vacated."

Olivia sat up straight, words darting from her mouth

before she could stop them. "Sage can't be fired without board approval."

Jets interrupted. "We're not talking about academy business right now." She tapped her temple with her finger as if thinking deep thoughts. "My first question is where were you between four and four thirty on Friday, October 8, the day Dave Franco was killed?"

"I worked at the office all day," he said with confidence.

"Students saw you at the top of the cliff right before Dave's fall," argued Janis.

Cox looked at her intently. "You have proof other than hearsay?"

"I have two witnesses. That's all I need."

Cox shrugged. "I often met with Dave after work in that spot. We got together early because of parent weekend. On most days we'd meet after school, sometimes for a beer and a smoke, if you must know. Blow off a little steam because teaching teens isn't exactly a walk in the park. Those kids can get on your nerves. Decompressing, that's what Dave and I did. A nice guy. I had no reason to kill him. It would be ridiculous to say I did."

"Sometimes you don't need a good reason, Mr. Cox. Sometimes a simple shove over a cliff is done in a moment of panic or fear. Maybe Dave knew something about you. And the best way to keep him quiet was to—"

"I tell you, with God as my witness, I did not kill Dave Franco!" Cox shifted in his chair, appearing agitated.

"Just calm down. I was only suggesting," said Janis in a persuasive voice. She fumbled with her folder and then leaned across the table. To Olivia's surprise she said, "Okay, Mr. Cox, you can go now. Stay close so that I can call you back if necessary. Have a nice day."

It didn't require another invitation for Rydell Cox to

stand. He hurried around the table, opened the door, and exited the room. The tang of his expensive cologne lingered afterward. Olivia stifled a polite sneeze in her elbow. Then she waved her hand in front of her nose. "Ralph Lauren?"

"Wouldn't know," Jets muttered.

Michael walked into the room. "So whodunit?" he asked with a slight grin.

"My bet is on Simon Court. He's sneaky and defensive and was seen with the deceased talking on the very spot he was pushed over." Olivia nodded, pleased with her own assessment.

Michael shook his head. "Kravitz was cagey with his responses, especially about that whole key deal."

Janis looked from Michael to Olivia. She turned to Olivia. "Tell Court and Kravitz they can go. I'm not going to arrest either one, at least for now."

"Okay," Olivia said, pushing herself up to standing. She headed out the door.

When she stuck her head into Kravitz's room, his eyes were closed.

"Mr. Kravitz," she called quietly.

Steel-blue eyes popped open. "All done, are we?" he asked in a pleasant voice.

"Officer Jets says you can go."

Around the corner in interview room three she found Simon Court still on his feet, pacing the room like a caged animal. "You can go," she told him, leaving the door open, not waiting for a response.

By the time she looked into Kravitz's interview room again, he'd already left.

"I said goodbye," Janis explained, as if she were talking about a house guest instead of a murder suspect.

Michael waited past the doors to the outer office. Olivia

called out, "Let's head back to the academy right away. Janis wants to check out the lockers."

Once at the academy they found Abbey Court sitting outside the auditorium. Kicking her heels underneath the wooden bench, she smiled as they came closer. "Hey, Olivia. Is this your boyfriend?"

Olivia glanced at Michael to see how he took the label. His face, inscrutable, left her no clue.

"He is my boyfriend. I want you to meet Michael Bellemare."

Abbey graciously held out her hand for Michael to take it in his. "Nice to meet you, Mr. Bellemare."

The formality of her response made Olivia wonder, *What is she up to?*

Michael dropped her hand quickly, turning toward Olivia. "I had a chance to hear the Tone Ranger performance last night. I was impressed."

"Were you?" Abbey's bright smile dimmed. "My father had the opposite reaction."

"I guess that was the point," Michael said. "Teach your parents well, the last verse."

"I suppose," Abbey said quietly.

Olivia sat next to the girl on the bench. "We wanted to talk to you about the day Dave Franco died. Thinking back —it was only a few days ago—you were the one who first called the constabulary to say you saw someone fall off the cliff."

Abbey twisted her hands in her lap. "I did see Dave tumble right over as if he were pushed. It was terrifying."

"Did you call for help right away?" asked Michael.

"I ran to get help and then I called on my cell," she said promptly. "Should I have done something different?"

Olivia patted her knee. "I don't think there was anything else you could have done."

"Okay, that's good." Abbey's bottom lip began to quiver.

"Is there something more you want to talk about?" asked Michael, sitting on her other side. He brought a supportive presence with his kind voice.

"I w-was afraid to say," stammered Abbey. "But now I see it might be important."

"What's that?" Olivia asked gently.

"Dave wasn't alone when he went over. Another person kind of, you know, didn't just stand by. They actually shoved him from behind."

Ducking her head to hide tears, Abbey kept talking. "I ran away because I was frightened and shocked."

"Tell us, Abbey. Who did you see shove Dave Franco over the cliff?" Michael asked.

"It was...oh I can't tell on her, I just can't." Abbey's voice wailed. "She did it. All I could do was run as fast as I could away from the cliff. I didn't want to get Anais in trouble." Abbey looked up with swollen red eyes. "We were so close up until then. I didn't want to be the one to tell the cops what I saw. I thought they'd figure it out themselves."

Olivia put her arm around the sobbing girl's shoulders.

"I have proof," Abbey added, "if you don't believe me. I have her boots."

"You mean her hiking boots?" Olivia asked.

"She threw them away in the trash a day later. I got them and saved them just in case."

"Both of the boots?" asked Olivia, thinking of Mayor Maguire's discovery. "Tell me where you've kept the evidence."

"In my locker in the Curated Cuisine pantry. I can show them to you now."

Olivia and Michael followed the girl as she marched across the path to the Curated Cuisine. On the way Olivia considered the possibilities.

Anais tossed her boots, afraid she'd be found out. If she pushed Dave off the cliff, then she must have been very angry. I'm still confused about what would make Anais angry enough to push someone to their death...

And then there's Abbey. She held back pertinent information, afraid that Anais would be discovered. Abbey kept the incriminating evidence in her locker. And then I wonder, did Simon Court or Cookie know about the boots?

Other than finding Dave's killer, Abbey had another motivation for not telling the police. If Anais was arrested, the Tone Rangers would lose their alto and their hopes for early admission. No college would touch them with a ten-foot pole. So Abbey just kept quiet.

Emerging from the woods, Olivia heard Janis Jets's voice from the kitchen back door. "I'm not gonna put cuffs on you right now, but I expect you to turn yourself in before six o'clock."

Jets came bursting out of the doorway, bumping right into Olivia.

"I've got what I needed," she announced, holding up a large plastic evidence bag with two hiking boots secured inside.

Anais came out the door next. White-faced and trembling, she said, "I called the grands. They were almost down the hill, but I caught them in time. We'll be at the constabulary within the hour."

"Good," said Jets with authority.

"I'm so sorry," cried Abbey, rushing past Jets to give Anais a hug.

Anais held her arms out in protest, her face flushed red with anger. "I don't know how my boots got in that locker. The police think I killed Dave and I didn't do it."

She did not wait for a response, making her way down the path toward the dormitory.

Abbey cried after her, "Even if you killed him, I'll still be your friend. Wait for me. Please, Anais!"

As she ran past, Michael reached out to grab her elbow. "Let her go," he told the flustered teen. "You can talk to her later. For now it's best to let Officer Jets take charge."

CHAPTER TWENTY-ONE

Olivia watched Anais Butler run away. "I am her only friend," Abbey said, her voice growing faint. The girl began to sob, her shoulders shaking and tears pouring down her cheeks.

Michael looked at Olivia and mouthed, *What do I do now?*

Olivia stepped closer to Abbey, placing an arm gently over the girl's shoulders. Michael stood back.

As Abbey brushed away her tears, her shoulders steadied and the sobbing stopped. She sniffed and patted her face with the sleeve of her shirt. Olivia dropped her arm as the girl finished composing herself.

Janis Jets sighed deeply. "Now that the crying is over, come into the kitchen. I want to ask you about those lockers."

"I have things to do," Abbey turned to leave, her customary impatience pulled back on like an old sweater.

Jets stopped her. "I have questions for everyone, and that includes you."

Abbey, taken by surprise, insisted, "I have nothing to do with this."

Janis ignored her protests, holding the door wide open for Abbey to walk through.

"You go first," Olivia told Abbey.

"Oh all right," Abbey mumbled, stepping toward the kitchen.

Once inside the walk-in pantry, Janis spoke. "You can stand over there."

Olivia stood between Michael and Abbey, facing the bank of multicolored lockers. One door had been left partially open, the key hanging from the lock.

"That's where we found the hiking boots," Janis explained. "I was told that was your locker." She pointed to Abbey, who nodded.

"They aren't my boots," Abbey explained. "I found them in the trash right after Anais dropped them. My window looks onto the courtyard, so I had a perfect view."

"Just to clarify, you're saying those boots were put in your locker by you."

"I knew they were evidence. Like I told Olivia and Michael, I saw Anais push Dave from the cliff. They were arguing, and when his back was turned she gave him a shove. So when I saw her trash the boots, I knew she was covering up for herself."

"Why didn't you mention this a few days ago when we were asking for any witnesses?" Janis Jets failed to disguise the impatience in her voice.

Abbey's eyes narrowed. "I didn't mean any harm. Anais is my friend and I didn't want to get her in trouble."

"I think pushing someone to their death hardly qualifies as trouble. More like homicide to me, and your little friend may be up for a long time of incarceration. You knew that, right? I may even arrest you for standing in the way of my inquiry, since it took so long for you to report what you saw to the police."

Abbey ducked her head.

Olivia turned her attention away from Abbey to stare at the boots Jets placed in the middle of the table. "May I look at those more closely?" she asked.

"Help yourself," said Janis.

Olivia took one boot, then the other in her hand. "One left, one right," she commented aloud. She inspected the bottom of each boot. "Both size 8½," she added, "most likely women's." She held them aloft to look at the soles.

The boots look equally worn, no distinguishing evidence that I can see.

"Has your forensics team looked these over yet?" she asked Jets.

"Not yet, just found them. Do you see something I missed?"

"So I didn't mention it," said Olivia, "but Mayor Maguire brought me a boot last night. I was right here in the kitchen. He wanted me to chase him and grab the boot. Eventually he released it to me. A size 8½ for a right foot that looked just like these." Olivia held up the pair of boots they'd found in the locker. "I mean, same style, same size, everything."

"Well that's a problem," Jets said. "Three boots...where's the fourth?"

She turned to Abbey. "Can you explain why there would be three boots?"

Abbey shook her head vehemently.

"Or do you know where the fourth boot can be found?" Michael asked.

"I have an idea," said Olivia, her eyes widening.

"Okay, what's the idea?" prompted Jets, looking at Olivia impatiently.

"Let me take Michael and I'll be back quickly. I think the other boot may be close by. Do you have one of those plastic bags? I'll put it in there so as not to contaminate evidence."

Jets reached into her pocket. "Here you go. Have at it. I'll stay and hang out with Abbey."

Olivia snatched the bag from Janis's hand and made her way to the door, Michael following close behind. When he caught up with her jogging along the path, he panted, "Mind filling me in on what you're thinking?"

Olivia didn't stop running. When she and Michael reached the dormitory the first thing they saw was a shaggy brown dog. "Hey, M&M," she called out. "I thought I might find you here."

Michael pulled up beside her. "I don't understand. Did you know Mayor Maguire would be here?"

Olivia bent over to catch her breath. "Did you look at Abbey when I brought up the third boot? She nearly keeled right over. Then it dawned on me that M&M might have found the fourth boot, only he didn't have room in his mouth for two. Once I took the first boot away from him, there was a good chance that he'd go back for the matching one."

"Is that why he's waiting outside the dorm?"

"He's waiting to sneak inside. I bet if we let him, he'll lead us right to where he found the first boot."

Olivia used her key card to unlock the door to the dormitory. As she predicted, Mayor Maguire rushed past, his tail wagging like a tour guide's flag.

"Just follow him," Olivia told Michael.

Once in the entryway, the dog took a right turn, heading for the stairway to the second floor. Michael and Olivia followed. Making another right turn, Mayor Maguire trotted halfway down the hall and stopped. He turned to face door 214 on the left.

Michael arrived first, pointing to the name attached to the door. "Well look what we have here. Abbey Court's room."

"We can't just break in," said Olivia reaching for the doorknob.

"Looks like that won't be necessary," commented Michael as he saw the knob turn under her grasp.

Mayor Maguire brushed past Olivia and Michael. In the room, he ignored the bed with its rumpled sheets, moving straight to the closet with the closed sliding door. He sat down, waiting for Olivia.

She slid the door back. M&M stood and then ducked under the row of clothing, his rump and tail sticking out. She heard a thump followed by a rustle coming from the corner of the closet.

Before she could dive in after the mayor, he turned around, his body draped in a maxi dress that hung precariously from a wire hanger. His tail wagged.

"Look what you found!" Olivia cried, stooping down to pat his head.

Mayor Maguire grinned, keeping the hiking boot firmly clasped in his mouth.

"Here doggie, doggie," said Michael. "Bring me the boot."

Mayor Maguire walked out of the closet, his tail waving in triumph. He scrunched down on his front paws to give a playful growl, the boot still clasped in his jaws.

"I feel guilty taking away his discovery," Olivia told Michael. "He's so delighted with himself and he just wants to play." She knelt in front of the dog to pat his head. "It's okay, M&M. I'll play with you later. I really need to have that boot."

Mayor Maguire growled again, this time showing her the side of his face as if to say, "I don't do later. Play now!"

"Oh hell, I'll give him my shoe if that helps. Grab the boot," Michael said, reaching down to untie his sneaker.

Mayor Maguire looked to Michael, his eyes focused on the hand that tugged off the shoe. Dropping the boot from his mouth, the dog walked over to sniff the shoe in Michael's hand.

"Good doggie," Michael mumbled. "Of course this is a better toy. Let that other one go. We can play with this one." Michael drew his hand back and gently tossed his shoe into the closet. Mayor Maguire bounded after the shoe while Olivia stooped to pick up the discarded boot.

"Into the evidence bag you go," she said, then sealing the top.

The mayor pushed his way out of the closet, this time holding Michael's shoe, ready for his game.

"Are you going to let him keep his new toy?" asked Olivia, staring at Michael's feet, one shoe on and one shoe off.

"I'll give him both shoes and a steak for dinner if he solved who murdered Dave," commented Michael wryly.

Back in the Curated Cuisine's pantry, Olivia and Michael found Janis Jets hovering over Simon and Abbey Court. The father and daughter sat at the round table, glaring at Janis.

"My attorney is on his way," Court announced.

Jets darted a glance at Olivia and Michael. Then she told Court, "Sure, bring on your attorney and anyone else. Let's have a party. But first I think Olivia is holding some more evidence in her hand." Jets turned to Olivia. "So tell me everything."

Olivia explained where they found the shoe and how Michael sacrificed his favorite sneaker.

"Your socks are dirty," Jets told Michael. Then she smiled. Holding up the boot in the bag for a better look, she said, "It's a left shoe, size 8½."

"Four shoes, two lefts, two rights, and size 8½," summarized Olivia. "Dave helped all the Tone Rangers buy hiking boots. It was part of his tutoring strategy, to keep the kids moving, especially when they wanted to talk about what was bothering them."

"So these are Abbey's boots and those are Anais's boots..."

"Both girls wear the same size," concluded Michael.

"We have footprints at the top of the cliff indicating someone scuffled with Dave before they shoved him over the side," Jets said thoughtfully.

"*Those* are my boots, the ones from my closet," blurted Abbey. "The other ones belong to Anais. She pushed Dave, like I said."

Jets stared at the distraught girl. "So why don't you try on the boots. We can see if they fit and check the wear on the soles."

Her father leaned over the table to slap his hand over her mouth. "Shut up, you stupid girl. Don't talk until our attorney gets here. I warned you already."

Olivia felt anger rise up in the back of her throat. "Keep your hands off her," she exclaimed, but not before Janis Jets stepped to the table, leaning in to insert herself between the father and daughter. She turned her head, speaking to Simon Court. "I don't like the way you handle this girl and I'm going to separate you both for her safety." She tapped a number on her phone and held it to her ear.

"Yep, it's me. I need an advocate from Child Protective Services. I want to interview a minor about a murder and her parent isn't capable of holding his temper."

Simon Court's face grew red with fury. "You can't tell me how to talk to my own daughter," he hollered, standing. He shoved Janis Jets and her cell phone dropped to the floor.

"Oh yes she can," came a voice from the kitchen.

Charles Kravitz stood in the doorway, glaring at Simon Court. To Olivia's surprise, two other men stood right behind him. Like matching bookends, both men wore black suits, crisp white shirts, and dark neckties.

As if they'd rehearsed, each one held up a badge with their right hands. The one on the right announced, "Simon Court, you are under arrest for racketeering, money laundering, conspiracy to defraud the US government, and obstruction of justice. You have the right to remain silent."

Olivia's jaw dropped as Charles Kravitz stepped aside, allowing the two men to wrestle Simon Court into handcuffs. Unable to free himself, Court bent over at the waist as the two men dragged him from the kitchen.

His head swung around as he shouted at Olivia. "You couldn't mind your own business, could you, even after I warned you about that sister of yours. Cox should have killed you when he had the chance. One twist of your skinny neck, that's all it would have taken."

"Get him out of here," Jets commanded.

Olivia's hand moved upward, her fingers touching her neck. When she spoke, her voice sounded shaky. "I never saw that coming, those FBI guys and Cookie."

Jets ignored Olivia's words. She sat next to Abbey. "I know this must be a shock to you," she said to the girl with the trembling bottom lip. "Someone will be here to help you through the confession. You know who really pushed Dave, don't you."

"You can't arrest my daddy. No one can. He always wins," cried Abbey.

No sooner did Abbey stop talking than a woman bustled into the room. "I happened to be in Lily Rock for a day retreat and got a call from Officer Janis Jets. I'm from Child Protective Services for a teen named Abbey Court."

Abbey looked up. "They arrested my daddy," she said, her eyes darting back and forth.

The woman, who wore a clerical collar, sat down across from Abbey. "We can sort this out together," she said in a calm voice.

"I want to tell the truth, I do," admitted Abbey. "I only wanted to help Daddy with his business. He cared a lot about the students, getting them into the right universities. Dave got in his way. He tried to talk us out of the tutoring."

"What do you mean?" asked Janis.

"Dave told each of us that we needed to go to college on our own terms. Even if we scored high on the tests and got in because of the music auditions, that didn't mean we'd be okay once we got to college. He said he saw lots of kids whose parents pulled strings, but the kids ended up being miserable after their acceptance. He didn't want us to be unhappy, so we'd hike and talk as he tried to convince us."

"But he didn't convince you?" asked Janis.

"I couldn't back out. My dad was in charge of all the admission work. I told Daddy about Dave separating each of the Tone Rangers to talk to them about their futures." She paused, as if remembering. "Daddy got so angry. It didn't take long for the Tone Rangers to change their minds about early admission. As soon as Legend cracked, they even decided to vote me out as the Tone Ranger leader. That stupid Legend. She didn't want Dave to take the admissions test for her either. Something about a guilty conscience. Who cares about that? Once you're in, no one even asks about that stuff."

"And then Raleigh even told me they wanted to go to community college instead, to figure things out. Imagine, a community college after all those years their parents paid for Daddy to get them into Harvard.

"So when Dave invited me for a hike and we stopped near the cliff, I just figured, go with your instincts. That's what Dave always said, so I did. I pushed him off the cliff. Right over he went. And then I ran. I couldn't bear to see him land. I just kept running."

Abbey looked up at Olivia, then down at her hands. "I knew I'd left some bootprints at the top of the cliff, so I took Anais's. I put mine in the back of the closet and put her boots in my locker for safe keeping." She pointed to the pastel-pink locker with the key still in the door. "The police didn't focus on us as suspects, so I thought I'd be okay."

Abbey looked Olivia with anger in her eyes. "Except for you." She pointed to Olivia. "You were so nosey and always around asking questions. That's how she found out!" Now Abbey glared at Janis Jets. She sighed and continued to speak, her voice calmer.

"When you told me there was a third boot, I knew I was done. I finally told Daddy. He didn't seem that mad. Daddy said his lawyer would keep me out of jail." A dazed look came over Abbey's face. She looked around the room at the eyes of everyone watching her.

"I want my daddy," she cried.

The child advocate reached into her pocket, coming up with a business card. She handed it to Jets. "I think that's enough interviewing for now. Here's my card so that you can get in touch with me. May I arrange for Abbey's accommodations while you figure out the next step?"

Olivia noticed that the woman avoided using the word "jail".

Jets tucked the card in her back pocket. "Make the arrangements." She ushered Abbey to her feet; the girl trembled, barely able to stand.

As they left the pantry for the kitchen exit, Olivia took Michael's arm, leaning against him for support. "I had no idea about Simon Court, did you?"

"I had my suspicions," he admitted. "Janis told me a little about the FBI's operation."

"So Janis knew," Olivia realized. "That's why she's been acting so odd."

"Right, she knew. But she couldn't let you in on the sting because she had to keep you safe. That's why she wanted you to work with the teens, to keep you out of the way. Plus she couldn't cover all of the suspects herself."

Olivia heard banging coming from the central kitchen and dropped Michael's arm to walk toward the noise. She found Cookie wrapped in his white apron, standing in front of three huge kettles on the stove. He chopped onions and celery and slid them into each of the pots, using his knife with speed and authority.

Cookie looked over to Olivia. "If ever there was a need for soup, this is the time. What a week!"

"Do you need help?" offered Olivia, admiring his knife skills.

"What I need is a night out with my girlfriend. This place is making me nuts." Cookie smiled, continuing to wield his knife. "Come on back tomorrow and there will be soup for you and Mike."

Olivia turned to go, but then came back around. "There's just one thing I want to know. Are you working with the FBI?"

Cookie smiled. "The FBI contacted me last spring, since I have a high security clearance with the Navy. I told them I'd do this one job. I managed to convince Dave Franco that he should work with me by the middle of summer. As his handler I appealed to his inner sense of right and wrong. At first he didn't realize that Simon Court swindled parents and universities with his college admission scams.

"Court manipulated those families. He knew right where the weak spot was. Parents would do anything to guarantee their child early admission to a prestigious university. And I mean anything. Anais's family alone donated millions to a fake charity for underprivileged children in Mexico. Of course, all of that dough went into Court's company via back channels and laundered money."

"Was the paperwork you mentioned in the park about the laundered money?" Olivia asked. She flushed and then added, "I overheard you the day you dropped the key."

"He didn't want an electronic trail that the feds would find on a computer. Court was old-school that way. He used a lot of papers and forged signatures which parents would give to the students and they'd leave them in a locker to be retrieved when Court visited the campus. I was supposed to keep my eye on the people coming and going and report to him if anything looked fishy."

Olivia leaned forward, fascinated with Cookie's story. "That explains so much. No wonder the FBI arrested Court on so many charges."

"The case moved along faster when we involved the local police."

"So Janis was part of the investigation?"

"She went undercover as a corrupt cop, dating Rydell Cox, taping their conversations." Kravitz smiled at Olivia.

"How was that exactly?"

Kravitz dipped his face into a soup kettle. He turned down the heat. "I'd better stop talking for now. Everything else about the case is on a need-to-know basis."

Olivia shrugged. "I've heard that before. I guess I know all I want to about this particular situation. I'm heading home."

Cookie brandished his knife over his head as a goodbye gesture.

"To us," Michael said with a smile, leaning over the table and tapping his wine glass to Olivia's sparkling water.

"We finally managed our dinner," she responded with a grin.

"What I want to know," Michael said, "is how the FBI managed to get enough information to arrest Court."

"They must have done some wiretapping," Olivia said, sipping her drink. "That's how the FBI works, though I'm hardly an authority."

"That's probably how Dave got involved," Michael added, smiling at her over the rim of his glass. "Cookie put a wire on him and then he engaged in conversations that implicated Court and his illegal plan."

Olivia closed her menu and set it aside. "After all of this,

I am so happy we finally got out for a night." An irresistible aroma came from the kitchen. She inhaled deeply. "Garlic and mushrooms, just the smell makes my mouth water."

"I'm going with the rack of lamb with the risotto."

"I'll have the scampi for my main course. Do you want to split a salad?" she asked.

He nodded. Michael folded his menu, laying it on top of Olivia's. "Finally we got our first date," Michael said. He took her hand in his across the table. "So I'm your boyfriend now. Is it official?"

She nodded, the warmth of his grasp bringing goose-bumps to her arm. "It's official."

"Then there's no more running away from Lily Rock." He stopped for a sip of wine. "The way I figure it is that our biggest decision is your place or mine."

"No more running, at least not without an explanation," she promised.

"No more running away it is. I'm ignoring the explana-tion part."

Breathing deeply, she ran her finger back and forth over his wrist.

I feel so contented and alive.

Since the waiter had left them alone, they looked into each other's eyes. Michael smiled. "So what will happen to the other Tone Rangers now that they're missing their girl soprano?"

"From what I can tell, Anais will go home with her grands. She wants to finish high school closer to her family. And Raleigh will stay to graduate. Without the pressure of early admission, they may go to community college. Raleigh wants to work in a bakery. As for Legend, I think she may still get early admission. Of all the Tone Rangers, Legend has a solo voice and talent in music arranging."

"Has anyone spoken to Linnea since the arrest? Michael asked.

"Janis told me her mother is coming to stay with her until the baby arrives. Five thousand dollars were raised at the recital from parent donations. That will help some."

Olivia sipped her sparkling water, remembering her last conversation with Dave.

"I guess Dave had been nervous for weeks. Linnea was worried. She thought it was about the baby, but she now realizes wearing a wire for the FBI must have been a staggering responsibility. I think Dave knew he was in danger. He may have been worried that he wouldn't be around to raise his own child."

"Turns out Dave was right," Michael said, his voice dropping with emotion. Before Olivia raised her glass to offer a toast for Dave, she heard a loud voice coming from the front of the restaurant.

"Well, if it isn't Ms. Amateur Sleuth and her boyfriend." Olivia's head jerked up. "Imagine meeting you two here." Janis Jets stood next to their table. She wore her skin-tight leather pants with the low-cut cobalt-blue top. Her hair, a mass of curls, flowed around her thin shoulders.

She's on a date. Surely she's not still undercover with that Rydell Cox.

A man came from behind Janis. He stood a good three inches shorter. Cookie Kravitz placed his large palm at the small of Janis's back. "Small town," he mumbled to Michael and Olivia, a huge grin on his face.

"What?" Olivia glared at Janis. "I thought you were dating Cox!"

"Please, I'm not an idiot," said Janis, flicked her hair off her shoulder. "Cookie and I have been together for months now. He originally moved to Lily Rock for the FBI investigation, but now he's staying for me."

"Does that mean you aren't taking another job?" Olivia exclaimed.

"Don't be such an idiot. I'm a Lily Rock resident through and through. On the one hand, I only pretended to look for another job as part of my undercover persona. On the other hand, I didn't want you asking too many questions in general. I figured if you thought I was leaving you'd back off."

Kravitz moved his hand from Janis back to lift her chin for a kiss. "We've got to have dinner now, so talk to you two later," he said, staring into Janis's eyes.

Before they could be escorted to their table, Olivia injected one more question. "Do I need to show up for work tomorrow morning?"

Janis Jets blinked. "I forgot to tell you. You're fired. Now stop bothering me."

Olivia turned to Michael, who had just finished pouring his second glass of wine. He barely disguised his smile.

"You want me to be unemployed?"

"I want you to be safe. The constabulary job is too close to the action," he said.

The corner of Olivia's mouth tightened. "We can talk about that later."

"I still don't know why you need a job," he said. "You've got lots of money. Why not take off a few months and see how you like it."

Olivia felt herself smile. "I might do that. Working at the constabulary turned out to be more trouble than I bargained for. Now that Sage and I have settled Marla's estate, she may not want to return to the academy as the head, so we're both unemployed at the same time. Now we can book more gigs for Sweet Four O'Clock."

She raised her glass to Michael, who raised his. "I'll drink to that!" he said, the warmth in his voice bringing a flush to her cheeks.

He took another sip and then added, "Like I was saying earlier, your place or mine?"

READ ON FOR A SNEAK PEEK OF...

Excerpt from Chapter One
A Thymely Death
Lily Rock Mystery Book Four

Olivia heard the bell above the door jingle as it closed behind her. Standing in the middle of the bakery, she examined it, checking out every nook and cranny. The carefully placed tables and chairs, each more distinct than the next, caught her eye first. "You've been antiquing," she commented to Cookie.

He smiled, watching her appreciate his choices.

Olivia kept commenting. "I like the way you took all of these tables and chairs and refinished them in the same oak stain. They look intentional but not the same." She turned to face him. "Thyme Out is a great name for a bakery."

"Since I bake with herbs and spices, it felt suitable. I like that play on words. What do you think?"

"It works, especially with the new place next door. Mother Earth and Thyme Out—very Lily Rock."

"Yeah, about the lady next door," Cookie started. Then as if thinking better of it, he changed the subject, a vague look coming to his eyes.

Cookie has some opinions about that woman.

Before Olivia could ask, Cookie cleared his throat. "The Mother Earth owner did a lot of work taking out dirt, adding dirt, taking out trees, adding trees. I'm kind of curious how things ended up."

"I haven't met her," said Olivia. "I'd like to know if she's planning on a nursery or a garden, or a venue that looks like a combination of both. She got her plans past the town council. That's amazing considering the people here hate any tree being removed."

"I know, I learned that the hard way." Cookie nodded. "I got rid of a large overgrown bush in the parking lot behind the kitchen, and you would have thought I'd stolen a puppy from Mayor Maguire and sold her on the black market. Big brouhaha. We finally worked it out. I planted four smaller bushes to replace the ugly old one."

"I bet Meadow convinced the town council planning committee to let this one go," Olivia remarked. "She's often the most rational of the Old Rockers."

"I believe it was Meadow who helped negotiate the impasse. Funny the old townies call themselves the Old Rockers. They must have been something back in the day."

A shrill voice interrupted Olivia's laugh.

"Help me! Come quick."

A woman stood in the doorway of the bakery, frantically waving her arms in the air. When Olivia and Cookie turned to look at her, her eyes landed on Cookie. "I need a man. There's a dead..." She burst into tears.

GET A FREE SHORT STORY

Join my newsletter to get the latest news about the Lily Rock Mystery Series, Welcome to Lily Rock Holiday Novella Series, and the Redondo and Rose Neighbors in Crime Series.

Along with contests, discounts, giveaways, and events, I'll send you *Meadow's Hat*, a free short story download.

Signup on bonniehardywrites.com/newsletter

ALSO BY BONNIE HARDY

Lily Rock Mystery Series

Cozy Mystery Books

Olivia Greer's trip to the mountain town of Lily Rock turns out quite differently than the getaway she expected. Her friend is found dead and she ends up being the prime suspect in the murder. With the help of Mayor Maguire, the town's labradoodle, and Michael Bellemare, the famous hunky architect, she comes to discover deep connections to the town that she could never have anticipated. Love. Laughter. Whodunit. Join Olivia as she begins her journey of self discovery.

Welcome to Lily Rock Holiday Mystery Series

Holiday Cozy Mystery Novellas

As an homage to the holiday classic film, *It's a Wonderful Life,* Bonnie Hardy contemplates what the small town of Lily Rock was like before the arrival of Olivia Greer. In this prequel spin-off series, you'll enjoy fresh adventures with holiday themes and learn the backstories of the characters you've come to know and love.

Redondo and Rose Neighbors in Crime

He's a mentalist. She's a doula. They are neighbor's in crime.

In this new series by Bonnie Hardy, Neighbors Rex Redondo and Vivienne Rose are entangled in the investigation of who murdered the woman floating in Viv's swimming pool. Playing Bogart to her Bacall, Rex and Viv solve the mystery and explore their mid-life romance in a setting reminiscent of Old Hollywood.

ACKNOWLEDGEMENTS

I want to thank my small and mighty family who stood by me this past fall at the book fair, talking to people about Lily Rock. Emily you are a gifted entrepreneur and Bill, aren't you glad we nixed the ten year plan?

And finally thank you, dear readers.

ABOUT THE AUTHOR

Born and raised in Los Angeles, Bonnie Hardy is an educator, curriculum writer, musician, and preacher. A lover of libraries and literacy, Bonnie directed a literacy center in her home town.

A retired military spouse, she's lived and worked in Washington DC, No. Virginia, Maryland, San Diego, and Twentynine Palms. She's also packed and unpacked more times than she cares to count.

Bonnie has published in *Christian Century, Presence: An International Journal for Spiritual Direction,* and with *Pilgrim Press.*

When not planting flowers and baking cookies, she's sitting at her computer plotting her next cozy mystery.

You can connect with Bonnie at
bonniehardywrites.com

www.ingramcontent.com/pod-product-compliance
Lightning Source LLC
Chambersburg PA
CBHW050825190726
48286CB00007B/1989